THE
MASTERPIECE

CHIEMEKA NICELY

Zoe

You have greatness within don't be afraid to share your light with the world

First published in the UK 2018 by Nicely Publishing

Revised edition 2022

Copyright © Chiemeka Nicely 2022

British Library cataloguing in publication Data. A catalogue
record for this book is available from the British Library.

Paperback: ISBN: 978-1-8383682-6-5

To my family for their love and support.

&

To those willing to see through the fabrication bestowed upon them.

WELCOME TO ACIRFA

The Genapians (Gen-a-pi-ens).

Every species known to man were aware of them in the 9nth dimension. They spoke of them in their bed time stories. Taught children from their early years right through to adulthood about their importance. They were classed as the *Others* many wanted to identify with.

There were mixed voices about their existence; some filled with love and light; others, most, envy and jealousy. Above all, the one distinction that separated them from the Genapians was the Blue Star. They believed its sole purpose was to activate specific codes in their DNA, heightening their perception, elevating their consciousness — more than 40% brain consumption. Their abilities as a result were so superior that they were beyond the understanding and imagination of most civilisations. To be in total unification with their vessel and their environment, *God on the physical plane and God in the sky* – there was no separation. For the music they played in their stride to actualise their divine purpose paired with mental resilience, they were the eminent threats to the other species progress or the legends unmatched to reality.

Genapa had Six Kingdoms for Six Dynasties across the Super-continent. Each dynasty specialised in STEM: Science, Technology, Engineering, and Mathematics. The Sixth Kingdom always in the Beyond with spirituality as their system for advancement and enquiry rooted itself with the natural laws. To govern their being with order and integrity, righteousness and gratitude. To flow with the cycles and rhythms of nature: living forward, not backward or upside down. This was the only way their infrastructure could remain intact, forever blessed and protected by the Supreme Deities they respected and appreciated as reflections of themselves.

The Second Dynasty was famously known for their tapestries, sophisticated models that stood tall to the sky even ran deep beneath the earth. They utilised mathematics and engineering, the construction of exquisite designs in alignment with the stars; signs they had not entirely forgotten themselves, they had chosen instead to hide and move with the evolving times. Pyramids, for example; giant structures of red and black earth sheltered their former Kings and Queens in tombs that also contained the infinite knowledge passed down by their Ancestors. A beauty they were even in blind-darkness. Their skills, rich culture, inspired their annual 'Visionary' day which honoured and celebrated their peoples' talents and the Supreme Deities for bestowing such gifts upon them.

The Third, Fourth, and Fifth Kingdoms mined their underground materials: Copper, Amethyst, the stabilising stone Carnelian, and Jasper rocks. These they studied, theorised, invented new technologies to harness their power, interweaving them into jewellery and clothing. Each faction within their respective dynasties would wear a specific colour and design to characterise the level of skill they had acquired and the value and belief system they adhered to. Some would be worshippers of Sun Ra, others taking a liken to the 48 laws of power noted by Ma'at.

The First Dynasty, however, was the most developed out of the six Dynasties. They had that heavenly-kingdom shinning with magnificence in the north; walls even thick enough to stop a stampede of elephants, an avalanche of bombs and missiles. Their technology ...

A range of weaponry from the mind-link, carbon lion-claw bracelet, spears enhanced with kinetic energy to magnetic earrings that heightened their abilities. The Silver Rings of the Elite Supreme Warrior Clan, a super-computer used to communicate with the other warriors, created virtual simulations, and acted as a recording device through the eyes of its host.

To live as such, mighty and integrated with technology, the First Dynasty had to make sacrifices; sacrifices the Sixth Dynasty would have rather they hadn't made. And thus began the bad blood between the dynasties.

Thus began the upending conflict that would stretch their unity to the depths of separation ...

Despite all the dynasties advancements, there was once a time where Genapa suffered through darkness. A seeming chaos that upset the balance they were all meant to uphold. A period of great embarrassment and despair.

What had caused this? Who were involved?

From a standing of glory to a fall enough to set them back a generation or two, why did this have to happen?

It's the cycle of things, what rises must collapse. What was unseen had to be brought to light. What was unspoken had to be handed a microphone. The scales of balance had long since been tipping, so with their involvement, their arrival, the chaos they brought till this day — a reset was due.

The returning of the divine. The remembrance of truth. The rebirth of the Enlightened.

"The most reliable way to predict the future is to create it."
- Abraham Lincoln

I

KIMARR, GENAPA

{Calista}

Fight or flight?

The former has always been encouraged, but right now the latter was a must.

The strangers materialised from nothingness, gathering around me like a pack of hungry wolves, eyes ready for their feast.

For miles, the earth screamed for nutrients, as a web of cracks sprouted like alfalfa across its fragile skin. Steep hills with the occasional eyesore of crumbling huts were visible through naked trees, their fruit lost within death's phantom.

The Sixth Dynasty's Palace still bore the scars of the war, blood and ashes trailing around every chunk of stone. After all these years, it is the only reminder of what was and what could have been. The kingdom's black walls still remained pockmarked, with straws of roots weaving through its crevices. The once elegant palace tilted beneath engraved, crumbled pillars, it was a pity it had become liken to rubble.

When it fell, the hearts of the people must have crushed with it. Even the statue of the Dynastic Emblem of a Lion's head with a Cobra wrapped in its hair had become disfigured by Ma'at's side, one leg folded beneath her. The goddess of truth, justice, cosmic order; her yellow-brown skin chipped with red rocks, oh the sight of dried blood everywhere, my stomach churned. The one thing intact as though the only hope and willpower of the people who once occupied this space was the model golden staff. The one every dynasty had with the Red Sunstone pieced at the centre of the top loop.

With every step I took, my breath hung like a fog in the air. Wading not just through the disaster but the memory of their past crawling along my skin, this was the first sign that nothing was as it appeared. The second — a gravitational shift.

A ghost-like blizzard of energy danced across the land with a seeming content sweeping rocks off the ground, and I mere inches on-and-off the earth. Then a high-pitched frequency, deafening to the ear, my hands cupping them, could not dull the sound nor relieve the bubbles that pressed my eardrums. Even my eyes, as they began to dizzy, I thought it best to give my head a shake, to snap out of the spell-like sensation, but my legs were weakening at the knees too. For all of this to happen at once, I must have travelled too close to something, a part of Kimarr that had been untouched since this devastation. To be firm; to be calm in mind — I needed to be. So, with both hands pressed to my heart, a deep breath drawing from my chest, it was better to remember why I was here. As a matter of urgency, why I had crossed the lands and seas to uncover a truth guarded. Such earthly tricks would not send me scurrying back to Aelburn.

Defiant, gaze forward, unwavering, I proceeded.

From the moment I crossed the border, my bare feet wading through the River Elin and its red soil to set foot on the deserted Kimarr, a vague feeling of unease crawled over my skin with a quiver. My ankle beads rattled amplifying my concerns. Despite the stories about the Sixth Dynasty's disappearance after the Civil War, it felt surreal to be here; strange energy hinted at life here — the unseen wandering. Anyone who had set foot on Kimarr within a decade would have thought it too; an overwhelming feeling of pure Ka, energy and spirit, infused with pain and misery. It burned my tongue –- a metallic taste staining my saliva, twisting my insides into fists. It took a lot not to vomit on the very ground where death had marked its territory. It was at this moment that I knew ...

I was not alone.

When they come, the sky opens baring its soul with a tremendous downpour of rain. Thereafter, in an erratic pattern striking the earth, blinding-red flashes. Luckily, not so close to have me worried. Nonetheless, with the shadows that near, I crouch one arm protecting my front, the other gripping the Jasper-hilt sword at my waist. To the eerie stillness, the only disturbance is the beating rain followed by my slow exhale. When they close in, dread shifts my weight from one foot to the other. A sudden wind slapped my shoulder-length plaits with small silver beads into my face.

The trail of fire in my eyes, the red lightning picturing once more, "Ah."

The rumbles thump with my heart. *Turn back*, it shouted. *Evade the oncoming group. I have no business being here. My assignment should be marked as a FAIL.*

Yet, in honour of my father, my mentor's philosophy too, "Fear is an illusion; false evidence appearing real." I needed to find reassurance in these words but, their weapons ...

Strapped onto their backs, ranging from the basics of axes and spears to whips and knives. Those were very real. So was their shadow. A black coat of fur shimmering silver with the Blue Star's reflection in its eyes. Water dripping from its whiskers, its paws splashing in the mini sinkholes behind its masters.

"Panther." I gasp, never seen up-close, mesmerising, royal in its stance.

They are all male with a skin tone unlike any other. Very different from the shades of black-brown, foreign but strange, I assume they are people of the ice rather than the Red Sun. How else would you explain their excessively pale skin with a subtle red tint to it? If not for this variation, I would have thought they were bloodless. And when they bare their teeth, in I guess an attempt at a smile, the sharpness, looking is enough to slice me. If not for their broad nose and thick lips, I would have thought they were an entirely different species. Despite this they hold some form of beauty, maybe not so long ago they held more a likeness to the original black man than the diluted version before me.

About eight of them stand tall with unkempt hair defying gravity. Their loincloths decorated with mini black beads accentuate their bulging thighs.

"You're trespassing," the one standing across from me, his hoarse voice carrying with the wind and the cacophony of the rain. His bloodshot eyes watch me like a lion does its prey, unfazed through the mist of the downpour. Under his gaze, my claw-choker neck jumpsuit feels stripped to nakedness. They skim across my two beauty spots nestling, almost sheltering, beneath my full lips. Then to my sun-kissed complexion over the prominence of my cheekbones. Mere metres from each other we mirror our differences. I imagine the energy around me is captivating, alluring even; I always attract what I should not. He takes a deep breath as if my presence would invigorate his life; his mind a projection of images explode through my sight. Images of a woman much darker than I, her features blurred, his true love I suppose. "How? How can I see his thoughts?"

When the images fade, the only thing remaining, "he thinks I'm exceptional." His thoughts touch my lips, utilising my mouth instead of his. "To be surprised I have made the trip, would be an understatement. There's a plan ..."

The short link between us severs.

"What plan? What do I have to do with it?" The glint in his eyes, our encounter ... my eyes widen.

When he rolls his neck, a long scar running from his chin to the base of his throat becomes visible. His companions; each holding the same mark, "Clones?" My jaw slacks. He does not bear the mark of the Eye of Horus, yet he so easily conjures multiple reflections of himself. Looking at my own, he couldn't possibly be an Elite Supreme Warrior.

I clear my throat. "If you could just let me pass, then I'll be on my way."

"You are a long way from home," he whispers in a sing-song voice. Then he holds out his hand, tasting the rain as it speaks to him, or maybe bridging the energy gap between us. His panther prowls closer to his side, sparkling like an unstable portal. "This was no accident -–" he pauses "-– intentional." Sweat slithers down my back with his every word.

The sky darkens.

"We have been expecting you."

The relief in his voice, it does something. The questions brimming in my heart.

A trap?

This assignment ... did Father ... am I to be taught a lesson?

The panther growls and fuses with its master. In a blur, I cut the guy to my right a burst of blue light exploding a path to follow. He disperses. Gravity's pull weakens. I leap every other step, arms trying to balance me in my flight. All the while, I click my fingers; only sparks, I needed more than that.

ching

Their swords unsheathed, the remaining seven slice the air. From my periphery, four of them split into two on either side running ahead of me. "Such speed ..." I think fast. Pressing two fingers into my Eye of Horus, I call upon a portal. A gold streak sauntered forward to the stream of water in reach. I galloped then placed two feet together, vaulting off. My arms caught my knees and I tug-to-flip into the lake. The water separated with the parting of my hands. The black hole that should have swirled me through ... "Ugh." I gulp the salty water, heaving my body to the surface. An excruciating pain ripped through my calf. All around me, my blood dirtied the water even more. The rock that had cut me I forced away.

With a throbbing hand, I feel for the gash that is widening by the second.

How strange, where had the portal gone?

The water licks my wound; everything solid becomes so soft it seems to melt before me. The low tide I yield to. His figures looming over me brings a chill to my spine.

In a sprint, the seven become one. The image of his panther occasionally pushes through the barrier of his flesh. His lips distort into a smirk. I squeeze a blink unable to get rid of his ripple-like reflection.

"S-stay back!" The echo of my voice hadn't travelled further than the bank of the river. I throw my hands up, tensing, pushing until finally spirals of black tentacles wrapped around my fingers.

"The Blue Flame." His eyes light up.

Just about more than sparks, flickers of baby flames. More. I need more. Clenching my teeth, my eyes watering, "More." It felt like I was begging myself to do the bare minimum. This is me, the Blue Flame, why now do I defect at what I'm good at? If Father could see me ... he'd be more than disappointed.

"Ssh —-" he crouches.

"No, no not like this." The tears in my eyes.

"It will soon be over."

My fingertips vibrate, with a sizzle my Blue Flame becomes smoke.

"What do you want from me?" My tongue slurs, heavy along the bottom of my lip. In the lake, my reflection wavers, loud and clear it tells me I should have listened, *I should have stayed where I was, in Aelburn.*

He jumps into the water and scrapes me up just before I collapse. A spark ignites between us as our skins rub.

For a second, I forget whose embrace I am in, as I stare into his brown eyes. A man with a depth to his soul, an obligation to those he serves. He must perform like everyone else.

Protect.

Empower.

Awaken.

Just as quickly as the spark had approached, it disappeared, leaving me void of emotion, void of thoughts. Our connection lost. The darkness cocoons my inner flickering flame.

"You will soon find out."

My blade falls from my hands into the lake. Light passes through it as new territory claims it as its own amongst two-toned rocks. The sky with quick succession closes back up and the red lightning strikes taking us with it.

"We cannot become what we want by remaining what we are."

2

{Calista}

I'm sitting on the floor but I may as well be in an ice box, bolted away under lock and key. There's no ventilation just a stale air of all that would be classed as rotten and dead. I swallow remembering a similar time when the cold had trapped within my body, paralysing every inch of my tissues, organs. Though I was half-conscious, its moments like these that puts me back into that time, reliving a memory I'd glue my eyes shut to forget. Being here with a cramp settling in my legs, I am helpless to my mind. Numb and like stiff meat, like then when my body temperature had dropped below zero. Sometimes I wonder what would have happened if the voices that called to me hadn't lent a hand. If my Blue Flame hadn't surfaced at that vital moment, protecting my heart, my brain, giving me another chance to live.

Why then had my greatest asset rescued me and not now when the stranger took me?

After embarking on my first solo assignment, did I make the right choice setting foot on Kimarr? With my back at a wall in some strange room, maybe I should have only dreamt of the Sixth Kingdom and left it at that.

I cannot tell whether it's pass midnight or the sun is high in the sky. The ceiling for all I know is open yet closed, in a weird abyss of darkness. I wince as a sensation twists around my wrists. The only heat radiates from shackles as thick as a bar of gold. I can tell it's rusty from the way it burns, if I could see so far up I know the skin around would be raw and tender. Just to twist a few fingers away, my skin would split. From where the chains hang, something solid must be holding my arms above my head. It's not so secure as a trail of water and debris leaks into my already damp scalp. I sigh, the last bit of strength I held giving in my arms. Still, something isn't right.

"Where is he?" I could not hear my voice.

I lift my head just a little, my eyes performing the rest of movement around the room until I settle on the person concealed yet seen enough through the dark. Something of theirs is scratching at the ground. More than that, maybe with their fingers, at a speed enough to dizzy. Their pattern, "what is that?" I mouth. I couldn't make out anything besides their bowed head. Whatever their mind had issued to create, it was doing something; commanding the four walls to close in. Like the shuffling of panels in a maze, the sides move first, then the one behind me and the figure, then back again. Each time the walls slapped us closer I anticipated my heart exploding through my throat. When the walls halt, moulding to one smooth wall forming a circle, I hold my breath. Right up until —

A blue glow ignited.

The markings, they were fives. Upside down. Back-to-front. Hectic scribbles, all shapes and sizes of overlapping fives. And with the entrance of light, darkness retraces from my face. Like a magnet, the blue light dabs at the corners of my jaw, kisses my lips even. But when it skips to my eyes, a shrill stirs in me. The light a vacuum sucks the sound I beg to be released. I gape. One by one my senses are being stolen from me. First sound, now touch. The stabbing in my eyes, then nothing. The gripping of my jaw, then nothing. I, a still painting to be observed. The figure rocks out of their seat. Their hands covered in dirt, press into my knees, my shoulders, before I know it they're gripping my face. With their nails digging into my tender skin, I worry my eyes would be next. I'd lose my sight. And it would all have been because of the blue light. The Blue Flame I've lived my entire life with, watering my gaze, had come to harm me after we had been each other's twin. The Blue Flame, the Blue Star at its greatest on Acirfa, "what had I done that was so wrong?" The small sound that escapes me, a plea, rattles my chains. The figure closes my mouth and starts to release their hold, but its face — colour is forcing its features to take shape. A familiar oval, full lips, chocolate-brown skin.

My pulse pounds at my neck. Deja Vu? A dream? My fluttering eyes; reeling into the wall.

Me.

I was looking at me. The one who had come with the light.

Me.

The one who should not be here but has fought to squeeze where they should not.

Me.

The one I thought to hide.

A mark rests on my forehead: a Phoenix with the Eye of Horus in the Red Sun above its head. It winks; she presses her palms together and becomes an array of lunatic bats.

From the symbol alone, I have doubts. It was weird seeing myself that way with a light that seemed hideous in my eyes. The colours of fiery-red, calming-blue, to have both — impossible. But there was a darkness besides the bats.

The bats …

As soon as they had freed from her form, I could hear their wings flutter. Their rhythmic flap trapping, rebounding the air in my face. The droplets of water … plow … plow … plow … horrifying music. What was coming?

And their eyes, beady, focused on its target.

Me.

I rattle my chains with a new ferocity, all previous pain absent.

I must leave.

"Somebody —"

They won't budge as if sealed by the bats intentions. Nothing moves except them. The swarm of bats watch me with their teeth elongating tasting their future meal before dining in the present.

"Somebody help me!"

They advance. I scream as their wings cut into my skin, digging deeper than my flesh. They claw their way through me, it and I become one. Its wings stretch across my skin like wet paint covering me in a cocoon of dried wax.

The blue glow flees from my face disappearing with the number five.

I raise my head from my chest. Giving the room a once over, the great difference is it is fully lit. What I saw I confirm as a waking dream. The remnants still invade my mind; the feeling would be hard to shake. Invasion is the correct word as I question myself even more, such as: *what are you afraid of Cali?* What is so real I cannot accept it as False Evidence Appearing Real? From her mark, to having my face, to the bats penetrating my skin, what strange prophecy had befallen me? I'm no good at deciphering dreams, what I do know though, they are always an extension of the information we process in our reality.

This confinement I'm still present in, where there were walls there are bars of steel. It looks to be crumbling, as thick as the poles may be; some form of green glow circulates it, perhaps the reason why it still holds together. The ground is uneven, sloping down to what looks like three levels, give or take. The row in front contain two people minimum. The pathetic dim light hides their faces. The smell of burning flesh, vomit and reeking body odours stains the air. No matter where I redirect my nose, I cannot rid myself of death's presence. The walls are caked with a brown substance tiny fissures sprouting from it like weeds.

With slow and controlled movements, I yank at my chains. A stream of crushed rocks drips into my hair.

"Would not do that." A child's voice drifts to my ears. Jabbing my eyes around the room, I search for her until I locate two small eyes under the bottom bunk bed. Cloaked in the dark, she bathes in its glory. A glorious compliment to her skin. If not for her eyes I would have thought she was an extension of its embrace. Her small hands rest under her chin as she rocks her head like the chiming of the hands on a wooden clock. When the hook in the wall drops into my lap, she whispers, "they are coming for you."

I squint my eyes, cocking my head to the side. She crawls closer into the light.

"Who are they?"

Her bald head, tattooed with ancient symbols of swirls and animals, snaps to the gate as footsteps are heard coming into the room on the ground floor. Her birthmark I suppose, some form of badge: a phoenix dancing with a partial eclipse is visible near the periphery of her forehead.

"Who are they?" I repeat tapping my feet for a response she holds back on. She presses her hand behind and pushes back into the shadows.

"No … don't –-"

Her silver eyes remain.

Two sets of feet, one in shoes, appear at our cell gate.

"She's awake," he exclaims. "Tamari, her chains."

A pair of black shoes come into my line of vision. My fingers circle the screw at the end of my chains and carefully whip it out in search of the new comer's face. It misses, he steps back, and the other person catches it with finesse. He pulls, hot needles stabbed my wrists, curling my fingers to fists. Like his panther, he moves without a sound. The stranger, Tamari, clenches his jaw and stiffly shakes his head, dropping the screw to his feet. My hands suspend in the air for a moment longer then groan to my knees.

"This is kidnapping you know." Through the silence, I curse myself for sounding so hoarse; weak in the face of those I wished to confront.

Tamari grabs my wrists and stares at the shackles. They moan, casting around my skin. In his eyes, a blue ring erases, a minuscule sample of what the Blue Star's energy can do. Just as impressive is how easily he commands it without faltering under its purity. Usually a subject is needed to act as an intermediary, the most prominent example is technology but he makes it seem far more remarkable — like his body is the technology.

He shoves a bottle into my hand. I want to fill the water in my mouth and spit it into their faces, but the grating of my bones in my trachea restrains me.

Don't they know who I am?

The newcomer steps forward into the light; the water separates to beads, small ragged breaths escape my throat.

Tamari snatches the bottle from my closed fists. His companion, "I know him", not personally, but my father Emperor Rameses, at one point showed me his picture. A charming young man who commands strength and confidence with just the stern look in his eyes. With a strong posture as firm as tree roots, he was not a man to pick a fight with. Back to his eyes, a never-ending burning fire dancing across his gaze, I am the one to see the challenge he wills anyone to take up and accept in a heartbeat. The fire: my calling.

His eyes glisten. "What's the matter?" A taunting, crooked smile raises his cheeks. "You look like you've seen a ghost."

I lick my lips; maybe I have. Unlike Tamari, he has a skin tone similar to my own, more black-blue than dark brown. It reminds me of Dakarai's, just as smooth. Questions bubble in my mind, but none touch my tongue. This is strange. Never have I been speechless. My mind and my mouth have always run as though in a constant flow of debate. But sitting here looking up at him as if I am a scullion deeply disturbs me. We both have the same status and yet to be treated as anything less has my body tensing. I try to communicate my contumacy with my eyes. He seems to notice and laughs. It reminds me of that horrid dry laugh my father would use when I embarrass myself in my attempts to impress him during close combat.

Once again, Tamari shakes his head. He looked less frightening than before, almost ... safe. I banish the thought immediately, looks have a way in deceiving you. My father's words come to mind: *they all disappeared, a ghost in the wind,*

My vision starts to blur.

They both turn and leave, locking me inside. I look at his shiny black shoes my eyes lazy.

"Soon it will all make sense. You are here for a purpose far greater than you are yet to understand."

"Hell is empty, and all the devils are here"
— Shakespeare

3

{Calista}

Y ou know that feeling, when an opportunity arises; a swell of excitement yet sinking of courage in your stomach; I felt that. The news couldn't have come any sooner: Father issuing new assignments. The ones I usually got seemed so worthless in comparison, mediocre duties always kept inside Aelburn. Never transcending outside and so my yearning to see and experience far beyond the First Dynasty grew by day turning into night and the sun renewing through the moon. It had already been decided, one day I would prove myself, not just to my people the ones I serve but to Father — the hardest one to please. These assignments, however, were spoken of a week earlier than its date to be distributed to the Elite Supreme Warriors. We never knew where such information was being acquired to perform our duties and when the word special was paired with assignments, I just couldn't withstand dishonouring my character. I became that creep, that bandit sticking to the dark, going where I should not — Father's territory.

I timed my mischievous act just right. While Father was out in our community on official business with his security detail, Mother in her quarters in the palace with friends, and no one around to miss me, I crossed the line one should have the self-restraint and discipline to resist. Through his study, to his desk draw. Father was predictable depending on what you were searching for. To my surprise, they weren't anywhere on his desk. That said a lot, these weren't anything we'd tackled before. I looked to his bookcase, the spines of the books were in alphabetical order at least to the centre right where they reversed. Not just the letters but also the books upside down with some contained in holographic-sheets. *Subtle, Father, not enough for me,* I had thought. I ran my fingers along the top of each book to the bottom. There was a spritzing sound like the opening of a fizzy drink. I looked behind me, a moment's pause, *no one would notice would they?* Then in front, orbs of light swirled to life: *just a quick look,* I settled, tip-toeing down the narrow glass steps. From then onwards everything was straight forward, the orbs would lead me to stand in front of a mirror. Different from what I had seen, this looking-glass was shaped like a spade, thorns wrapped around its base scattering at the corners. They were wild and despite their prickliness, I wasn't going to stop, even though I knew thorns represented hardship, sin and sorrow; Father was definitely linked. *What were his crimes to have sprouted such a harsh plant not far from his chambers?*

As I continued to look in the mirror, a blue light shone, beckoning me to caress its surface. My fingers reached out for the glass expecting to feel a hard exterior, it was jelly-like, allowing my hand to pass through. This simple metamorphosis reminded me of Rimorr, also known as the Mirror Realm. I never knew Father had such capabilities, it was rumoured, to access a whole realm and contain a piece of it that person had to have unlocked the ability of transgression. And something more to do with physics and cycles. On the other side of the 'jelly', my hand felt around to an envelope. I pulled it through and slowly pried around the seal. Inside were two papyrus tablets. The letters were written in invisible ink but with my Blue Flame they leapt into the air. Only two assignments outside Aelburn; one to Kimarr, the other, beyond the veil protecting Acirfa.

Everything happened for a reason, if I had known that day what I know now, I would have played safe; not tampered with the assignments. At least had a partner to travel with if it had already been determined I'd be off to Kimarr. With Dakarai or Khari's assistance, Tamari wouldn't have grabbed me.

Ah the consequences ...

There's a long trill from the ground floor sounding right into my ears as if implanted in my brain. They activate the locks and all cell gates slide open. I rest my head against the wall, chin up, and make no efforts to inquire about what would be taking place in the moments to come. Still, I watch them. The people that exit their cells, they shuffle along with their backs hunched and chains swinging to the ground. Their eyes focused on the steps down, I seem invisible to their world. There are women, men, children, no limit from the young to the elderly. One thing I rate them on is their perfect unison; mindless zombies, detached from a master's strings. They were in no hurry but from the small hands tugging on mine, I ought to be. With a strength unmatched to her small build, she kicked my leg into action and whipped me to the back of the line. My cell-mate, she spared me no attention, just held onto my wrist. The only doors bolted from the outside swing open, not even a second had passed and they moved.

My free hand I hold in front of my face, expecting the sun to blind me. There is no difference. I create some space between my fingers. Grey. Dull. That is the sky. A historic painting, no life present, if boring was a thing it would be that. The sky. A blanket of clouds. Judging from its thickness, the night sky or the Red Sun wouldn't be able to peek through.

Since stepping outside, the faces concealed before reveal faces of wet rags; not a smile nor a breath of positivity in the energy they just about manage to drag their feet with. My cell-mate loosens her grip and I take one step forward through a gap between two women. They continue walking unaffected to my intrusion. Still curious whether they are faking it or not, I wave my hands over their eyes. Neither of them   stumble. I look to my hand wondering if I am truly a ghost, then stifled a chuckle. At this point I wouldn't be surprised if they had a programmable chip in their backs following the code of those keeping them in this daze.

I step back to the young girl's side skimming over the torn paper to broken glass and cigarette butts littering the sunken roads we walk. The shadows that tower over our path are from caved in buildings. That seems to be the design, they don't crumble neither, all of them bending to the same point above us as though we are the heart and they the ribcage. The blocks around them are surrounded by armed soldiers similar to Tamari; the only difference is they wear close-fitted hoodies, loose trousers and their only weapons, a baton and a gun hooked across their chest. Though small, the greatest weapons and technology were just that; I glance at my silver ring in comparison. The women have their hair slicked back in a bun, whereas the men have their faces covered up to their eyes. Their outfits, I like, giving me ninja but special agents vibe. Though not so impressive in contrast to our warrior attire, they do give off a chilling aura. They hold my eye contact; if I continued looking I figured I'd become like those in front.

Speaking of front, I skid to a stop leaning back. "A waterfall." The girl runs behind me, pushing me on. "That's where they are taking us."

Much worse, it's massive, shrouded in green fog.

"No, I can't ..."

"You have no choice," she retorts.

When everyone breaks formation, she eases off me. They squeal, rushing to drink the water hands cupped to their mouths. Many submerge their bodies under, the thick grime and one would imagine stench, rolls over the cuts and grazes on their shoulders, elbows and knees. The water a mixture of clear, grey and red, I bite my bottom lip just thinking about all the toxins they are allowing into their stomachs. Being this cruel to themselves, feeling desperation, something I feel too, I wander closer. Licking my lips, how good it would feel to wet my throat, swallow something more than stale saliva. A yearning, to look pass the impurities, lose myself in this disgusting, primitive state. I raise a hand. The water pools in the middle, then elevates, closer and closer to my lips. So close, the stench starts to bother me. That's all it took for me to throw it away, back to where it came from.

"I just can't do that to myself." My shoulders cave.

The person beside me, a little too excited slapped at the water, some sprayed onto my face. The hesitation I felt before, swipes away with my tongue on my bottom lip. Mistake. I should have used my hands. No, they were wet too. The taste, just like the smell, revolting. Like a panting dog, I hanged my tongue out, spitting, spitting anything that swelled on top. Gritty, I bend up my face, "could this get any worse?"

I suppose to these people, who only know this way of life, they can trick their minds into believing this is fresh, healthy water, but from where I come from this would be on the opposite end of it. For a waterfall to be so defiled, this must mean the people in charge lack the innate connection to take care of Mother Nature's child.

Seconds later, my chains are yanked — beyond the waterfall. I jerk shuddering from the freezing water; the memories that surface, gasping I cower. The restriction of my throat, hands, thrashing about; my "help" bubbling through the water. Drowning. Again. Slipping away from life into the pits of darkness. Yet, a hand pressing against mine, her face in line with my vision ...

The nightmare fades.

I had collapsed to my knees. She stares, a solemn expression, no wide eyes, no questions voicing. When she helps me to my feet my first thought is to look to the sky. My heart relaxing. The sky a pitiful expression of my clouded mind, "I want to go home." The cry of wanting to return to the walls that have always kept me safe, with my loved ones and companions, "I want Dakarai to wipe this all away as if it were only a terrible dream." My shoulders remain low.

Our scenery has improved to a corridor of glass panels, on the other side there are rooms containing beds and chairs, alcohol and whirling lights. The ground is paved with limestone patterned with black arrows. Not a single soldier is in sight — unless they had taken off their uniform. I wipe my eyes dry with the back of my hand. Their skin is the same as Tamari, albinos', if not paler, blue veins running through their faces. In this open room, I squint -– not in confusion, but in disbelief. Everywhere, the scrawny naked bodies of couples are 'making the beast with two backs', oblivious to all around them, maybe well aware, this is the show they have been advised to put on. I clench my jaw refusing the bile up my throat. The dim red-light guiding us pass them doesn't help. From my studies about Earth, I'm convinced this is their representation of hell; temptation in its most sickening form. Slaves to their uncontrollable desires, as they engage in constant intercourse, bound in matrimony with their evolved savage nature. A sick cycle to be in complete submission to. A couple of times, I make the same mistake again, looking into their bloodshot eyes. I regretted the move immediately. The men, in particular, run their pierced tongues along their sharp teeth and fingers.

"Disgusting."

"Mhm" the girl agreed. I go to cover her eyes. "Nothing new, look at the ground if you have to." I wanted to follow her advice until I heard the cheers, the curses and my whole focus zoomed into the gladiator stadium. Where people were scarce before the waterfall, in here, there are too many to narrow down to the thousands. Live and in the flesh, they are feasting on the objects of their excitement. Out of their seats, stamping their feet, I just about make it to the empty stands we are ushered to, closest to the stage, in one piece. Two fighters beat each other senseless. The smaller male with a cleanly shaven head kicks dirt into his opponent's face thus prying on his arm.

"Ooou," the crowd goes as his arm limped from its socket.

I know these tactics: deceive and then attack outside of the pattern you trick your opponent into following. The ruthless and more agile kind, where their eyes follow the bait, falling short, exposing their defence. The big guy rushes at his opponent as he snaps his arm back into position. In a swift move, the small guy catches his opponent in a headlock and breaks his neck. They both fall to the ground, and the crowd goes quiet.

"I guess everyone was expecting the bigger guy to win. Understandable. But muscle isn't everything. Still ..."

"The bigger guy was just big for nothing." My thoughts are finished from a zombie, he had snapped from the spell.

Two soldiers lower the barrier, removing the winner and the dead body. A loud horn blows, two more people are thrown out onto the battlefield; one muscular guy with bruises that seem to form an extra layer of skin and a meagre brown-skinned girl with shoulder-length silver hair. The horn blows again; they circle each other like wild hyenas. When they attack, I'm at the edge of our barrier, gripping the metal tight. Springing to action, she works his legs, her arms on guard. Though they are thick, she seems to have the power of an ox, every kick, from the bottom of her feet to the top loosening his flesh. The slaps alone has me wincing. His arms unlike hers are strong and wherever possible he gives her a good beaten. As they advance then back off the blood trail thickens till their feet are covered in it.

On the timer hanging in the air, the digits read two minutes; the fight ends.

I expected it to finish much sooner despite their obvious differences. A man of his calibre, so tall and heavy, shouldn't be fighting a woman of a smaller and lighter build but the way she dealt with him and the roaring of the crowd, gender didn't matter. All that did was who could satisfy them plus win.

When the muscular guy fell, the thud was deafening. The chained around me weren't surprised, some huffed, others moved to the back of us. It's clear everyone was familiar with her. From the way she had held his head, smashing it in to no end on the ground, jamming her fingers into his eye sockets, she was a beast. Ruthless, her humanity, where was it? Regardless of such savagery, I couldn't look away, I had to see this side in all its horror, I had to be prepared for what more I would encounter. Even when his skull turned to pulp, her hands retained the tingling from the constant hammering. The blood that dripped from her fingertips she wiped onto her chest.

When she bows before the crowd, her hold over me breaks.

She stands there, soaking up her triumph, hands to the sky bathing in the water they flash at her. The cruel smile smeared with blood, I watch paint across her face. If Dorian Gray had a twin, it would be her.

She licks her lips, the savage still apparent.

I stiffen. Her gaze, she is looking at me. I, amongst thousands and thousands of people, she turns her body to attend to. And with becoming aware of me, her smile took on a new form, so wide with eyes so dark. A challenge. A new fascination. An opportunity.

"She's found her target." A teenage girl, probably a year or two younger than me backs away. "Better you than me."

"She can try," I mutter under my breath. "Test an Elite Supreme Warrior and see what happens." In the face of such courage, a quiet voice at the back of my mind whispers, *she has killed though, I am pure, hueman, all morals and values go out the window with her.*

After her full assessment, she shifted to the man that seemed to matter most amongst the crowd. Still wearing his shiny black shoes with his royal attire slung across one arm covering the other.

"Who knew the dead could fit so perfectly into the living?"

A ripple. Perfect-not. His image is tearing. Something struggling to hide, would not be kept at bay any longer — the real person the crowd marvels at rather than the man I see. The true leader and ultimate savage of this world. He rises, one after the other, everyone bows in his direction. Except for me. By bowing to your kidnapper, you give him the power to control you. "What kind of princess would I be if I embarrassed myself in that way?" I grit my teeth.

Although my mind scrambles to make sense of this deception or reality, I know one thing for sure, I have done what no one else has. Even though I'm smack in the middle of it, wanting to be as far away from this place as possible, I still manage to relish in the thought that I will be the first to bring news of their survival ... or a somewhat partial one.

This was the assignment: uncover the truth to the Sixth Dynasty's disappearance, whoever has survived report back to my superiors. The first step has been taken; the Sixth Dynasty lives. So far, at least one has shown his face. Joy swells in my heart as I picture the pleased look on my father's face, I would be worthy of his approval from then onwards. I would be much more than a pretty face, and a Princess of the

First Dynasty; as capable as a man. The sly smile on my face doesn't last long.

A sack is shoved over my head. Once again, I'm held captive in the dark.

Tamari kicks my knee, I buckle from the force. The chains around my hands scorch the well-polished floor. My eyes roll, grinding my jaw. I may not be bowing to The Prince, but I am for sure at his feet. With increasing boredom, I click my tongue trying to make as much noise as possible to irritate him. He doesn't show the slightest bit of emotion. My thoughts exactly, "even the living could still be dead inside."

He flashes me a smile meant to warm my heart as it would other girls. A boyish grin with small dimples not far from his jawline.

"How did you like the entertainment, Princess Calista?" He with utter care pours fresh, crystallised-brown liquor into his thin glass. He swirls and smells it before taking a sip. His gaze falls to mine with the same darkness I had witnessed in every one of his citizens. Or shall I say, prisoners?

"You know who I am?" I look him up from toe-to-head. If that's what he calls entertainment, who knows what he calls education, probably an arrow through the heart for every question answered incorrectly. Ah, that's right he's a fake, who knows what role he is playing.

"You think a lot, I'm sure you have many questions. Ask away." A chair of light shoots from the ground welcoming him to sit.

Like hell I do. I project my thoughts with the pressing of my lips.

"What am I doing here? Where am I?"

"And she speaks ... you almost had me worried there." He holds his breath for a moment before continuing. "You already know, Kimarr, after all, it was you who found *us*, not the other way around."

I scowl.

"Am I a fool? Kimarr is deserted, has no vegetation and walking zombies. This place, has albinos, addicted to pleasures and hold fights for entertainment."

"I know this is all very hard to believe, but that's the way we've designed it. Soon enough you will see things the way we intend it. We have big plans for you."

"I don't care. This is a violation of my rights. No one should be treated like this, especially me. When my family catches wind of this, they will most certainly have your head."

His chair tips him into my face, a finger sliding under my jaw. "But will they find out, that is the question?" It's smooth but rough. I don't want to think about the blood that has pooled on them. He grips my jaw, squashing my lips together, holding it in a position to meet his gaze.

"By the time I am done with you, you are going to thank us for our concern." My mind flickers back to when Tamari noted they had been expecting me. Whatever they want me for, it doesn't look like they are just getting started. Something tells me what they have planned began a long time ago.

"We'll be in touch."

"He who does not look ahead, remains behind."
— African proverb

4
EARTH

{Dakarai}

S tepping beyond the veil protecting Acirfa onto Earth is the easy part. The hard part, echoed in my heart all the problems of my inner world settling upon one person. I squeezed my palms together at the thought that she might not be safe, that she got herself into a bind once again. And with her brother Khari by my side, this only makes my heartache worse. It is always better for her to be accompanied by at least one of us on these assignments, not that she doesn't have the ability, she did succeed in becoming an Elite Supreme Warrior, it's just. She's a woman after all.

Tears prickle in my eyes as autumn's breeze welcomes us. Orange-red leaves scurry to the far corners of the worn-out grey pavements. Graffiti mauls the withered walls stretching pass the reach of the streetlights. The paint drips with monstrosity rather than beauty, the only decent attraction are the holographic discs of light illuminating them from the base. The street light beside us flickers, shadows dancing through its hands. A full moon floats across the cloudless sky.

The portal we arrived through shimmers out of sight with the invisible veil.

"Earth." I tasted the word. The one most like ours but a baby in comparison. From our teachings to our reality on this foreign plane, we'll get first-hand experience. "Let's see how great, or shambolic, Earth can be."

We roll down our sleeves covering our Eye of Horus, flipping our hoods over our heads. In one of the holographic discs, I use as a mirror to alter my appearance. The aim is to look older, fit the role I've been given on Earth. Being eighteen years of age, not a hair on my babyface, this is necessary. Just a few tweaks here and there: chiselled jaw always work, and a bit of a stubble, nothing dramatic.

Khari chuckles, rubbing his hands together, blowing into them like a technician does his laptop after it has gathered a considerable amount of dust through its fan.

"You are alright, you already look your assigned age."

"It is not my fault you cannot grow a few hairs. Do not worry my brother, you will get there." Chuckles again, "I doubt any time soon."

I laugh off his sarcasm.

It seems we haven't prepared adequately for this drastic change in the weather. Knowing of Earth's temperatures and being subjected to them are two different things in comparison to what we are used to on Genapa. When it was cold, it wasn't enough to wear more than a t-shirt let alone wear layers upon layers of clothing, our skins were thick enough. Or maybe that was just Aelburn.

We have landed in London, England. The passengers we spot walking by have their hands thrust deep into their jogger pockets, searching for any bit of warmth that could soothe their tired muscles.

As we exit the alley onto Rushey Green Road, a strong scent of tobacco and weed hangs around us. I bury my nose in my hoodie, almost coughing from its thick cloud. A group of boys with their belts below their waists and hats that shield their stoned eyes nod in our direction. We return the gesture, settling into our cover with ease. They cross the road and disappear under the statue of the big black cat. Men and women, dressed smart, pour into the Broadway theatre. They laugh and chat loud enough for everyone within a two-mile radius to hear every word of their conversation. The cars zooming by over the speed limit, trying to beat the traffic light before it changes to red, is like a quiet new born baby in comparison.

Even through all of that noise, I still slip back into my mind.

How is she doing? Calista, she refused to disclose the nature of her assignment. Such an act of defiance, it really irked me then. From going to sharing everything about these things, to absolute silence really left a hood over my eyes. To not see her, feel the certainty that she would make it through this time. Ah the feeling ... like a ticking bomb in my brain.

What did she have to hide?

The look she gave me when I tried to press the answer out of her. The shrugging of her shoulders, raising them as high as the top of her pointed ears, her arms spread wide, eyes rolled to the ceiling.

"Leave it alone Dakarai," she had sighed. And when I didn't she slipped her fingers around my neck, playing with the thick cornrows that rested on my shoulders, her lips inches from my ears.

"Calista." My jaw clenched, I faltered. She knew my ears were sensitive, she played such weakness to her advantage, even so I would not forget — what she secretly swore not to reveal.

This is the first time we've been separated on assignments. It is strange, almost like she has deserted me. There's a vacant space by my side, a constant reminder of our unpleasant separation.

From that day when her family took mine in, and I laid eyes on the thick curls framing her oval-shaped face, the inquisitive stare in her light brown eyes, I knew this was the beginning of something wholesome. Something I had been deprived of. I was enfolded in a loving embrace as if I was a long-lost sibling of theirs. It helped after the life I had lived.

Khari touches my shoulder; I snap back to reality.

The first Earthling we encounter happens to be my neighbour. When we walk into our apartment on the ninth floor, she is coming out of her own. A quizzical look displayed across her face -— eyes small, eyebrows lowered.

"Her vibe ..."

"Chilling, yet soothing," Khari agreed.

"Something is off as if she wears a mask amongst these humans but is not from around here."

Khari straightens enjoying her inquisitive stare. A smirk plays across his lips as he admires her curvy figure, a knuckle pressed to his mouth. Her small black heels click together as she smooths her pencil skirt.

The girls back home loved Khari, so in his eyes, he didn't think the females here would be any different. Once a player always a player, or as he likes to call it ... a man who has a way with women. Being the Prince of the First Dynasty, even without such a title, his charisma and robust character are a real draw for any woman that lays eyes on him. This one, however, appears immune to his charms.

Her silver-grey eyes notices the way Khari's thick reddish-brown locks rub against his defined jaw as he removes his hood. Khari caresses the half-formed stubble around his mouth. She continues to admire his broad shoulders and his six-foot-three build as she folds her arms across her chest. Khari's dark brown eyes stares into hers – much further than her physical form. When she shifts her attention, unlinking whatever union they had, her arms loosen. I release an, "ah" knowing she has found her target, smiling at the baby hairs fraying at my hairline. The stud earring in my right ear glistens in the ceiling light, almost willing her to take that step I know she refrains from.

"Hi, I'm Tahir." Khari steps out of the doorway, his gloved hand outstretched. She cocks her head to the side, a smile parting her full brown lips. "You don't look like a Tahir," she says with a honeyed voice that paralleled her midnight skin. Khari lets out a low chuckle.

She slips her bare hand in his as her eyes meet mine. "And you are?"

I place my hand on Khari's shoulder steering him into the apartment. "By the looks of it, your new neighbour." My eyes slip to her blazer, a name tag reading: Maliyah. I give her the satisfaction of knowing my name, proceeding to shrug, "Michael." She makes a sound of disbelief, shaking her head. Whether she believes us or not, that doesn't matter. She flicks her bone straight hair over her shoulders taking off.

I shiver, something is definitely not right about her. Somehow while looking at her silhouette in the distance, Calista came to mind. "How uncanny."

"Let's get to it."

Inside, there's a square box Khari empties out on the small table. Our false identities are tucked into envelopes. Khari is Tahir Moore, a bartender/mixologist. I'm Detective Michael Williams. Since Khari is twenty-four, he doesn't need to do much to fit into his role.

We create a mood board with the description of the assignment at its centre. The task:

"To observe and monitor the Earthlings, looking out for potential threats to Genapa, Acirfa."

"Easy enough, right? Not even close." I doubted even before leaving Aelburn.

"I wonder what is concealed, Father is trying to unravel. Why else would he send us?"

"I heard there may be confidential information that was leaked concerning how to infiltrate Acirfa. This doesn't make much sense, the shield is supposed to be impenetrable with the Blue star sealing the gates. But. If this is true, how did they get it, are they from our world?"

Khari presses his knuckles with his thumbs. "By all means, whoever they are, they must stay far away from Genapa."

Later, when my head touches my pillow, it doesn't matter that I'm in an unfamiliar environment. My body melts into the mattress, dripping into the other world — the dream realm. The place I visit every night to no end; a constant that has been in my life since that disaster. The purple haze circulating my head, dances across my eyes. Then sifting through my fingers. The dream, within a dream, that has always been a nightmare. The haze illuminating my black veins remains as a reminder of how I've been tortured, tainted, taunted through my powerlessness.

Red sand caked between my toes; a boy shouts my name. His arms powering him forward, my heart explodes through my ears. He's doing something, waving, mouthing, but how could I move when the thing I see; the eyes that pierce my heart paralyses my mind. The cruel smile twisting his lips. The red-light aimed at my head. A beam of danger, death, despair.

To move.

To dodge.

To make great efforts to survive.

How can I when my kingdom is in ruins? My people served a cold separation from life. The animals hearts bombed out of their chests. Who am I to survive as the sole heir to a throne decimated? Who am I?

His hand outstretched, head shaking with a firm no, my value — I am hopeless.

When the trigger releases, silent, I welcome it through the smoke it erupts from. The bullet zipping through the air.

This is to be it; the end. This madness; destruction; abomination will cease. Everything will reset.

I close my eyes.

By the sheer force of its power I'm knocked to the ground. But the weight of it rolled off me.

"No." I twitch onto my side, the realisation hitting me. The life I wished to sacrifice had been replaced with another. My custodian, "Tadaaki, why?" His body lifeless, I shake it, the tears falling like meteors. "It was supposed to be me."

My trembling hands tried to cover his still eyes. My vision blurring, that's all I picture. His corpse; his death; his murder.

The aching hole in my heart forces me awake. He was like my brother first before custodian. To take my place in blood, the oath we made in honour of our brotherhood, I would beg the deities to return him to me. "It wasn't fair. My kingdom falling. His death. Someone must pay."

My motto is always move forward never back, yet this memory drags me back to the past as if there is a lesson to learn.

A time when I was physically inexperienced, incapable of even protecting myself. What could I learn from the one who pointed with such precision and execution after invading my home? Why must I learn anything at all?

From that day forward, since the First Dynasty took me in, I have pushed myself past my limits to at least become half the man Tadaaki was becoming. I would never deny myself again, make the same mistake; devalue my worth; my purpose in this level of existence.

I will be a protector of my people.

"Don't judge my chapter by the story you walked in on."

5

{Dakarai}

I t has been a month since our arrival on Earth.
Khari has been busy at the nightclub in Canary Wharf,
chatting up the ladies keeping drunkards at bay. I've worked
alongside my fellow intelligence mates solving homicides
and drug crimes. As fas as our assignment, it is a work in
progress. I'm beginning to think there might not be anything
after all. Maybe I'm a little too eager to get back home. Maybe
I'd hate to find something that would hold my attention
much more.

The majority of our time is spent interacting with the
Earthlings. I have had the distasteful pleasure in becoming
acquainted with Maliyah. She isn't what I expected, in fact,
the more we speak, the more she enters my space, the more
she reminds me of Calista. As such, because of their similarity
she's become ... manageable.

She has this youth to her but a mysterious glow of age and
wisdom. So when she told me a couple weeks back, "live a
little," and I believe she used the phrase, "YOLO: you only
live once," I couldn't help but laugh. She had noticed, how
uptight I was, all work and only work. Sleep, eat, exercise, and
survey the streets. For a young man, it was understandable

that she felt I needed to loosen up. My only thoughts were: "The sooner this assignment is over the quicker I can get to Calista." I know, I should be serious about this but the way my palms itched every night, there were no coincidences, something was up.

Still, Maliyah always amused me. If only she knew what was on my mind, she'd be less likely to run her mouth about people's lives she could not begin to understand. She would go to work every day and still find energy to be up in my business. I often wondered:

"How would it look, the thing or person Khari and I have been searching for? Would it be under our noses or yet to make its move?" This inspired me to let her closer. Close enough to ask her about the symbols around her neck and shoulder, to which she brushed them off as only tattoos she had gotten over the years. The ink, however, was golden, but in the light appeared black and to shift as though alive. Egyptian symbols, Adinkra symbols, there was really no limit other than they could only originate from Africa. Africa on Earth but when flipped be liken to what we have on Acirfa. Despite this, she was sneaky, I felt she was getting more out of me than I her. Like when she noted my apartment had an element of secrecy to it. Just the standard furniture -— settee, dinning table, cooker, bed -— white walls really.

"I'm a simple man." Was the only explanation I offered. She couldn't deny there were such people out there; many Earthlings had adopted the philosophy of minimalism.

Those symbols though, even without her under my observation pop into my mind. It wasn't just what I saw but the feeling of what was unseen. When I get some time I'm going to have to run an identity check on her, the Earth way and the Genapian way.

Incoming transmission.

I put down my cup of tea looking from our mood board to my opened hand, my Silver Ring jumping with a call and notification icon.

"Tahir ..."

"I'm sending over a video, get here as soon as you can." His feed cuts.

Video received. Opening.

The video starts from when Khari noticed her. I slip on a black jacket, with black gloves, grab my keys and take the first lift down to the car park. The lock releases and I hop on starting the engine on my motorbike.

Destination: WGA, Canary Wharf.

My Silver Ring connected to my helmet, on route, I let it play as I zip in and out of traffic.

It is a busy night at the nightclub. Khari had noticed a female in a hoodie approach the bar. She stood out in a club themed with suits and ties, heels and dresses.

"Her clothes is kind of a sign something is wrong but not enough," I mutter.

Her fingernails are clean, trimmed, the sides long, the top short. There is a gold band ring around her middle finger, she isn't homeless I take it. When she removes her hood, revealing her greenish-grey eyes, Khari in a trance, excuses himself from a customer. Her eyes become like the parting of two seas as a goddess makes her entrance.

"Smart brake activated."

Beeeeep!

I lurch forward, my front wheel evading his front tire.

"Oi, watch it." The man shouts his cigarette dropping ash down his shirt. His free hand over his window twitches to give me the finger. He speeds off.

"That was close." I shake my head banishing her eyes as the red warning light fades from my helmet screen.

"What can I get you, beautiful?" Khari's smile is wide as he throws the hand towel over his shoulders. She rubs her hands over her face, huffing.

"A gin martini please."

"Mysterious, I like it. Coming right up."

The young woman turned just enough to still be facing Khari but using her peripheral to find someone else. A man, not far from an exit door to her right his glass raised with one corner of his lip. The overhead lights reflecting in his eyes forced them to grow small. With his other hand he tipped his cowboy hat. She returned to the bar, "careful there," Khari chuckled, drawing back the v-shaped glass he slid to her on a napkin. He registered her nervousness as did I but she played it off, picking it up from its neck. She dips a finger, swirling the liquid.

"Thank you, Khari," she whispers.

His eyebrow's knit together; I jam my brakes.

"Sorry you must have me confused; my name is Tahir." Removing one hand from the counter, he pointed at his name tag. She smiled shaking her head.

That's when he had called me, his finger wriggling in the motion of riding a bike. It initiated our emergency signal. Had Khari been compromised? Still, I wondered, this was a little too easy. For her to know his name just like that. Her eyes, it had to have something to do with it.

"I need your help; they're hunting me," she grabbed his arm, a grey mark spreading like a rash from his wrist to his elbow. Toxic is the only word for such a reaction. This woman must be toxic; her eyes have also shifted from green to a sickening grey.

Revving my engine, I take off with even greater urgency.

There is something about the way her hand flexes around his forearm, the stress in and around her eyes. Khari has always been cautious of people touching him without warning, so when he starts to pull away, her touch or maybe her eyes, the haste, has him squeezing the counter top.

She looks at the man still watching her, whispering, "meet me around back in twenty minutes." Then disappears through the crowd.

A few words are left on the napkin, and the mark on Khari's arm fades. The language -– if he could call it that -– are a bunch of upside-down numbers and letters. They form a spiral with four lines extended from the centre diagonally with the ends finished in tight curls.

When I burst into the club, uttering a few excuse mes around dancing men and women on my way downstairs to the underground section, Khari slips the napkin into his back pocket. A customer pulls him away and he gives me a nod. There isn't much to assess; the energy she should have left behind is vacant. No buzzing skims my ears, not even the hairs on my neck stand on end. Everyone has a magnetic field, some energy to identify them by no matter what species they are.

"Anything?" Khari raps a knuckle on the counter.

"She must have cloaked but given how edgy she was, I doubt it." I zero in on the grey mark that has reappeared as a coded message. Khari compares the design to that on the napkin.

"I've never seen code like that. If Aziza were here, would she know?"

"Who lil sis, as one of the top Scholar student in Aelburn I wouldn't put it pass her. When we get more info I'll send her something to work on. For now, let's head out, it's a good thing my break just starts."

We go through the fire escape and spot her like a feral cat scratching her skin till it is more than red. Just the sight has my skin feeling a little irritated. In comparison to what I viewed earlier, the differences are astonishing. The one out here is bothered by the cars blowing their horns, tires screeching, even the faint drops of water from the building roof. And her eyes, the light has gone out. She's moving, but passive in her own body. Trapped like a scared animal running from its predator; she can feel a presence; smell what awaits her. When I touch her shoulder, she jumps back like she had been shocked with barbed wire.

"Great, you're here Dakarai." Hope fills her voice. My eyes narrow as she continues. "I've only got a few minutes."

I overlook her knowledge of my identity and switch to detective mode. "Start with your name and why you are here?"

"I'm Sarah. This company ... my life is in danger."

"Maybe we should find somewhere safe we could talk, I can get you some water to calm your nerves." Khari tries to catch her eyes, they only look behind her.

"Here is fine, Khari. I haven't got much time." She circles to a dumpster and rattles her fingers on its handle. Then she clenches her fist, her sweaty palms squeaking. "The SYSTEM it must be stopped. I can shut it down. Get you all out. Calista ... even her ... she needs to be here too."

The mention of Calista piques both of our interests. It still comes as a shock that she knows information no Earthling could have guessed.

"You don't believe me, I get it, but we aren't meant to be here. This..." She stops, her eyes redden with the tears that has taken a breather at the surface. "He's here." The streetlight at the end of the alley bursts, light and fragments of glass spraying the ground. I spin to guard her, Khari a little ahead of me.

"Do you hear that?" I whisper. Amongst the people walking by laughing in the distance and bottles smashing against the ground, there is a cutting sound -– the sharpening of a blade mixed with a grinding machine. We stare, through the darkness, it is hard to make out anything. I'm seconds away from activating my Eye of Horus. Sarah goes ballistic swivelling with no bearing she smashes into my back. She screams. A voice she hears I begin to hear.

"Sarah. You were warned." It sang, then shouted. If I could see him his mouth it would be wide open dripping with saliva.

"We are out of time." Her breath falls from her lips.

Zing.

That sound; a blade. It cuts through the air. The moment it glinted just skinning my ears it penetrated her neck. She slumped into my arms, quaking with her skin shrivelling up. A young body aged to a corpse that should be long decomposed.

"The codes are everything." Her last words, eyes glossing over. Her lips had not moved, she had spoken directly into our mind.

Who was she?

Who had sought to kill her?

A shadow catches in our peripheral; Khari bolts after a man running away from the scene. He frisbees his hat behind him, Khari jumps kicking up on the wall to land on his feet. It implodes in a dustbin. I follow Khari using his eyes through his Silver Ring. He triples his steps a couple metres, hooks the man by his collar and thrust him high up against a wall.

"Who are you?" Khari isn't breathing half as heavily as the man. Still, once he relaxes, not a word. Khari tightens his grip, using a hand to pat him down for his weapon. The deeper he searches, the hollower the pockets get. When he looks back into the man's eyes, they have lost their humanity; an empty shell. They are as deep and gaping as his pockets. All Khari sees is dark holes. The biggest of them all is the man's mouth. Something grips him. I widen my eyes, what could it be? Something unseen. It moves like a protective resistance to Khari's attempts to stand strong, maintain his hold. A repelling force that couldn't be counteracted with strength alone. "Hang on, I'm coming."

"No, stay with her!" Khari stumbles back, his hands drop to his side.

The man laughs, his mouth stretching, the tonsils at the back of his throat shaking. But there's a light, where he swallows — Khari leans in, I hold my breath. A sea of codes; white and blue cyphers. It wasn't light at all. And something is feeding off it, a virus, it's black and gooey. They appear to have a symbiotic relationship.

"What is that thing?" I gasp.

"Not a man for sure." Khari drags one foot back, one hand crossing his chest. "I shouldn't have questioned her sanity. All these codes. What are you?"

The thing, bows his head, his moon-eyes lifted. "I'm The Messenger." Its voice, a human possessed with a dark soul, sticks as if submerged in water. It shakes off the wall, his foot elongating as it strides to Khari. Sarah seems heavier in my arms, I move her to the ground.

"I'm The Messenger; message delivered." It claps its hands in Khari's face, he pivots kicking his back foot forward striking his head. It goes through. Then "Boo."

I couldn't tell whether the sound came from its mouth, one thing I knew, his head — its deflating. What undefined features it had pressed to mush. Khari cursed, two-stepping back as his dripping face, body, like runny paint on a canvas fell to the ground in a pool of slimy skin. The droplets of water along the concrete floor it sucks up, transforms with, swirling down the drain.

A bright light cuts across my eyes.

"Tahir..." I shield my face from the grey light emitting from Sarah's body. "You need to see this."

Khari uses the wind to portal back. I lift the bottom of her hoodie, a blurred barcode lines her spine. It focuses, her name is an acronym: *Signed Android Relaying A Hijack.*

"Hijack?" Khari squats to get a closer look. He hovers a hand.

"Don't tell me ... android ... hijack? She's not human."

Something bangs into a dustbin, tipping over glass and plastic bottles. The culprit a cat, its fur grows tall then it disappears as a shadow through the wall. Weird. Cats can do such things?

"Let's figure this out back at the apartment. Being out here —" Khari's eyes scan the walls. Earth love's their surveillance, especially the hidden-in-plain-sight kind, so I get it. Fixing her clothes, I roll her onto her back. "This looks bad."

It does but what she said holds more weight. It pulls at my thoughts, playing tricks, did we hear correctly? This mention of a SYSTEM. I'm no Tech N9ne so it's difficult to pull up records on the Unidatabase to cross-reference this across the galaxy. Either way, could this be the link to our assignment? It does sound like some virtual stuff, not an imminent threat to our planet.

Still, must our reality be questioned? That is what she meant right, this SYSTEM, something tangible that holds us where we are now?

This reminds me of the dream I had that night we first arrived on Earth. Shortly after my nightmare, it felt like I had slipped into a coma. My eyes sealed shut; my body collapsed against my pillows. And where my mind had taken me, a memory or just a dream, wherever I was, being strapped to a metal chair was where it all started and ended. I was not alone, there were other metal chairs with limp bodies, I just about made this out through the mirror I gazed up at. The lights were bright, blinding. The walls were white, glassy. I had this feeling of being watched; I wanted to turn my head; stop the aches stabbing my eyes. Yet, being confined, the only clear thing I could focus on was the needle in a gloved hand moving in on my neck. The liquid squirting when pressed. I moaned, "what are you doing to me? Let me go." But there was no sound, just silence, my lips glued. The needle in my neck. That's where it ended. At least I thought it did when I woke up gasping.

Khari stands. "You drove the motorbike right?"

"Yeah, why?"

"I will catch an uber, you make your way back. I've got something to check."

"Wait, you cannot leave me like this. I've got a body and Maliyah, what if I run into her?"

"So cloak, that is nothing you cannot handle my brother."

He slaps my back grinning, taking off thereafter before I could get in another word.

Reluctantly, I wave a hand shielding her body, locate my motorbike and make my way back.

"Speak less than you know, have more than you show."
- Shakespeare

6

{Dakarai}

Khari didn't return home that night. Wherever he had disappeared to, my mind was too preoccupied to ask. After all, I was alone in our apartment with a sort-of-dead-yet-inactive-body. She had not changed since that night. Her barcode, insignia whatever had dimmed but behind my eyes whenever I looked at her, I couldn't shake it from my thoughts. Of all colours, why grey? Gloomy, sad, all the lower grade emotions I'd rather not be reminded of, why did it have to be grey? Our strange meeting, how else to describe it, grey, something lacking?

That night too, tossing and turning, too alert to fall asleep, I travelled to the living room, stood in front of our mood board and wrote till I collapsed. Right there, not far off from her body covered with a blanket. If anyone were to ask me what I had scribbled, I would have said, "I don't know." The trance I was in was like a headache and it stayed that way. The only thing worthy of being recalled, always at the forefront of my mind, the nightmare; his hollow eyes, gaping mouth, his voice that spiked my heart. The message he said to be delivered, what was it?

That's what I wrote in clear bold letters.

What was the message?

It had passed us in a blur.

Was it really meant for our ears, Sarah's, or someone, something concealed?

"Dakarai?" Someone shakes my shoulders. A little too rough, whatever, it was necessary, I was slipping again. "You don't look so good." Slipping back into my mind, while my body remained on autopilot.

"Khari?" He hooked an arm through mine straightened me up in the settee. "When did you get here?"

Had it been days or weeks since I last saw him?

"Not long ago. What is all this?" The scattered paper around the mood board he picked up one after the other, some he gave a little shake, pressing them out. He clips them to the edge of the board, runs a finger down to the centre. Tap. His finger. My heart. The one question I couldn't keep at bay: *What was the message?*

"Good to see you are alright though." My voice sounded strange to my ears like someone else had taken control, pushing buttons that were alien to me.

"Yeah ..." He's more focused on the board. "When did you do all this? It looks ..."

"Scary." I swallowed dragging myself to stand beside him. He's nodding, then shaking his head. "That, but ..." Whatever he wanted to say he left it drifting in the air. It didn't matter, I probably would have done the same.

Everything I had written was in capitals, it covered the top sheet of the paper. Everything concerning Earth, nothing for Acirfa. Everything that was confusing; nothing that held answers.

"What's the White Room?"

"Something." I mutter. "Something scary."

In the mirror, hanging on the wall, I stare at my appearance. Red eyes, eyelids sliding further and further; maybe I was the scary one. After that night, what am I becoming? There's an itch I cannot scratch, a thorn in my side; I see but I'm blindfolded. This SYSTEM ...

"This SYSTEM she mentioned, you seem to have a lot of thoughts about it." He drew the connection between the White Room, the SYSTEM and Sarah; a triangle. The empty space inside, my only focus, it tugs like it's the master pulling my strings. Khari stretches past my peripheral, the living room blurs pushing me forward. Something's ringing, someone's calling my name, but there's something through the whiteness, something opaque. Yet, if I squint, move closer would be transparent. The eyes I feel watching me, they'd step to me with a hand of information. Whatever I was missing, the murky waters in my brain; the resolution they offer. My hand lifting of its own accord, awaiting what comes from the invisible. Something soft swipes along the lines of my palms; white paint. It swirls, activating with its own life, curling into a ball. It rolls between my thumb and finger. I close one eye to zoom in on the string of green snaking along it with. They're like a train of codes. Glowing. Separating with vibrated spikes, combining with names and numbers all muddled. When it collapses almost at the same rate as my breath as a tightness grips my chest, there it is — the needle. The one that had appeared before, oozing with green codes.

Aim.

Shoot.

I jump back.

"Dakarai? Did you hear me?"

The needle is gone. "Huh?" I wipe the sweat from my brow, glimpsing my reflection then my hands. Nothing had changed. What was that?

"Your phone, it has been ringing."

My watch showed two missed calls. There's a notification, a text. It reads: Michael I don't know where you are right now why you can't pick up the phone. Regardless, I need you in my office ASAP.

An immediate call into his office. "This cannot be good."

"What isn't?"

I pat Khari's shoulder grabbing my jacket. "Gotta shoot, my lieutenant ... will catch up with you later."

"You sure you are well enough to ..."

The door slams behind me. In my right mind or not, this could not be delayed.

The traffic wasn't bad on my way to Gipsy Hill. I parked my bike, released my helmet from my head and lightly jogged into the police station. Greeting a few colleagues with mornings and hellos up the stairs on my way up to the third floor, I wondered what could be a matter of urgency. So far, my true identity has remained a secret. I haven't allowed any of my intelligence mates too close to even get a sniff; as far as my Silver Ring and everything else goes, it is all cloaked. The Earthlings can only see as far as there five senses. All is well there. The ones that are welcoming I make sure to build a good rapport with, the others well when they are up to their old tricks, I don't bite, not even a flinch. Like this one guy, always cracking his dry, pathetic banter, I usually brush him off with an applause. He loves it, always got his fingers hooked into his belt sticking his small belly out. The way I could grill him ...

One thing I can tell you, they all value skills, as they should. This is no profession to be messing around in. Lives are at stake every day and as the protective body of this city, duty holds the same importance as an Elite Supreme Warrior. Any slacking, one of your intelligence mates will be on your case before your lieutenant. Though I'm not here to please anyone, it is nice to hear about my competence.

I scan my fingerprint and enter our office. He is the first one craning his neck from his computer, his mouth clapping as I head for my desk to down half a bottle of water.

"Oi-oi, late night last night, where you been then ay? All red in the cheeks, don't tell me you're high?"

The only female, a shade lighter than me, pops out from her screen raising her eyebrows, nodding to the lieutenant's office. "He doesn't look so good."

"Yeah, you must have blew his trumpet this morning."

Inhale-exhale. I'm at his door, two raps with my knuckles, I'm in. My palms start to tingle.

"Come in, have a seat Detective Michael." His voice is soft, light-hearted much different to his usual authoritative and booming self. His tone is almost hushed as if the ears outside would be able to hear, when the blinds are closed and his sound-blocking device is already on. His eyes had yet to meet mine; the lump in my throat I struggle to swallow. This is the first time I've been in here with the doors closed. The open space where the sun normally makes its bed on the floor and the grey walls covered with holographic panels seemed too small. Grey, I'm really getting sick of that colour.

"What's up lieutenant, is everything alright?" I slip into the chair opposite him, keeping the unease out of my voice. He sucks in air through his mouth, stands to perch on the right side of his desk, one hand under his jaw the other swivelling the desktop to me.

"This showed up on my desk early this morning. What do you make of it?"

The look in Lieutenant Johnson's eyes reminds me of my Master Teachers' when disciplining unruly behaviour; not listening or ignoring instructions. Trouble has reached me. They scrutinise, the glare of a detective questioning his suspect. The chair seemed much harder now, the padding non-existent. Any comfort to settle the growing tingles, any diversion from the twisted truth I will be presented with, what did my Master Teachers' say?

"Play it cool."

"No matter how nerve-wracking it may be. No one can see how you are inside unless you give that away."

"Move through what is seeking you."

Move through it, I assure myself, licking my bottom lip.

He taps the computer screen. The blurred image shuffles to the beginning. I settle a hand on my leg.

Stay calm.

Just like I had guessed; Earth and their hidden surveillance. CCTV rolls the clip of Khari and I encounter with The Messenger and Sarah. The paranormal elements are misplaced; Earth hasn't advanced thus far. The device that had penetrated her throat, became a bullet; a natural death it seemed. The video thankfully cut when she fell into my arms.

There was no further evidence. The perpetrator gone in the wind.

This is sloppy of me. I should have checked the scene, I should have ...

"Detective Michael, at first, I couldn't make sense of it ... so I visited the scene myself to keep this all under wraps. Outside WGA, right? To my surprise, no body, no blood. Clean. So ... choose your next words carefully."

My eyes couldn't lift from the screen and I feared his eyes couldn't move from my throat where I strained to swallow.

"That night, Thursday 29th October 9:40 PM, what happened?"

This whole situation, this coincidence. I could clear it all up just like that with the snap of the finger. Make it all go away. Lieutenant would conk out for a bit, wake up slightly dizzy, a drunken feeling like he had gone to a rave with some mates and took it a bit too far. My face even he wouldn't be able to identify; Khari's too. We'd become a miscellaneous file; no one would know how it got there; no one would wonder what it really meant. Heck, it would feel like a virus taking over their whole database.

This situation, I glance at my Silver Ring and lion-claw bracelet. Disappear. Poof, a magic trick. That's what this could be. Even still, the fact would remain. Deep in my conscious, subconscious. Everything happens for a reason, right?

"Michael ..."

These events, no matter how strange, they've played this way for a reason. The grey walls look closer now, a thin sheet stretching from its bottom to its top. Similar to the veil a bride wears at her wedding. Though no ordinary veil, it contorts at its centre. Sinking into an abyss, a space of darkness. Then with light; the codes; the SYSTEM in text.

Everything happens for a reason; a system has a programme. To be aware of it; to be asleep to its methodology. What to do? Submit to what continues to follow or erase?

"Nothing." The lie slipped out of my mouth, so smooth, I bit the inside of my cheek. Lies. They never end well. They must be covered. Remembered. Strengthened. Lies ... I have never told one.

Lieutenant rubs his eyes dragging the skin down to his jaw then clasps his hands on his knee. I lean in, hands rubbing my thighs under the desk.

"Where is the body?"

"The video is fake."

The twitch that jumped from his left eye, I urged myself to continue.

"There was an assailant yes, but, no one died."

He couldn't stop staring; I couldn't keep still. My left leg bouncing. My heart just banging in my chest.

"You need some water, Detective Michael."

I wanted to decline. I wanted to ease off a bit on the acting. Wanted to do many things, but when your body is completely drained and your mind is offset from its equilibrium, all self-control just goes.

"Yeah mate, I'll get you that water."

I shake my head. "No."

He points a finger at me, presses his tongue to the middle of his top lip. "The state of you ..."

"Something did happen that night ok. I couldn't write a report because it's all fragmented. I can't tell fabrication from reality but all I hear is this mention of a SYSTEM."

His hand stops inches away from his door handle.

"This SYSTEM that has me imprisoned in it, that woman, hell lieutenant maybe even you. The man, assailant, he said she had escaped and he came with a message to take her back dead or alive."

"Detective Michael." He's pinching the bridge of his nose. "I'm sorry to hear this has happened to you but I'm going to need your badge."

The words I speak hold all my inner truth but of course to the ignorant, the none-the-wiser, it would be utter nonsense. The firmness of his jaw, the conviction in his eyes; the hard evidence he believed, the video he showed, it couldn't have been tampered with. That's what he thought even after checking the scene, the placement of the camera, lieutenant, "you've got to believe me."

"You looked fine earlier but this ... enough. I wasn't born yesterday and the fact that you thought you could insult me with nonsense about a system every blooming person could be trapped in. This is the 21st century. There have been many systems in place, monetary, service, you name 'em. I'm not buying this crap."

I feel his rage. His pride. Everything he wanted to hang over my head and force into my ears from behind me. A subordinate like me; the disdain just rubbing him out making him seem so insignificant. But maybe I'm just reading my own feelings. I should have just opted for the easy escape; the erase. The route always advised by my Master Teachers' when your back is against the wall. But with these things, nothing is truly erased, true to the natural order of balance and cycles, it always returns when you least expect it. So, having travelled so far, my hand red, the only course of action is none. Let the programme continue. Let whatever is meant to be, BE. Whether I believe or not, I'll play.

"Are you saying I'm frontin'?"

"Frontin', lying, whatever yes Detective Michael. You know what else I found at the scene."

He strides back over, unlocks the bottom draw at his desk and lifts out a see-through wallet. The contents: a single bullet. So small and long it might as well be a needle, but the rear end is lit up with a red circle.

"How'd you explain this?"

"The assailant." I shrug.

"It has your fingerprints."

I slam my hands on his desk, look him dead in the eyes. That cockiness, that smirk of resolution, gotcha it says.

"You said there was nothing at the scene, no blood."

"A pretty damn good job."

"You think a cleaning crew was hired to destroy ..."

He wags his finger. "No crew. A one man's job, maybe even two. Who was the other bloke?"

"Lieutenant, the SYSTEM, it's playing its tricks. My fingerprints aren't on whatever that is because I have never seen that in my life. It's not real."

He rubs the slippery material between his fingers then laughs. "That's a good one." Taking a seat on his chair he holds his free hand out. "Your badge Detective Michael, now?"

Sure.

I remove and weigh the small thing in my palm.

"I thought there was trust between us, this whole unit in fact. Whatever you're hiding under this fake facade of insanity, I'm going to give you some time to give me the truth." He pauses plucking the metal I did nothing to grasp. "You're suspended until further notice."

Compromised, for sake of a better word; that's me. Compromised, in more ways than one. He didn't need to kick me out, I was on my way out anyways. Lifting the grey walls with me, rippling the blinds, stirring the evidence he held in his hands and the unit's database. Every detail since my entry to my exit, even sucking out the voices that trailed behind me. If I looked back it would be chaos, but if I saw through their eyes, they only watched Detective Michael with a hand clutching his head stumbling out the office. Nothing more. Nothing about our conversation. Nothing about what had gone missing.

"Speak so that I may see you" - Socrates

7

{Calista}

In the prison house, the zombie-people are full of life, their stomachs almost too. On the ground floor, the food they're eating have this familiar scent to it like baked patties. Crisp, full of vegetable and peppery filling. The only light joy to my misery has my mouth watering. To taste what my mother loved to bake, be filled with warmth, love, care, just the appreciation of art that could be eaten. And captured in this blissful memory I'm stood in front of the winners of their fight. The broadest smiles on their faces, if they had wings they'd be soaring out of this place. Maybe this is as close to real food as it gets. I've seen what they serve them, I've only been here two days according to my wall strokes and the food never changes except for today. Always mush, it should be named vomit, it certainly looked like it. My hands limp at my side, I see pass them. I miss eating and drinking without restriction. I miss breathing in fresh air. I miss it all; freedom.

I stretch for a patty on one of the dusty trays; two fingers pinching the sides. The dust upsets my stomach, but the eagerness to taste real food motivates me to look beyond its surroundings. Lifting, I lick the cracks in my lip, but the excitement is fleeting. A whack on my hand, the sting; who dared? My eyes narrowed, I hold back the wince — there is no room for weakness in a hole filled with murderers. When I find my disturber, skimming over her bloodied feet to her cool eyes the set scowl on my face could not vanish. The grin that dances across her thick lips, the kind I should wipe away. Of arrogance. Her silver hair, how I'd love to return the slap to her head. She dared ... murderer or not ... I am not her toy. The white marks around her eyes crinkle.

"That's not for you. You did not earn it." She speaks to me as if I am a child and I have no mind of my own.

"Says who? Do you even know who I am?" Her attitude stinks, I resist the urge to turn my head focusing on what she stands in the middle of; the one taste that could energise me. With a sneer, she whispers, "it does not matter, everyone here is a nobody, and you are not excluded from the bunch." Up in my face, a small step, she towers a head taller. *"Do you know who I am?"* The light plays its tricks to her advantage increasing the ego she inflates.

"A nobody." I laugh walking over to a table. Standing there any longer I was sure she'd be asking for a fight. And with my stomach growling I was not about to have her know of my current weakness. Sadly, the ones closest their eyes flock to me when they hear the strange sound. I cover my lower half as if its pain is on show. The sighs though, a sad song sang by many rested in my heart; another day in this hole. My cellmate across from me stirs the slob on her tray. Supposedly, it is chickpea stew; I think not. They must think we are fools to believe anything they say.

"So, what did you do to end up in here?"

She looks at me tapping the table. I didn't think she would reply, but still, I had to try. She shrugs her shoulders. I exhale and run on the table with my chipped nails. It doesn't take much for me to get bored. When I'm not training, I am hanging out with my family, painting, or doing something creative. But here the possibilities are minimal. Through my off-beat gallops, the girl gets creative. Her small finger outlines her name in her food.

Myah.

"That is a lovely name." She smiles. The kind I like. The kind that should be returned. Not just polite but friendly. Out of the corner of my eye, I see the silver-haired girl approach me again.

What did I do to deserve her attention?

Maybe it is my radiant aura. She makes a show of circling me before she speaks.

"You know you are going to have to cut your hair." The bones she calls fingers she curls around my plaits. I stiffened that instant. No one ... something swelled in my chest. Like I have been violated, my skirt lifted by a vile beast. To touch my hair without asking first, to take it upon yourself to do as you please; I hold and swallow. All the distress and anger that cramped in my chest I hold in my rooted feet. Eyes staring at her shadow asleep on our table. Reel it back in. Unwind but stay on guard.

"By the looks of yours, I'd say I am quite fine." Hers, nothing a little flame can't handle; test me again. I dare you.

"Not nearly enough unless you want them to be used as reins on the battlefield."

My retaliation: a smirk. "I much prefer blades if I ever make it out there."

"Oh, you will, I will make sure of it." She tugs on my hair once more, and the fire that shouldn't be contained ignites within. In one move, I spin around and grab her hair, hauling it to the side. My nails deep in her scalp, the light above swoons over her cheek. She laughs licking her lips. I had failed; the puppet tormented by the one holding the strings.

"Missy has a temper. You might want to save that for the battlefield." I clench my jaw tearing her hair more my way. The pain doesn't seem to bother her. This is no surprise. She is the female joker after all. Paint her lips red and dye her hair green and you wouldn't be able to tell the difference. But, there's a twitch in her left hand. As she notice me trying to get a better look she forces it behind her. Remember that inflated ego, now that hand, what does she hide? As cruel as this world is, she is a Genapian, bred and climatized to this environment — her innocence I hope still lives. The one that has had to hide, had to cloak with a boastful manner. She the one I see like The Prince, covers another.

Tamari out of nowhere, separates us in a flash.

"You know the rules. Save it for the battlefield."

She gives me a final look, the savagery returning to her eyes. A burning desire I match. She to cover herself more with a kill; I to expose the root of that twitch. And so I smile, take a bite into the patty and continue on. Taking a seat, smiling, watching her back away still facing me. Knowing I've been her target since we've locked eyes, enlisted to her imaginary list; to be her next opponent. The idea might not be so bad.

"Embrace the God within you."

8

{Calista}

W hen it first manifested, I was about twelve. It took over my body not one inch after the other; at once, like I was covered in gasoline and a small flame had become a wildfire. I shook then, falling to my knees, and on the wet soil where I thought it would spread it did not. Though, they thought it would. My father. My peers. All the eyes that watched me, all the eyes that took several steps back half-turning away. I had only breathed and that breath came with fire. Well, the Blue Flame. One of my peers who had enough courage took a bucket and splashed me with some water. The Blue Flame only grew taller, they, heaved further away.

When I looked to my hands, through the tears that burned, the black spirals that didn't look half bad, the mixture between light and dark blue, all I thought, "beautiful. What was to be feared?" And so as my tears dried and I took that stand, I carried on walking. Out of our open training room. They must have thought I'd turn on them but they were no longer my focus. Why did I have to care for their reaction? The Blue Flame, Mother had told me about it. That was enough to make my steps light, to go to her for more answers.

She always said while her eyes were to the sky, "the Blue Flame is more than energy; a whole new life force that balances the host it inhabits." She could teach me control, teach me anything, if I could lend her my ear.

So since that day, whenever I showed for training, I became the stranger no one wanted to pair with. The darkness was their friend. They feared much more than injury; they feared the stories that were told in the villages, of the past, of the nightmares that could overtake their dreams. This was all irony to me. One of the first teachings for any initiate training for the ESW clan: fear is nothing. FEAR: false evidence appearing real. Move through it; stand firm. Who I had become to them, a challenge they should have taken advantage of, they evaded. If I were one of the Master Teachers, I would have taken note of their unworthiness even as a warrior-in-training.

I had had my challenge once before, it was Father who delivered it. At the top of a cliff, where the bottom could not be seen, only an endless stream of water and billowing white smoke. He wanted me to only see him, to breathe, prepare myself mentally; to take flight without caution; to feel and move past the five senses. But ever since I saw below to the light push he gave me, my heart was already in maniac mode gripping the cages of my ribcage shouting to be freed. So as I fell heavy against the air, the blur of colours to my side and up, I held on rather than let go. And when I smacked into the water, I knew something had snapped. Too delirious to feel the pain that should have jerked me above the surface I sank.

That day had always haunted me, though it was nothing in comparison to what my peers had gone through at least it happened and I survived.

Those that embraced my change were the children in the village. They welcomed me with bows, jumps and dances. One thing they always wanted from me: a trick. Though that was not its purpose, I performed to their cheers. A few harmless fireworks, established stars, and animals like cats rolling in the red soil and birds soaring low then high. I only stopped when their parents called for them to, "get away from me." "Come inside."

To the majority, the Blue Flame was a reminder of the spirituality they once supported and lived by. So, when they saw me walking amongst them, the Blue Flame lapping at my heels, they would rush back inside their huts or curse the sky where the Blue Star never hid. My heart did lower from time-to-time, it made me feel alien. Like I no longer had any place in my community; like Aelburn could no longer be my home, for the people always had something negative to say. I had not harmed one of them. Yet, the possibility could always be near. They always thought; they almost always prayed would happen. Then they'd really have something to bawl for.

After absorbing all that rejection, my body did feel bruised, so I frequently sought the company of Mother. To grow from my ignorance about the extent of my energy; to know of its origin. Throughout history, there have been kings, queens, princesses, and princes who carried the Blue Flame, some killed and banished for being a bearer, others glorified as it was the epitome of our God-like nature.

It represented our Supreme consciousness from which we had forgotten who we were.

Mother enlightened me about a legend that spoke of the Blue Flame combining with kundalini: the awakening of Neter. The Legend of Bluka.

Seated in her sacred space, her garden, plants of all sizes surrounding us, the sun extending its embrace and running its fingers through her waist-length thick locks. She burned some incense and sage, fanning it around us. The range of crystals from amethyst, Lapis Lazuli, Emerald, to White Quartz she arranged in a spiralling format between us. She instructed me to inhale from my diaphragm then exhale. There was silence for a while as she guided us through meditation. Once we were at peace, unified she spoke of the Legend of Bluka. Of the first men and women who attained spiritual enlightenment, unlocking their Godly, Neter nature. One with the Supreme and protectors of the land they served Mother Nature and the Universe. This was a time where everyone was regal, where the dynasties didn't exist — there was balance. They assimilated their purpose through finding and understanding self. But to take it that step further, the Dynastic Emblem would embody all that was pure and symbiotic in this world.

The Cobra symbolised hidden wisdom as well as the protector of royalty. When threatened, the Cobra would stand tall, extend its hood, and protect its home and itself. By nature, it is venomous and hypnotic. The Cobra also represented fertility and the creative life force. Life would continuously seek to evolve and create offsprings that would continue the cycle of Ma'at's virtues, as well as take on some of the roles of Scholars, ESW, Nurturers, and Merchants. The Lion held strength, courage, leadership and enhanced the masculine energy while nurturing the feminine.

Bluka in its simplest form was the universal consciousness unrestricted to the hueman vessel. It was sectioned off into two parts. The Blue Flame, when fused with kundalini, ensured balance within the vessel the Neter spirit inhabited. For this to be a permanent state the seven energy points of the hueman body had to be unblocked. The masculine and feminine energies needed to flow through the body as one.

Those that were true to this cycle levelled to Supreme Deities, performed specific roles as they watched over their people. Examples of these were Ori the spiritual and intuitive one; Ogun the warrior God of iron, labour, politics, sacrifice, and technology; Oshun the Goddess of beauty, love, femininity, fertility, and divinity of rivers; Ibeji the sacred twins, male and female, of youth and vitality; Yemoja, Mother Deity of mankind and God of the sea; Ra, God of the sun. Thousands, upon thousands more that untethered from Acirfa travelling as mythology and bed-time stories across the universe.

Mother believed the legend to be real and that I was gifted enough to awaken Bluka. The start would be simple: to do for self, embrace truth rather than ignore it.

Ignorance wiped from the slate as I remember who I am supposed to be before Father made me into who he thought I should be.

I needed to love myself.

"Nowadays people know the price of everything and the value of nothing."
- Oscar Wilde

9

{Calista}

Life, something in abundance, here, it is taken so easily. Taken without second thought, its value so minimal, its purpose half-lived. Everyday life is robbed of a full term; every day I grow sick to my stomach experiencing the Fight to the Death, or as I like to call it, the Savage Games.

Today, they let us out our cages, out the hole, out into the back yard. Here, life is seen differently, it is not just the environment, it's the impact it has on them. Like they have nothing better to do than kill. Like they could rot so effortlessly, without a care for their bodies, their minds. This hamster wheel they are constantly at top speed on, out here they crash.

To watch them with my own eyes and not be told stories first, it's a new kind of feeling, like I had not shown enough gratitude and respect to Mother Nature, my parents, my community while I lived blessed within the walls of Aelburn. From the scent of new clothes I received daily to maintain my honourable image, to the jewellery of protection I was adorned with from head-to-feet to the food I could devour with ease, what is the meaning of life if you have not lived outside your bubble?

What is the true price and value of everything if you know nothing?

For my father's approval, I sought higher than his price; determination and discipline. And the value of such a thing, the value of his consideration, I knew no such thing. I had only seen his admiration for his family, the factions he held great pride in. Would his approval be the same like him awarding the trainees who had persevered and become anointed as an ESW? What I desired did I already have it or what I wanted something so childish it shouldn't even be expressed? Father, the most dignified of his people, the one who must be for the people before he must be for himself; had I asked for too much? Me being allowed to become an ESW despite being a princess, was that enough?

In Aelburn because of him, our people rarely ever suffered. Maybe I was just shielded from the horrors of life; maybe I was too young to understand. Either way, the atmosphere was always pleasant with a few ignorant fools who couldn't settle their anger, accept that they were wrong. Not to mention if their ego and pride were attacked, they would act like children, shouting and cussing over the simplest of things. Some would even gravitate to violence, at which times members of the ESW Clan would intervene. There was a zero-tolerance policy in our community, you disobey the regal family and disrespect the laws, you were cast out after one single warning. There was not to be any blood spilt without justifiable cause. If you so much as breathed a word of hatred and disloyalty, Father would know of it. He had eyes everywhere. It was a small price to pay for him extending his hand to ensure they lived stress-free without having to be concerned with whether they would live to eat and see another day.

Here, my heart aches. This need to help where maybe I should not. To think much more than myself, my assignment, see the eyes that have lost hope and submitted themselves completely to this world. But I could not keep the pity from my gaze, *how life could change*, I sigh.

The silver-haired girl I pitied the most. After close observation from the Savage Games to moments like these I see the peace she has always been on the look out for. So, I come a foot closer to understanding why she loves the Savage Games; why it is her only escape from a world so loud and ruthless. To find some solace in the noise where it is the loudest. If that were me, I probably wouldn't have half as much courage as her. She may have a streak of evil and a coldness to her character, but underneath it all, she is just trying to survive.

But strangely enough, in this distance, my back against a bench the scars that pattern her back, I scratch my nails against my palm. If I could gather all who had mauled her precious skin, damaged her in ways her mind and soul could not comprehend, I would strangle them. Slice each and every one of their throats. Make them get a dose of their own medicine. The right, no one gave them such right. I crack my hand down into the earth. Immediately after I gasp, ashamed of having such vicious and vile thoughts. The truth still remains the scars are liken to whiplashes, several upon several non-stop. Her blood is still within its cracks.

"They will get what they are due."

She pulls her shirt over her head and I did not have to activate my Eye of Horus to hear her wince. A tear, I almost shed a tear. When she turns, her eyes and mine aligned, they don't look so bad. The savage amiss, only the girl who has grown up too soon in a world that deems her anything but human. An animal under their command, and they parade her for it as if it is something to be fulfilled by rather than disgusted.

She sits alone, away from her followers — those who would rather stick to her than be faced with their own thoughts. Her legs crossed. She looks away, I figured her mind had taken her somewhere else far away from the truth of this reality. Her hands shake as she holds them out in front of her. I wondered what she was seeing then her hand flashed with blood, all that she had collected after her crusade with death.

"Hours before the beginning of the daily Savage Games, they call this a breather?" I mutter to myself.

The air is polluted with the smoke of raw tobacco. Out here, inside, neither air was better or worse, they both burn my chest the same. I could really get sick out here, my life is worth more than this experience. My body itches for a clean shower. The closest I've gotten to one is when I stepped beyond the waterfall.

After the girl's hands stop shaking, the life returns to her eyes.

She gets up and looks at me.

"What are you looking at?" she snarls.

"I see you. You are not as menacing as you think."

The distance between us is much smaller now. I've stepped to her too.

"What would you know, you don't even know me? I am a nobody, isn't that right?" Her nails dig into her palms; the moderate breeze rustles her hair.

The defeatist talk. The beat down to the ground talk. The self-fulling prophecy they have all given themselves.

"You are somebody." As I am a princess, you are a hueman worthy of life's blessings, not man's twisted games. Would she understand me if I continued with this?

She laughs.

I guess not.

She brushes her thin shoulders against mine, enough weight for me to half-step back, as she walks back to the prison house.

"We should go." Myah slithers up behind me, touching my arm. I follow her gaze to a shadow stepping out from behind a building. The tallest of them all, out of place in this filthy world. He stands under the streetlight, the litter scurrying away from his pointed shoes. One of his hands in his trouser pocket, the other ruffling his neck-length straight hair. He must have felt my gaze because he turns around with swiftness and walks in my direction. His feet too light for the ground, almost as if he is walking on water or merely levitating. When he stops, as does my breath, he cocks his head, fingering his full beard. I wonder; what he is thinking?

Can he see me?

What is a man like him doing around here?

Something creeps into my heart; he has a familiar face. A slash vertically across both his eyes. His skin entirely drained of blood. I've heard the stories about him. Most notably, from the Civil War.

"We need to ..." Myah is pulling on my arm. Persistent. I must listen. Walk away. Turn my back. A simple thing has become so hard to do. This struggle, it waters my eyes. My vision still clear, he has become the subject of my canvas. The one my lens focus on. Because.

He is The Kutawala.

The coloniser who led the invasion into Acirfa. Memories of the stories the villagers told with such disgust and anger flood in through my ears. Their shouts and spits shaking my hand. This ruthless monster murdered thousands of Genapians without mercy or compassion. The deadly bombs his army used, disintegrated the plants and purged the land with their envy. He is the one who now enslaves the Sixth Dynasty. The one, who at the time, took down the Five Kingdoms with the element of surprise.

The Devil his people marvel at.

"Intoxicated with madness, I am in love with my sadness."

10

{Calista}

I hear their voices. Whose do I speak of? I do not know but they are everywhere. Just taking up space, transforming into that which they should not be. Some gruff, some high, many crying, many yelling. They lash my mind, stretch back the lids of my eyes. What must I see through feeling pain?

A hand to my temple, I massage, I jab. "Make it stop." Then I'm rocking, the voices jangling as my head swiftly goes from left-to-right, right-to-left. Up. Down. This constant shaking all about. To the cold floor, my forehead presses into, kneading, brushing.

"Stop." The tremble of my voice, I cannot hear through their screams. Their spits of fire, blood. But there's one, the quietest I should not hear. The grumbles that follow, the stamps, clinking of metal. Her voice; I lift my head.

Breathe.

A grey cloud climbs to my eyes, filled with static, a fury like a storm. The tension that drives through my bones; the ghosts that unearth from the walls; the hands bursting through the cracks in the floor. They fly through me; their coldness, lack of empathy, humanity. I jolt with their presence, heavily fall to my back and fail to exhale. This weight. So heavy. The cloud swoops in claws through my eyes; darkness. The voices remain echoing.

I hate you.

You burned my village.

How can you be so cruel?

I wish I were dead. So, kill me already.

A chorus of anguish. Desire for revenge. To gather as one conflicted soul in the middle of war. I don't want to be here. Who has forced me here?

Nothing is worth our pain but the blood of the Devil who has brought us Hell.

Through the fire that rises, the huts caving in their might, desperate bodies jumping through its destruction, that voice, a mother's continues.

The price too cheap, his death alone too minor for the charge, his crimes, it must not be resolved so quickly. A sanction as heavy as his must be paid in parts. Who shall do it?

Who shall do it? They scream forcing me to my knees covering my ears. At the centre of chaos; eyes squeezed shut as though they are in my face, still I see what they want. Their bodies; taking shape, their eyes glassy with the disastrous scene. The men, woman and children that build from the dirt, faces expressing their yearning to survive, they fracture, splinter to their feet in bones to ashes. Continuing the cycle through the flames, they rebuild. But one image; one man, always in the background mighty upon his airborne slab of metal soars far and wide through the outskirts of the kingdoms. One army of inhuemane beings at his disposal trampling on Mother Nature leaving behind their residue of green magic and the cries of the living departing to their dishonourable deaths. Those that fought as valiant as they may be, the eminent truth came crashing down that: what was meant to be would be. The end of a blissful era had concluded. And with its arrival the beginning of the tipping of balance into chaos, death, destruction. The return to darkness.

The Civil War -— why here, why now?

I crawl to a stand at the centre of the village burned to the ground.

The bodies piled on top of bodies. Animals scurrying to any place without The Kutawala and his Albinos.

Amongst the teary-eyed children, the faint voice I'm sure I had heard she stares at her reflection in a pool of water. Her eyes I see this world through. She grasps at the ground dirt shoved into her nails. Tears and snot racing down her face and dripping onto her collarbone. She lets out a heartfelt bawl, racking her small chest. The ground shakes with the explosion of the bombs. A green fire lights up the dead. She bangs on the field with closed fists, barely being able to control her spurts of anger. Her family: Father, Mother, and little brother's bodies slowly turn to ash. When she rises out of her crouched position, through her watery gaze, she stares at The Kutawala. Her heart to stone; face emotionless.

The tears that fell; the hands that readied. She drives her feet into the ground, kicks off and is off. Breezing through the smoke, clawing through the flames, leaping over the splintered branches. Through his masterpiece; through what he would call a victorious moment. Zeroed in on his face then his chest, I snap from her body back to the shell of mine and watch him catch her in his focus.

My mouth drops; his features they lift admiring her courage. I start to fan the smoke, make a gesture for her to stop; this would not end well. Her emotions all over the place, the trap she was galloping into at full speed.

NO.

Impulse over strategy.

NO.

Loss and desperation.

NO, I shout. And his toothy-grin ...

"After stamping out our light now – I must do the same to you."

She crosses her hand in front of her rotating her fists to the sky. Red fire encases her hands, solidifies around her copper gauntlets. The white tribal marks at her eyes spin like a Ferris wheel. She jumps with her fist drawn back. He dodges, spreads his fingers like he's throwing a frisbee. Upon release, the small ball shifts into a metal rod and slaps itself around her neck. Immediately, she's thrust to her knees, arms pinned to her side.

"You killed my family. Now I am going to kill you."

"Save it, little girl, you are not a worthy opponent. Be happy that I'm allowing you to see another day."

"Another day is more misery and pain added to my soul."

The sheer strength and power, she was definitely fierce during her younger years; a force to be feared; a force whose use had become contained.

She pushes through the weight, wobbling to a stand. *"Sekhmet, give me strength."* She calls upon the warrior Goddess, 'She who Mauls', 'The mistress of Slaughter'. She answers her call with the manifestation of a golden sun disk ringed above her head.

"The balance must be restored. Evil wiped from the slate." Her teeth gritted, Sekhmet's flame roars out of her. She kicks off, imprinting the soil as she zig-zags. Her fire licking at the air, advancing her steps at thrice the speed she started off with. Her nails elongated. She slashes them across his eyes.

In the moments that she took to get to him, I was amazed and he seemed so too, for she held him captive in the spot where he felt the most safe: connected to his metal board. The gashes, I gaped, he too, the blood dripping onto his open palm. His face hardened as did his fists around a metal button. A pulse rippled through the device locked to her neck. A cyclone of fire whirls around her. When it dies, she collapses.

The images splinters, her face, him stood over her. My hands in the air I quickly lowered them to my face; teary. But my eyes were moving, past the walls and the floor. Across from my cell, there she is. The silver-haired girl, she's the reason for The Kutawala's scar. Her manifestation of supreme power, she did that. No wonder she has survived since then. Drying my tears with the back of my hand, her eyes flock to me from the wall she bounced a ball at. The same look she gave him she gives to me. A murderous gaze. I'm guilty of visiting her past; invading her privacy without permission. How will she move now?

She flexes her fingers, cuts her eyes, before turning her back on me. After all I've seen her do, what has been taken from her by the one who leads the Savage Games, that day, what I felt outside -— to survive isn't all she wants. Her anger is her fuel but she has been in this state for too long. It must be tiring. She's wearing away. Deteriorating mentally and physically. That question: *Who shall do it?* Wasn't only vengeance. Much more. Our introduction to each other is symbolic.

What must I do for her?

Who must I become in that instance?

I shrink against the wall; the noise has returned, this time I give in. A while later warm hands pull on my wrists.

"Calista. Follow my voice."

Can't.

There's too much.

Voices everywhere.

"Listen. Control it."

Drowning. Stifled.

"You can do this."

A gust of inspiration floats me up; the voices fall to my feet. I quickly gulp in the air.

"That's it."

The Prince stands, his eyes following my every move. When he's sure I am back to normal, he let's go. I almost wish he hadn't just in case they wanted to creep back in.

"What happened?"

"You are like me. A psychic. You just experienced your power revealing itself as it levelled up."

What now? The bearer of the Blue Flame as well as a psychic?

"How?" I ask, but somehow, I know it makes sense. I've had migraines and after I overcame them I would feel like I've read a whole book on a person just by looking at them. It was like that time I first met Dakarai. I didn't need to touch him to know he was suffering. It wasn't the lifeless look in his eyes, he just spoke to me. I could feel his pain all at once and I wanted to console him. I think that's why I connect with him on a deeper level than I do with my siblings -— the attraction was pure and needed. Without knowing, I had created a mental link with him, I felt what he felt, and he caught a few tender feelings when I was in trouble. Call it a bit of intuition if you will. But this sounds more like psychic-empathy.

"How do you control it?"

"A lot of practice. You will get there soon enough. But this is great news, you are awakening."

Awakening for what though?

"To live is the rarest thing in the world. Most people exist, that is all."
- Oscar Wilde

||

{Calista}

"Train ... get up ... I can ..."

My elbows give and my chin smashes into the rock-hard pillow. Luckily, I had not made it to the floor, I have not found the strength within me yet to make it so far. Something so easy, with the constant crying of my stomach, has become so difficult. Laziness, I clock my tongue, I never thought this is what I would have become. If Mother, Brother, even one of my Master Teachers were to flick my ear I wouldn't budge. Would just lay there in a right state, crumbled at their feet. Today unlike any other day, my motivation has thinned. The people around me, it's the energy they carry, intoxicating, I struggle to maintain my vigour. If I could just get a peak of the Red Sun, the Blue Star I would rejuvenate like a back-up generator. I rub my fingers together, click them after; nothing. I had always thought it strange, that day since I met Tamari till now, I couldn't get my flame on. Some damper; some block; what inhibits me, something external or internal?

Through the thin mattress, fingers poke my sides.

"Ow." Every jab like a needle, in avoiding, I roll to the ground. "Ah, if I had been eating correctly, breakfast, lunch and dinner I would not be so weak."

She pulls herself from the darkness and climbs the steps to the top bunker. I imagine she held some kind of smirk, it must have been funny using this cheap trick to get me to move. She has said the bare minimum since she told me her name though she is always in my company. I guess I am more 'me' than the rest. As my shadow, she often tugs on my little finger. When I asked her again why she was here, she said, "being punished for not listening, my being here is a secret." She had not held a finger to her lips, nor looked me in the eye. But that wasn't what touched me. "They may see a girl but they cannot really see me. Only you can." I had pointed at myself to be sure, she offered no further confirmation, those words alone were to be heard and interpreted as I saw fit.

The floor is too sticky to stay on for too long. I shift to a cobra pose, pushing off the ground, loosening my back muscles, bending in the direction my legs point. It feels good, to stretch, to release. I take in a deep breath.

Mother used to hold these sessions where my siblings and I had to attend daily. Aziza was always eager to enter first and be at the centre. My younger brother would be the drag and Khari and I were somewhat unbothered. After our training, this was a little breather and we didn't mind the family bonding time. The sessions would always vary from meditation with affirmation to yoga for mobility and strength. All in all, the calming of the mind and body. The establishing of a flow. In this space under Mother's protection we were guided, appreciated, loved and most importantly safe. Safe to express. Safe to Be. So, it was always noted we think before we act, find better ways to respond, refraining from reacting with violence as a default.

After I performed a cat-cow sequence, as I breathed in my chest-dipped back-arched to breathe out my back-rounded. Now I've pushed into a downward facing dog. A V-shape with my hands pressing my shoulders away from my ears on the ground and the back of my foot reaching down. I round into a plank and then take my feet in sitting cross-legged. My hands, one drawn to my stomach the other to my heart, I clock in with my rhythm. The flow in and out of my breath; the tune in and out of my surroundings. The observation and dismissal of thoughts. A thrum that overtakes the leaks, scraping of the bars and chatter around. Vibration, the peaceful movement of my Blue Flame, of the universe.

The minutes that go by, I do little to register. But something would come to disturb my peace, a shame, of course it wouldn't last long. And that disturbance it galloped into my lap then fed into my lowering hands. Nails, claw against my cell bars. I need not guess whose presence has found mine.

"You trying to teleport out of here?" She laughs, stepping into my cell.

If that were a possibility, would I still be here?

It still baffles me how my Eye of Horus fails to manifest a portal, to even perform its basic function: light up upon command. Whatever disrupted its frequency could be the same thing that circulates in the air with an electric charge and green glow.

"What do you want?" I whisper.

"Just checking in, making sure you are still alive."

"I am not that easy to kill, now if you would ..." I stretch my hand inviting her to leave. She brushes by inspecting my wall.

"What you counting for?" She traces her fingers around the engravings. Strokes of triangles and circles contained in a box.

"Maybe till the day I get out of here, or the day you get your fight."

"The first one, not a chance, but the last, you may find it to be much sooner. But now, guess who I will be fighting?" She shifts her gaze up. This boils my blood. Oddly enough, the girl reminds me of my skills peer, Casandra. Our relationship; frenemies.

She always tried her hardest to insult me, the cheek, I had never met someone so bold in my face. As if we were on levelled ground and she could throw me off any game effortlessly. The times that it worked it was because no one else had dared, no one had enough courage to test a princess. So, being that she was my first, this is hard for me to say but, she had found a soft spot. Where I lost my face numerous of times, lashing out, calling on anger when my thoughts demanded otherwise. This was down to my innocence but also my lack of control with the Blue Flame growing day-by-day. When we'd fight, she would win through my outbursts; I'd win when I blocked her out. When I had also fuelled my anger into my fists and gave her a right beaten.

I remember the first day I managed this.

It started with her favourite words; *The Emperor's greatest disappointment.* It burned much more that time and I don't know why. Maybe because my every fight, Father settled with a disapproving look, no matter how much I had improved. I was the only one who couldn't please him. Aziza got lucky, she didn't get the pressure, she survived all the heartache and physical injuries by choosing her own path. That of a Scholar. She was allowed to; I could only choose what Father wanted of me. To be strong; to be tough; to have the skills required to be more than what a princess would be. To be a warrior. Aziza became a leader in her field and was known for her vast abilities to recall at rapid speeds. I, even after their pressures had relaxed, could not stop. The fire had already been lit within and the journey wasn't much of a hindrance. I admit, I began to love it, feeling powerful. Having a sense of prominence on the leader boards. But Father, his face always at the back of my mind. Never impressed, like that day.

I took the burn I had received from Casandra and moulded it to serve me. My mind blocked everything out, and I allowed my anger to lead. I performed moves I didn't dare to execute on the VR. Steps that could fatally wound my opponent. In a dance, our feet and hands moved in sync circling each other's body, but not managing to latch onto one another. I stopped all of her attacks with the slope of my forearm. She could have knocked me unconscious and I barely noticed the shocked look that passed across her face as I countered. My only focus: our hands and legs. When the time came, I jumped onto her shoulders and threw us to the ground; rolling my legs into a lock around her neck, pulling her arm towards me, palms faced outward. As the noise leaked back in; everyone was cheering. The moment Casandra tapped at the ground, I released her and made eye contact with Father. He huffed, that same pressed expression built a tick in my jaw. He rose from his throne and exited the training arena, never looking back. I watched him leave collapsing with distress. My right hand started to shake. I knew what this meant. Beside the mat, Dakarai outstretched his aura. My body wanted to calm down to which my mind had resisted. The anger's temptation, so powerful, I wanted to let it go. Cassandra crawled away from me her eyes to the spirals travelling up my hands. But Dakarai, he saved them all that day, if not for his help, the arena would have been ablaze and my Blue Flame wouldn't have just stopped as a few spurts from my fingertips.

The look in Myah's eyes isn't one of fear, but I know, she shouldn't have to go through this. There should be rules, limits to who could enter. No matter the hellish state of this place, the children ...

"Why her?"

"Oh, you would be surprised how strong she is. Don't let her innocence and age fool you. She is more than capable." She runs her fingers along the bed rails. After she makes a full turn, she flicks her fingers in my direction.

"Unless you advocate to be her saviour."

The game she plays, she just might have a heart. Myah is just a pawn she chooses to exploit to kick me closer on her board. Games, when others have the upper hand I'd rather deflect, stand down. But choices, when there is little to none, would the end result still be the same, or could it be changed?

Hours later, Tamari is at my cell gate. He slithers inside watching me as he rests against a wall.

"Watch your back." His words somehow, I expected. Something I've already had in mind. It comes to no surprise he finally utters them after recycling them over and over in his thoughts. The unspoken truth in this environment; any sane person would know this.

"I've got this covered." My eyes to the ground.

"I am talking about Tamika, she is a tricky one," he says as if I had asked for an explanation.

"The one who mauled The Kutawala. The one who challenges me. So that's her name. It sounds a lot more pleasant than she looks, certainly not very befitting for her character." But then I wonder which character am I talking about, the one she has developed over time as a means for her survival, or the person she was before her world fell apart?

As the minutes go by, there's this weight on my chest I try to relieve with deep sighs; waning thoughts that the day would just end already. A hand brushes my shoulders. Snapped from my thoughts the odd sensation has me shrivelling away from his touch. Some form of vibration different from travelling through portals. A zap without the ticklish feeling. Tamari's presence I had forgotten came with purpose.

"Just who I want to see."

The Prince stands throwing a crystal ball from one hand to the next. The inside shimmering with purple and black energy contained within jelly-like hexagons overlapping itself. The blend of colours blinds me enough to look away and still see its remnants wherever I redirect my gaze.

"This won't take long." He circles me, his spins projecting multiple balls spaced out to a halo just above my neck. Though I am not at his feet and my head does have to raise to meet his, my hands hover over my eyes. And before I could mention my discomfort he rushes to his point.

"I hear Tamika has provided you with a proposition. Do you want to know what I advise?"

Not really.

With my silence, he resumes.

"Don't fight her." That plain and simple?

"I wonder why you think I should not, I thought you would be giddy with excitement."

"Maybe, but I assure you, you won't like what comes next."

"Care to elaborate?" My two middle finger's part to view his expression – the same as when I first saw him. Twinkling. A man with all the answers and enough bait to get a reaction.

"Most definitely not. But if you do so infamously *not-listen*-to-great-advice, I will do so with pleasure."

He clicks his fingers; I'm back in my cell.

"I hate when he does that."

Just like Tamika, and supposedly everyone else, there are many games at play. As the only piece on the board without ties nor definite stake in this game, it is time I construct my own. Not to be a pawn though if they think me to be one, I can uphold the guise for some time.

"Don't fight her?" I spot Tamika in her cell. "Well then ..." Following her methods, I scrape my nails against her rails with a sweet smile – lips stretched to the point where they'd crack. She raises her eyebrow. I slam my leg in a high kick against her throat and hold it there with her back positioned against the wall. She grins, unsaid words ticking her off. Her lip's part, the sign I was waiting for. Her windpipe crushing at the cry of survival's plea, though she maintains her glee. Her hands balled at her sides counting the seconds down to her release.

"You want to fight?" The bulging of her eyes ensures me, more than anything; that's what she wants. "So, let's fight." I grind out then remove my leg.

"I pledge to be Myah's champion in a fight to the death with you, Tamika."

May the best woman win.

"Difficulties are meant to rouse, not discourage. The human spirit is to grow strong by conflict."
William Ellery Channing

12

{Calista}

"**H**ere's a fight that should be very interesting. My fellow citizens, welcome to the arena our undefeated and most callous victor, Tamika. And the crowd goes wild as to be expected. I absolutely love it! Also welcoming a newcomer who goes by. No name. Mysterious, I like it. Let's hope she's mysterious enough to stay alive. We all know how these things work. Once you enter, your life is on the line. Literally. One tip: always protect your neck. Now, without further ado, let the battle commence! Mysterious girl, I wish you all the best. The Devil knows you are going to need it. This is hell."

And with that the barrier goes up, lighting bolts circling to the point above our heads. Before I was ushered out, I had made some alterations to my attire, stripping the arms into eight sheets. Four for each hand I wrapped around my knuckles. My precious necklace and ankle beads I secured beyond the zip to my thighs.

Tamika offers me her hand; she had cleaned it. Her intention to begin with seemed pure and I under the impression that it is courteous to shake your opponent's hand no matter the type of fight, I take it. Our hands squeezed; our eyes locked. Then her smile. Yanked forward, she thrusts her knee into my nose. I saw every inch of the move still; my nose leaks with blood.

A chorus of 'ous' and 'ahs' rolled in with pleasant cheers from the maniacs watching, eager to feast their eyes on more than a little blood.

"Oh, that's got to hurt. Our victor quickly starts the battle off. If her opponent doesn't step up her game anytime soon ..."

The commentator rattles on in the background, as I draw my hand across my face.

"How is your nose ... regal?"

I rush at her, arms flowing in front disguising my leg pushing to jab her in the eye. She stumbles a few paces, blinking.

"How is the eye?"

The smile that reappears, my attack was nothing, something to brush off and continue.

"Oh, you think I didn't know, princess? You smell of them."

There she goes again; my identity.

I step a couple paces back, enough to recalculate our space — guard up.

"What gave me away?"

She nods at my arm. "Your symbol of course. The Eye of Horus and the Ankh you wear around your neck. They may not be able to see it, but I can. I see everything."

"And who might you be?"

"Don't tell me you are still clueless. Ah, I guess I expected better from you."

She lowers a hand to lift one side of her vest. A red burn on her torso, the kind of pattern that could only be found in a certain tribe. This tribe once they had realised their gifts, sometimes even after birth, the mark would appear. A symbol of immortality, sight and oneness of the beyond; two bars crossed together with the Eye of Horus in the four circles.

"The Macho."

One of the, if not greatest, tribes to have lived closest to nature on the outskirt of Kimarr, in the mountains and rainforests. They held an impressive ability for sight much beyond the physical. They always kept to themselves, socialised rarely with their neighbours, they preferred to maintain their pure connection with self, nature, the universe. They were peaceful. I had to check if my mouth was open, they are a legend and I always was inspired by them. To reach greater heights, to be ...

"It's a shame how my people ended, wouldn't you agree?"

She lunges for my throat, both hands already revealing her move, gripping at the air she hoped would soon be replaced with my neck. Such a move, I was disappointed she didn't mask. I block spinning to an elbow shoved in her chin. I was sure I heard a crack, not just from the impact but her neck too.

"Don't you wonder, what death tastes like?"

I don't bite, still moving, still wanting to be as light as possible.

"You know, we are more alike that you realise, both products of our environment."

I pssh, "You are audacious and barbaric, I am nothing of the sorts."

She tiptoes in a dance she thought I wouldn't focus on, notice her objective to worry me with her proximity. Her small steps when matched with her words, I wouldn't be able to tell its increase in speed from spell. As if the two wouldn't go hand-in-hand. To move so quickly yet appear to slow down to a rock skipping over the water in slow motion with the spell light on her tongue. This distraction of hers, I wonder how much longer she can take to dance as if she has all the time in the world; I have all the time in the world. A move so simple, I grow tired of watching.

"At least we will be after today."

These words however pull me back to that dark thought I had from the start, tried hard to escape, tried to forget as it lingered like her shadow almost on top of mine. The kind of presence that had me knowing, in the end there will only be one victor. One death. I kill and become like her. She kills me, I end my purpose here. But rules, they can always be broken.

Her dance stops, shakes the earth with a final beat. The silence between us that stretches, holds the weight I wanted her to share. All the noise, all the eyes, nothing mattered for we are now in a place where only we two exist.

Her drooping eyelids filled with soil that has long been malnourished hangs like her worn-out vest.

"Do you know the story or the truth? Of my people, our people's end? Don't you wonder beyond The Kutawala, beyond the stories?"

I swallow.

I've concluded. The silly games are over.

"You should be ashamed, Princess of the First Dynasty, exploring my mind. Invading."

She didn't have to touch me, wear my body down with her punches, kicks. My fingers start to tingle.

"That was not my intention. It just happened."

"Just like how your people, *happened* to see but abandon."

"What do you mean?" Her fury, it pulls on my tongue.

"Where were your people when mine was murdered?" Her head tilted back; eyes more exposed than before, a peek of a tear cowers. "Of all the technology you keep in the sky, underground. *My people.* Where were *yours* when they promised with technology, with resources no matter the circumstance, whether we were inside your kingdom or not, they'd be at our disposal if an enemy were to launch an attack?"

I tried wetting my lips; the answer, I had none.

"Were we uncultured? Not civilised enough for you? The promise of a Genapian should be kept and held to the highest regard below that of our deities. Yet," she begins to move, lengthy strides.

I trip over my feet, scrambling back up dusting off the dirt in a frantic plea to still remain calm, unshaken by her emotional force.

"Answer me!"

"How can I? I was only a child. My only responsibility to this matter is that I am an extension of my father. His reasonings I've sought after as well. My being here, our meeting, it is only because I did something I should not have."

"You think you being here is a mistake. That assignment, it was always meant for you."

Her voice drops an octave. "For this moment."

I look away, the crowd blends back in. The Prince, the only face recognisable, he has his eyes glued to us. What he said, *don't fight her.* Why? She says *this moment.* What must I run from?

My shoulders drop. My eyes burn, the sting from a tear. I will shed that tear; those streams she cannot because they have been held back for so long. Maybe this is why I was placed here, to hear her truth.

"Your people were peaceful."

"Yet, this is how they ended." She makes a point crushing her hand. I didn't get it, her pain. I had only seen not lived it. To have gone through that, to have suffered, what could I as a mere princess, Elite Supreme Warrior do? This assignment, I am only just learning past the stories. But —

"If I must be responsible for my Elders' mistakes ..." The scary eyes in the crowd that began to draw, of excitement for pleasure, entertainment, a complete disregard of the beauty of life, I, "I will bear the shame. This will be my apology to you."

Tamika, today this will be my purpose.

My hands flattened to my side; I open my palms to her.

She lifts off into the air, hands above her. She slams into my chest, knocking me to my back. I roll over to my feet, but the same energy I started with it leaks into the ground. Her arms like scissors, she cuts at my side. My muscles though they tense, I do little to block, exposing enough to feel the weight of her frustration. The tears she has restricted since The Kutawala's introduction into her life. The desire for revenge.

Every blow.

Kick.

Slap.

The energy I should not consume.

All of it.

And when she stops, more swaying to her left, she bites down on her lip, stretching till her chin sharpens.

"Well, this isn't fun, is it? You are supposed to fight back! Am I a joke to you? Not worthy of your effort?"

"This is how I relieve your suffering." I spit blood, my breathing all over the place.

"No, this is how you look down on me. You are just like them. Only hide behind your technology, do you think I want your pity, apology, body to just do as I please?" She throws her hand wide. "That means nothing to me. This all ... nothing matters. I just want ..."

The four cannons along our perimeter shoots fire into the air, it spreads as a second layer to our barrier. The crowd on their feet roar even louder. Stamping, beating their chest, knocking into each other with the fuel they charge over to Tamika.

"Wow, this has got to be a record. It has been five minutes going on ten, and the fight is still in motion. Tamika is everything alright down there? This looks like child's play. It's time the battle got a lot more heated."

Water gushes out onto the battlefield. In less than two inhales-exhale, we are thigh-deep.

"I chose you for a reason. So, give me your all."

"Fine."

She smirks, her will to continue arrives with double her previous strength. Her emotion her greatest asset, she slices my skin. My hands, then my arms, luckily not my face.

"Will you not let it out? Why do you still hide it?"

Her legs glide against the current of the water as she sweeps my legs from under me.

"This is no place to let loose."

"I'd say there is no place better."

Our injuries are quite the pair, where mine are a cracked rib with a few bruises on my shoulder; hers are less serious around her left eye and right arm. Her tactics are ever-changing but since we began, they've always been to wound me as much as possible; endless attacks; little defence on my part. This move I don't mind; I'll also test her stamina.

She kicks herself up onto my back like she's saddling a horse, digs her knees into my sides, and unusually wraps her arms around my neck. She is like dead weight. No matter how hard I try to shake her off, she doesn't budge.

I drop to my knees, the water soothing my muscles, and jab my nails into her temple. Repeatedly, I stab, rocking her head back until she gives with a cry. Heaving her over my shoulder, she plonks to the ground. The opening she made through the water she travels back through. Her claws out, slicing and dicing the air, she misses to hook me as I worm around her strikes. But each time I moved back she advanced at double the speed before as if the water had rejuvenated her. When I spin to catch her neck between my calf and thigh in a high kick, she ducks and delivers what has made her become known as the 'undefeated champion'. My skin tears around my waist; I crash under water. I press the ground to get up; my arms fold.

This fight is not over.

What are you without your Blue Flame? You have her, stop playing around, do what needs to be done. The voice that targets, where Tamika is drowned out, the crowd and their murderous screams.

That voice, where does it come from?

"Be like a flower, survive the rain, but use it to grow."

13

{Calista}

They say change, it is supposed to take time. Get used to. But when it's instant and my muscles fail to operate, to protect, do something for my survival, shouldn't change have rescheduled their intervention?

I feel nothing but the water squeezing at my soon-to-be-corpse.

Tamika. Though I believe she looms over me, maybe ready to finish or assist me back on my feet to be the warrior she has chosen to challenge her, I cannot move. Don't want to move. For.

Change.

It might not have been as immediate as I think. Something had already started, began, but since when? This thing that has travelled with me, more than a follower trailing me at night. It whispers, it is subtle but with enough thought, it has always been with me. When I set out for Kimarr, when my skin and Tamari's touched. Maybe it was the spirits of the dead, rising with Tamika's anger, thirst for revenge, wrapping through my hair, penetrating my scalp. But how foolish of me to ignore its presence, think it was only my own. Dark thoughts. Thoughts I've never had before. Thoughts that were tempting to utter aloud. Thoughts that build with a mantra now, dancing, beating. It starts from my head but it's travelling done my spine, spreading through my blood.

This awakening I wish to voice through the water. The bests parts of me I lower, hide, the most chaotic. What should be controlled, disciplined.

My neurons fire, I burst through the water at its command. I land then shoot off in the opposite direction from where I had departed.

Where had my sense of self gone?

I am losing myself again.

So running, as if a cheetah were on my tail, eyes forward, arms at a 90-degree snapping like newton's cradle, what could that do for me when I run from myself?

That's right Cali, stall until you can't stall no more. There, a voice, not mine, loud, clear as day as if linked arm-in-arm. She's familiar with an elegant grace to her, like a female ready to present on the radio or sing a lullaby to a baby. The kind any man would stop to listen to and as a result I wished I had the potential to sound like. Feminine. And so, when these next words become embedded in my core, I buckle with hands on my knees and struggle to breathe.

Murder, not mercy.

"Running are we princess? Fine, go ahead, run like how The Kutawala told my family to just so they could bomb them from a distance. They didn't stand a chance. Why do you think you do?"

Not now, I beg.

"Be a wuss. Be weak. You cannot stop what is to come anyway. It is kill or be killed. You are going to have to kill me to finish the game!"

Listen ... I wanted for her to listen, for sound to cease. It had become too much with my irregular heart beat thumping in my ears. Too confused to speak, even muster some explanation for why I had suddenly become a coward, I squeeze my knees.

"They want the kill," she points at the crowd, "and as my duty, I must provide them with what they want. They don't call it the the Savage Games for no reason."

My back all of a sudden straightens. My control has slipped and there's this hunger. Not only Tamika's but mine. Hers. Her mantra, in my head, screaming.

"How can you be an Elite Supreme Warrior yet you cannot do what is necessary for your survival?"

Murder, not mercy.

"That is not what being an ESW is all about. I will not take a life."

Think, don't react. "Mercy, not murder." I roll the dreadful phrase to the tip of my tongue.

"We will see about that."

The air mocks me as Tamika hurdles forward with a fist pounding at my chest, the bulls eye: my heart. An unstoppable machine with boundless power pressuring my ribs.

Please don't let me do this. To uphold my sanity and moral code, please ... don't let me do this.

Sweat pools on my forehead as the pressure gives way to blood leaking from my chest.

You are not weak, my love. You are one of the strongest people I know. When you fall you get right back up, you never give up. I remember Dakarai's reassuring words. His touch as he consoled me after my heart tore in half when Father came to know I carried the Blue Flame. I wanted to give up becoming an Elite Supreme Warrior because I knew Father would always hold something against me. If it wasn't the Blue Flame, it was my inability to impress him in whatever form of fighting we were taught.

Here, with Tamika, my reason differs. I don't want another burden on my shoulders. Death is something that I believe would change me for the worst. She will have to kill me ...

Block. My wrists crossed, arms putting up one last attempt at a defence.

Is this what I truly want? Am I really about to give my life to a cause that does not serve nor respect me? A cause that would rather see us chained up like animals, killing one another rather than being the evolved regal beings that we are?

My mind goes into overdrive. Her thoughts and pain clearly pass through. What sticks out most of all is her passion for death. Her desire to become one with her Ancestors. "This is what you meant, our connection."

The outcome has been set, this is beyond the rule of this game. Beyond this world The Kutawala has established.

I want to ease her pain, not lose myself in her wrath.

I am not ready to die.

Murder, not mercy. She's back like she never left. The same persistence in thought matching Tamika's motivations and desires. Her face, her expression; there is no smile, just blood. Just a passion for power, to maintain her streak with death. To hold her pride in the face of The Kutawala who deserves all her vengeance. Who forced her into this state that has no end, with her only prayer being that the days would shorten?

But I, the closest thing to the opposite end she weighs on, holds what she desires much more than bloodlust.

As such, setting my eyes upon hers: this is not the same person I had entered the arena with. Her personality split; she wears two faces: her past and her present self.

With my legs in somewhat of a stretched squat, she drives her hand into my chest again meaning to pass through the barrier of my ribcage. The fact that she has not broken through, I almost smile knowing my Blue Flame has finally arrived.

Her behaviour mirrors a vampire going for the easy kill. Pull the heart out, and the host is dead. Teeth clenched, pressing harder and harder, she pushes me back. The parts of my ribcage that fracture, my Blue Flame mends.

"Do your worst."

I choose to let her release her anger some more. This is the least I can do for her troubles. I may not have been old enough to remember when horror descended upon Genapa, but right now I am bearing witness to its aftermath. I did not wish to know the extent of her issues but judging from her blows, they are more profound than mine ever were with my father.

Blood gushes from my nose. Her eyes water with every jab she thrusts into my body. When her muscles relax, she steps away from me, breath heavy on her swollen lips.

"Why does my life have to be like this?" she shouts, I'm the only one who hears her. "I am this way because I allow myself to be like this. Why do I choose to survive?"

"Release me from this life." The face that hides surfaces; the truth at full capacity.

And in retaliation. "Why must I be the one? Don't you wonder what that would do to me?"

"I chose you; the universe chose you. She chose you. That's the least you could do."

She, the one I hear, can Tamika see her?

A cold sensation slithers up my arm. A cramp fixates itself on my legs, the threat I had not safeguarded from adequately causes me to stumble. And with that stumble, my Blue Flame spreads through my blood spilling onto every inch of my body.

Murder is mercy. To kill is to release.

Even though she readily gives me permission to end it for her, her other half still attacks me with persistence. She faces her own battle within: one half wants the kill and the other wants the release.

At your hands, a merciful death. Her voice whispers again. A wintry-breeze with the intent to render one powerless to stop themselves from doing the unthinkable.

Murder in the form of mercy. The release. The reset. End her struggle.

No.

Yes.

I don't want no blood on my hands.

It is a small price to pay when you are chosen by the Blue Flame.

All control, she takes it, grinding my face like Tamika's. My hands grab her wrists, twist. They snap. She cries out and kicks at my hip. I grab her leg and break her ankle.

Continue. Release me.

She corrects herself and runs at me. I await her attack, closing my eyes, allowing my ears to be my eyes. She jumps in the air. I leap to meet her in the centre, my arms stretched wide. I chop down on something hard, warm, with all the anger I had consumed from her and many others who stood before her and lost their life in this arena. Our minds one, energy entwined.

The cry I expected, I only hear from my throat; a gargle of some sort filled with tears and blood. Then silence befalls me, at last from all around, at what seems to be the worst timing. I drop to the ground, mini tsunami's rushing away from me. On bended knee, her body falls behind. A dreadful crash into a crevice in the now drained arena. Slowly, I open my eyes and look at my hand as I rise, all hairs on my skin standing. The buzzing in my inner ear disturbs me the most as my reality slows to a little less than a turtle's pace. My fingers start to loosen. Her head tumbles from my hand. The sticky blood drips from my fingertips — a never-ending stream.

What have I done?

My mind is vacant of her thoughts. I wanted her to come back, explain why this was necessary, what we did together. Her disappearance at a time like now, why? What must I do now?

I heave, Tamika's lifeless eyes staring into mine. A feeling of constriction in my throat has me unable to empty the contents of my stomach. My ears they pulse as words punch their way into my mind.

Murderer.

Evil.

Monster.

But one stands out most of all.

Guilty.

One by one the crowd goes wild, and as I look to The Prince, he lifts from his chair, makes a point of smiling as he claps with everyone else.

I have released her only to take her place within her prison.

She got what she wanted; I did what needed to be done.

A feeling in my gut, a tear through the fabric of my existence, something ripped from my body has me falling to one knee. A blinding light passes through me. With a shaky hand I reach out. Above my head it travels, up, then distant but clearly moving with a sense of purpose and direction. My vision becomes spotty with darkness. While I've won the fight, I kneel, before death, before the savages. Before The Prince.

A disgrace to my race; a champion to theirs.

The making of a beast.

"Your perspective is always limited by how much you know, expand your knowledge, and you will transform your mind."

- Dr Bruce Lipton

14

{Calista}

Sweet incense tickles my nose, the one pleasant aroma I am more than content to have fill my atmosphere. Its strong scent seeps into every ache in my body. To feel calm, blissful, I almost forget I am not at home with Mother in her study. The urge to sleep, drift away from this reality, to enter a space of nothingness, peace; ah, I cannot, must resist. To evade the monstrosity I have become, relinquish my attachment to this vessel, this dreadful sin I harbour, the dishonour I have brought upon my family. My clan. I am not worthy of longing for a home to escape from myself too. To return now I would be ashamed.

The warmth radiating off of the candles circling me I wished they would shy away. I am undeserving of its embrace, my palms are still dirty with the outcome of the event that has passed.

The only door in the room creaks open inviting the world I should not know nor be a part of. In this new prison I find myself, how could he with not a care allow the light to creep in and tempt me to follow it?

"You ready?" Like an elderly person suffering from osteoporosis, I gradually rise out of the bed. Entranced by the light, I move with Tamari's hand at my elbow and cross the threshold I needed to hold me back.

"Welcome to the second round."

As if my life needed a dramatic play to shake me with enough laughter to liven up my low spirits, I hang my head and mutter words I wanted someone to hold a microphone to my mouth and announce.

I need answers but I also needed to be left alone.

Tamari removes his assistance and I plop into the chair opposite The Prince.

"I had to make you think. Why would I discourage you from fighting Tamika? What did I know, that you needed to know too? What is this all about?" His smile is of mystery and knowledge, it spins my mind closer to his.

"You have a purpose here. We didn't kidnap you; you willingly came to us. You felt that desire to take this assignment, and here you are."

Here I am? The master of my current condition but only a servant looking for the truth in others who would be the true masters.

"Empty words from an empty being." I croak.

He laughs. "I am very much alive."

"The rumours ... your death along with your people ... the Sixth Dynasty."

"Rumours that were half true," he sighs, barely audible. The memory of what they went through dances across his eyes. His fingers tap away at his lip like a pianist does his keys. With every tap, reliving the horrors of the past.

"How did you survive?"

I was lucky enough to have not suffered through that drastic nightmare. At a tender age, Father shielded me from the war as it tore through the dynasties one by one. I only know the stories, have felt nothing but distance from that matter, emotionally unable to feel what they felt. Only sympathy would seem like I did them a great injustice; to pity them would only push me further above them on that pedestal I'm sure some couldn't wait to destroy. For to be a part of the unity, brothers and sisters, and yet fade to the background and become onlookers was not only a great disrespect to ourselves but to our creators, Supreme Deities watching over us. I know this from how the villagers would talk, some with clear disdain at how treacherous we have become, others they didn't want to hear anything more. The past was the past, one that never should have taken place and as such in their present minds and situations — never did.

The Prince is clearly still antagonised. I wouldn't expect him to not be, his enemy still walks without pressure of an uprising. A young man stuck in the past where he lost virtually everything. His ascension to the throne, his people, his family, his understanding of who he was. He can never go back but, can he still go forward?

"We didn't survive," he breathes, still trapped in his memory. When his eyes travel to mine, I witness him snap back to reality. Anger replaces his pain. "Can't you see it? We merely lingered. I know you felt our energy on the land amongst the raw stench of death."

"What is with the brothel, cells, and regular Fight to the Death?"

"It was bestowed upon us, by The Kutawala and soon enough we began to accept it because that was all we had come to know. The bloodbath had smeared our memory of what we as people were trying to attain. Spiritual enlightenment — being one with the Supreme. The Civil War didn't end with our downfall, but it would have been better if it did. We are not the ones in control, we are just the face. Enslaved by the ones with a skin colour that is far from our own. The Kutawala holds us captive."

I have only seen him once, his demeanour did make me feel small but also ashamed that through all our advancements we couldn't defeat an enemy from beyond the sky.

"For a man enslaved, you seem free to me." I slump against the wooden backing.

He brushes off my sarcasm with a blink, his hands join on his knees. "You Calista are important."

Chosen, they all say. Only they would think so, no one else had said anything of the sort. Mother, however, only once when mentioning the Blue Flame.

"You hold the power to liberate us from our corrupted nature."

Another burden. I must carry a torch I never had the option in holding? "I see you are no better than them if you intend to use me to gain one up on them."

"I am nothing like them!" he roars, banging his fists on the table. As one who always keeps his cool, to reveal this side to him, I look away.

"You have me fooled as though you care for more than yourself, yet everyone I have encountered in this world has a plan for me. I must do and live up to what everyone wants of me. But what about me, what must I lose in myself to serve you? Why must I serve you at all?" My voice cracks, I'm gripping the loose material still bound around my knuckles, covered with blood. I had to disregard my moral code, for Tamika, for *her*, now I must do what — be a saviour?

His eyes they narrow.

I lean forward and whisper, "am I not a tool for you to take back your throne?"

A vein bulges in his neck.

"You see Calista, you don't know my story, my values. The throne is one thing but without our people it is meaningless. You don't know me as I know you. You haven't lived as I have. You know nothing of life but stories and more stories. You, though it may seem unfortunate, were born to be great. To be much more than this reality we share. Your ignorance that's exactly why you came."

Tamari folds his arm across his chest as he takes in a deep breath. I figure I am an open book to him. A Regal Custodian is trained to read one's mind through the energy they assert, body language also has a thing to do with it.

The Prince's words, they do sting. It's the truth I realised long ago but hearing it from someone other than myself, it hurts even more.

So, "tell me something I don't know."

"That voice you heard on the battlefield."

Yes, that voice, the one that remains silent.

"I need you to bring back my sister."

His sister ... she's dead.

As my eyebrows pinch together, an image I recalled when I first arrived. The woman that sat in front of me drawing the number five. She was me, but she wasn't me. That mark on her forehead. That Phoenix, I had seen it before on a holographic display. That symbol, right beside The Prince active on a face that was smiling.

My eyes twitch.

That face, why can't I remember?

I grip my chest, the feeling I felt on the battlefield, the yellow glow that had come from me it dangles above The Prince's hand.

My switch flips off; my hands start to shake with my Blue Flame brimming at the surface of my fingers. The marks the energy carries swirl to life, igniting spirals on my hand. My wounds heal, more than patching up my bruised and lacerated skin and as one who has crossed paths with death, I stand.

"You didn't?"

That's what it was, what had been ripped from my body.

"My Life Force, how could you?"

"A small price to pay for her return. For our plan to go smoothly."

"And you still expect me to help you."

"You will get it back Cali when you start your transitioning and gain clarity on where I am coming from. Walk the path of enlightenment into the darkness where all will be revealed." A shiver hurdles over my body as he calls me by my nickname, a right reserved for family. He outstretches his hand, expecting me to take it.

Awaken the Legend of Bluka.

Spiritual enlightenment, Bluka, his sister ... information overload, I'm massaging my temples.

"You threaten my whole existence. In the dark I'll be blind."

"You have always been in the dark." Tamari, his whisper; the truth. "This is different. The dark will elevate you."

"The truth will set you free if you allow her to push you past my actions."

Two sets of eyes watch me; my breath hitches in my throat. Not once do I look in either of their directions.

My existence stunted.

Avoid.

I begin to back away knocking the chair to the ground.

Flee.

There has to be another way.

Fear.

"I am not one of your chess pieces."

I rush through the wall. Arms raised shielding my body, my Blue Flame cloaks me. Air resistance exerts a substantial force as I push against the wind, spinning like a tornado from its eye.

"I thought you were done running Cali," The Prince shouts. "What's the moral code of Elite Supreme Warriors? We don't run, we face our reality headstrong, fight if necessary, and by all means with honour die for the cause. Yet you run. You avoid the truth I readily give to you, that's more than I can say for others."

Above, he stands between the broken walls with Tamari at his side. Then my heart does a little skid as a man walks through Tamari and jumps out of the building, a deep blue rolling off him in waves. The real ghost everyone is looking for. I fall to the ground like a meteor leaving a crater in my wake, followed by a tumbleweed roll, and a sprint in the opposite direction. I frantically search for the waterfalls. Where everything must rest. Leaping with a greater might to banish all the noise, to return to myself, to wake from this nightmare.

Over the past month, I had noticed something unusual. The waterfalls surround at least half of the land, but behind on the south side lies a weird energy field strangely like what the Earthlings called magic. A shadow that mirrors the likes of black holes. It creates a dome-like bubble that pulsates with a life of its own. If this is the gate out, to the *real world*, I must go through it. Its ripples become disturbed, soon enough, my reflection is staring at me. What I once looked like: clean clothes, skin, neat plaits with silver thread wrapped in my hair. A smile with eyes that were ready to explore and understand the unknown. Now it is only a partial semblance.

That's the way we've designed it.

I slap a hand over my mouth. No way. How is this possible? The mirror Father keeps, that jelly substance, it feels the same as this dome. This isn't Kimarr even if it is tethered to it. It's an alternate dimension. My reflection so easily manifests itself without me willing it to because the world must reveal itself. I must see what *she* wants me to.

The Mirror Realm: Rimorr.

Is The Kutawala really in control?

A shadow draws near. I turn my head. The king, The Prince's father, his shadow is here before he is and he is agile, moving faster than he should for someone of his age. His royal red robe blowing in the wind, determined.

Was he in that room all along?

This bubble, can I really leave?

He throws out his jazz hands and I feel the magnetic pull on my energy being sucked out like substance in a vacuum. Against the tide, I push forward, my form stretching and blurring while my reflection takes on its desired shape. A life of its own, pulling on the parts of me I am afraid to hold on to. My deepest emotions of not being in control, angered by other's plan, everything that could be breathed into this figure and ensure a loophole for my check-mate position.

With the last of my energy, as I fade to where they want me, my reflection shimmers through the barrier. It walks away with every ounce of freedom I become envious of.

Smiling.

"The most reliable way to predict the future is to create it."

15

{The Prince}

A week before Calista decided to take the assignment to Kimarr, I received a vision. It had been years since one of this magnitude had caused me to take a pause, sit in silence and try to rearrange my thoughts in a coherent manner. Worse the pressure on my mind didn't allow me to continue living the way I had among my broken people salvaging plans that were to be short-lived. How could I remain the same knowing what I knew of the past and the future that blew my reality subsequently wide open? No matter how overwhelming it was, it couldn't be ignored in my confinement where all that was coming into my awareness had to be picked through.

It was only right my physical body took a hit, undergoing a series of harsh sweats before settling into a coma. That twenty-four hours felt like the longest. It would only be broken after the message had sunk in its roots.

What helped most was that Tamari was by my side, he alone I suspected could fathom what I was going through. When he had his last test, I was there as company even if my mind was preoccupied by the book I was taking in. At that time, I didn't understand, the duty of a Regal Custodian and the cycles of transformation they had to go through. I couldn't see past the physical into the different strings playing in their mind. So having him there as more than a guardian, a brother, I felt secure enough to relax and allow the fire to take me over.

When she came to me, she had no face, disguised by the darkness we had once resided in as punishment for our disobedience and rebellion. Her voice, the only thing that set her apart from the Ancestors with the rhythmic sounds of the Shekere and the Djembe. The synchronicity of the music with my heart's joyful response meant her visit was pleasant but not entirely a surprise because secretly ... I had been expecting her. Deep in my subconscious mind, in the complex gene pool we both shared and the energies that birthed us both into this world, I knew she would return. I had wondered why it took her this long but remembering how we parted it was only right I dispelled my impatience along with the horrific images of her physical form destroying. One could only imagine how she moved on thereafter, her soul perhaps stalking the infinite planes of our existence, wandering aimlessly in search of attachment and reincarnation. Maybe even revenge. All the while, her purpose had yet to be fulfilled, it would be a great shame if she were to be restless forever until she found herself again.

The message my twin, Ramiyah, provided wasn't simple, it couldn't be, she had only granted me a snippet of what would be considered the whole. It required more than strategic planning, constant thinking and mental expansion. My character had to be altered, the ego I always kept in the palm of my hand, it had to stretch its skin over mine. I had to take on the shape of something that could challenge and defeat with more than strength; spiritual understandings. Nothing in this world had limits, ignorance had to be removed, my safety net destroyed, I had to be open to anything that came my way. Shed whatever armour of fear I had built around me, it was time she said *to step into your greatness.*

The three of us, a purpose far greater than ourselves, The Kutawala, we had to ensure her awakening. Calista's reprogramming, de-brainwashing; Ramiyah's rebirth. She had to be gathered, set free, she carried a change that was necessary, her time was now.

So the mission that was created with foresight, beyond the conceptualisation of time and space; death and rebirth. Aeons ago one prophesied this very thing: the ascension of hueman consciousness to its Neter state with the ability to survive within the hueman vessel without restrictions. This ascension would help us create and destroy at will with the power of the kundalini energy; more formidable when combined with its other half, the Blue Flame. The Legend of Bluka. Restoring balance and order and harmony with the universe and oneself, there was no other way but to turn a tale, a prophecy into reality. It would virtually destroy the fabrication we had all come to accept and jeopardise the infrastructure our Ancestors had built. Evil and good would become one, inseparable.

The mission: Calista had to enter her Lower Self.

A month later. Tamari and I plot against The Kutawala as usual, and strive to educate Calista with her purpose on

Kimarr. Over a long game of Aware, we discuss how we'll encourage her to understand from our perspective. Some of our actions may come across as aloof, but it'll be worth it in the end. Calista will come to know her reality for what it is, the truth unmasked in its entirety, the good and bad sides of life, starting with the Savage Games.

I make my move, picking up three beads spreading them over the next couple of holes on his side of the unfolded plank of wood.

Tamari scratches his jaw. "So, the Lower self, what is it to you?" Everyone interprets it differently but from what I've read and tried to download from nature it is much more than frequency.

"It is what the Earthlings call Hell. They have misinterpreted its true meaning to be something external and evil. They have given it a physical form in application with the so-called Devil Lucifer. Here the Lower Self is a state of mind, it has many variations from the chakras being blocked to one's perception and understanding of life which in turn develops their character and personality. Typically, the Lower Self holds the negative energies: desire, doubt, obsession, anxiety, ignorance."

"How does this apply to Calista moving forward?"

"In her Lower Self from there she will ascend. We will be her only voice of reason. It's a tricky thing to alter one's teachings about their reality. But at her lowest that will be her greatest test, it has to be, faced against her mind almost in isolation. She must decide to give up and default to her new reality or change and allow us to lead her. We've seen what people become when all they must know is how to survive."

"She comes from a different place, where everything seems perfect. What if she cannot handle it?"

"Doubt is a stage of the Lower Self, we are fluctuating to our Higher Selfs. She succeeded as an Elite Supreme Warrior, I hold the highest expectation though I should not. Now she resides in the unwelcoming cocoon of her mind after freeing Tamika, she is not alone, Ramiyah is with her. I may be her enemy having made the difficult decision in confiscating her Life Force but everything must continue onwards."

She will rise again as will my sister.

"Sometimes following your heart means losing your mind."

16

{Calista}

A cold metal around my wrists, a firm hand pressed against my head, I'm in the back of a self-driving car. The window is down but a thin mesh obstructs it.

People watch me, their noses pointing, tongues performing a twisted dance I'm sure spew nothing but criticism and judgement. It's alright though, I shrug, I couldn't care less what they thought. This is all a commotion I'm amused by. It's a pity they can't see past their ignorance and as a result rely on the notion that all youngsters of my generation are corrupt, out of control and are just living in the moment — for the rush. They wouldn't know the half of it. To generalise means to put death to individual characters whose righteousness goes unnoticed. Earthlings, presumptuous. That's not to say my own aren't the same but just the sheer confidence they maintain while believing themselves to be high and mighty, the closest to God who has all the answers for how one must live, all the rights from the wrongs. I can't help but rolls my eyes and laugh at the ridiculousness. Either way, I, Princess Calista of the First Dynasty am not the one they see, the one they know to be guilty of a petty crime.

The sirens on top of the police car wail the entire ride to the police station. I have a subtle ringing in my ears and a headache when hauled out and shoved through the glass doors. The station is busy like I'm sure they are used to, a few officials catch my eyes and I wink, not that they cared with the truck-load of work on their hands. I'm transferred to an interrogation room where my wrists are cuffed to a chain on the table before being left alone.

There are no visible cameras but that's not to say they are not watching. The walls are grey and one bright light dazzles my eyes every time I look at it above my head. There is a black screen that stretches from the door to cover half of the room.

A man finally walks in, the door swinging close without a sound, and sits opposite me with his hands clasped together on the table with what one would assume to be a menacing look. An act, I decide, to get me to crack quicker. Generally, in these types of situations, the interrogator will get straight to the point, wasting no time, but this one is different. Our eyes lock in a staring competition. My eyebrows inch up and I huff, silence tempting me to fracture its spell. I rattle my chains and smile, my patience for such a game long gone. The sooner we get started the sooner I leave. My chains don't clink long, the sound must have infuriated him; his hands are on them without another huff on my part.

"Who are you?" he asks with a soft voice that doesn't match his rough, untidy self. I guess he hasn't been home to look in the mirror and shave. The question mark slapped across his forehead forms a few scattered lines of age and fatigue.

"Who am I, that is a good question?" I look at the cameras, the ones blended in with the black screen, a faint red light showing they are recording. "I do not know. Who are you?"

I smile and match his hands now clasped together; body slightly hunched over the table. My eyes slip to the badge around his neck. "Detective Force ..."

He cuts me off at once, his tongue slithering out his mouth. "I've encountered many people like you before ..."

"Oh yes, do tell."

"... who think they know it all, are above the system and when caught doing their shenanigans can worm their way out of sanctions ..."

"Oh really, those thoughts never crossed my mind."

"Well, I'm going to be concise with this statement. There is no loophole. You commit a crime; it goes on your record."

Correction, I never committed a crime. I just happened to be in the wrong place at the right time, dressed as the perpetrator who naturally fled the scene.

"Go ahead and speak to me as if I am five and expect me to comply just because of your occupation. No matter what you say, detective," I boldly smile cocking my head to the side, "*I will get out of this.* You know why?"

He glances at the black screen. "I'm all ears, miss?"

"Because I am above the system. In fact, there is no trace of me *within* the system. This is, of course, why you started off this conversation asking me who I am and not saying 'you have the right to an attorney, Mary' if that was my name. Oh, and let's not forget the famous lines, *do you understand the extent of your crimes?*"

Silence. I must have said too much.

"You think you're smart, don't you?"

"I know I am, detective. This is why I practically *don't exist.*"

I sigh and lean back in my chair as far enough to not cause my wrists to strain with the cuffs.

"Why are you not in the system?" His quizzical look is one of desperation and frustration, it would have been best if I said nothing at all now I've garnered his unwanted attention. I just wanted to play with him, trigger an Earthling, maybe I've gone too far. There is no way he would understand.

My tongue curled and restrained; I hang my head. I only hope he will grow impatient with me; realise he has got the wrong one and know he cannot charge me with anything. Holding me any longer will be a waste of their resources, time and effort.

The minutes go by, him just staring, reading my false file and CCTV recording of the crime in action. My hair flowing to my chest I rock my head until something stabs my left temple. It flares, prickling and jabbing, pulling my attention away from my curled ends to the black screen. This method, this presence, no Earthling could perform. Only a Genapian. Only one I've already established a mind-link with.

Trained on the figure beyond the screen, his arms folded with an expressionless face. The detective retrieves a key from his pocket and opens the cuffs. My hands plop to the table, then my wrists rotate but until he makes a move, I will not. The person on the other side, he is all I see. He is the reason for my being here. But in the state that I'm in does he recognise me? "Did I mention, I am not from around here?" The words tumbled out of my mouth with no recognition. Maybe I still wanted to play the game, after all, I now have the eyes of the one I wanted.

"Clearly. I don't suppose this has an answer attached to it?" The detective drawls.

"I am afraid I don't kiss and tell. Who is that?" I point at the person on the other side of the glass.

The detective's eyes pierce my head, widened, wondering if I can see through the screen — something virtually impossible.

"What are you talking about?" *Don't tell me your sanity doesn't exist too?* he thought.

"The detective with the cornrows." I move to the screen tapping on the glass with my nails.

"Alright, I'm done." He is out the room in a flash, to stay with me any longer would drive him up the wall.

I press my ears against the glass and eavesdrop.

Detective Force shakes his head — a rattle toy that would lose all its beads if it wasn't contained. "You know you're not supposed to be here, right?"

"I know, just cover for me; it won't happen again." Detective Force fist bumps his colleague and motion for someone to cut the camera feed. His final words before he goes for some fresh air are, "she's delusional man."

The door opens again and he walks in straight to the chair. My eyes follow him, his eyes avoid mine altogether until I sit across from him. His mind open to me, I control my skill much better. It has always been this way with the help of technology though our connection is much more and now that my psychic abilities have revealed themselves it's like we are one thought. He has worries for me being here as well as concerns for his assignment. But for me to be here, now, when I should be elsewhere, he doesn't know what to think.

"Detective Michael, it has been quite a while since I last laid eyes on your handsome face." I laugh inside of course, putting on the poshest accent I can muster.

"What trouble have you gotten yourself into, my love?" A smile peeks at the corners of his lips as does my own at hearing his voice and my term of endearment. *My love.*

"Oh no sir, you must have me confused with somebody else, this situation is most definitely *not* what you think it is. I have been wrongly accused. I understand you have nothing to charge me with, so if you could kindly release me, that'll be most gracious of you sir." To talk like the Earthlings, all uppity and proper seems like a tease. If one of them ever heard me I'm sure they'd look at me sideways.

He stands and places his hands on the table. "Am I going to get an explanation?"

When you release me, I will tell you whatever you want to know. I whisper into his mind with all seriousness, the rhythm of my voice back on its regular beat, each word pronounced carefully.

"That is what I thought."

He escorts me out the room and pass the reception, no one notices us leave. It will be like I was never there. He leads me to his car, a Lexus LC black. The beauty of such a vehicle, I can only praise with a 'hmph' of satisfaction; our Master Teachers really 'hooked them up' for this assignment.

"Michael really, Dakarai?"

The traffic light turns red and he slows on the brake.

"It is just a cover, just like this is." He removes a hand from the steering wheel gesturing at my glamour. Not needing the hint twice, I remove and show my true self. "So, mind telling me what you are doing here Cali, aren't you supposed to be on your assignment?"

"I need your help actually." I look out the window responding with a little sniffle. I didn't want him to see my expression and me to see his disappointed one. He takes his eyes off the road for a second. "My love, look at me." There is tension in my neck — I refuse. A little ashamed I couldn't complete my assignment alone, I clench my jaw, but if I need help. I need help. Unity. Us Elite Supreme Warriors must depend on each other when in danger or in need of assistance. My love should be no exception. And so, despite the pang in my chest, I give in.

He sucks in his bottom lip between his teeth. "What's the problem?"

"Not here."

He mutters under his breath, "that serious."

When we reach his apartment, he flashes his key card at the scanner before walking up all nine flights of stairs to his floor. We near his door, a woman leaves her apartment opposite. She is looking down at first, rotating her neck. She spots our shadow and looks up; her face brightens then relaxes as she looks past Dakarai to me glued to his back.

"Hey Michael, who is this?"

He slots his key card in the hole unbothered by the question. "Why you so nosey man?"

"Damn boy you holding out on me again?" She shakes her head. "I don't believe we've had the pleasure of meeting, I'm Maliyah."

What did she mean again?

"Nailah." Her hand twitched as if wanting to put it out for me to shake, but she holds off. There is something odd about her that I cannot place. I guess because of this feeling it is better to give her my middle name. If our hands did meet, I am sure I would have gotten an answer to that feeling, but only at the expense of exposing myself. She strikes me as the type of person who could get under your skin just from a brief touch.

"Mali, I'll talk to you later."

Mali, is that how acquainted they've become?

Dakarai puts a hand on my waist and gently pushes me into his apartment. Even after inside, his hand remains.

"You want anything to drink?"

He disappears into his bedroom.

"Maybe some water."

"There should be some in the kitchen." He steps to me with a towel and his shirt off. I keep my eyes on his face, the face I've longed to see; the face that has changed so much.

"I'll take a quick shower then we'll talk after, make yourself at home."

He kisses my cheek but something is off, his energy, he tries to hide a lot, wear a brave face. Other than my news something else has been going on here on Earth. He's in the bathroom before I could tug on his arm.

Have I come in the middle of something?

Two hours till midnight.

"I think it is best if I tell you tomorrow." I spring from his sofa, push through the cramp in my thighs and trail the summit of his cheek, a stamp away from his eyes. His skin is shining with the light texture of shea butter but his brows are lowered, his eyes on mine.

Dakarai's hand slips under my arm pulling me to him. The safety of his hold, I want to escape, drift, forget all that has happened since our separation. Be vulnerable to admit my mistakes, my worries, my fears. The warmth to his grip, I limp in response.

"Why are you stalling Cali? What news do you bring?"

"It is late."

I break away; he reinforces his arms monkey-gripped around me. His face in mine, nowhere else to go boxed with truth and uncertainty, his eye contact I reciprocate.

"Show me if words are too much." The clouds between our foreheads thin, clearing in preparation to touch, third eye's aligned to transfer information.

"Seeing is much worst ... you will have questions ..."

"Naturally," he scoffs.

"I cannot answer them. There is stuff I don't know; my memory is fuzzy I ... my dreams only show fragments of what has happened."

This is most probably a side effect of me not taking the proper precaution to get here under short notice while my other half stays in Kimarr-Rimorr.

A second is all it takes, his head to bump my temple, the link for transfer broken. His breath on my earlobe, the question I knew he wanted answers for. "What are you saying, you should have told me about your assignment before I left?"

My heart nods.

But my voice. "If I did, we would probably both be in the same boat." My mind holds no such conviction. The Prince whatever he said, Dakarai and I, he probably would have found a way to separate us.

Dropped from his embrace, his hands rub up and down his face. "Nonsense." The expression is thrown and rotated with his neck then forced into my palms as they are covered with his. "My love, just tell me."

Burning, my desire, his, together we are a rock weathered by a stream, the dam useless to its current. Crumbling with every nook, I push up to his neck, squeeze, bury the dreadful voice I evict from my mind. Hoping he wouldn't hear, I whisper, "I'm dying."

THE KUTAWALAS

"Keep others in suspended terror: cultivate
an air of unpredictability."

T he Civil War wasn't the first time Acirfa was invaded.
There was another time, aeons ago, just when
Genapians were beginning to understand and advance their
technology beyond its roots in the earth. When the beings
of outer space stumbled upon their world, travelling infinite
light-years for this chance, this opportunity, it became
increasingly obvious. This was no coincidence. The way they
manoeuvred through the sky, their ships blinking into the
first layer, after decades, millenniums of research, of course
they wouldn't just stop there. Touching the sky was the first
part, landing and taking what they could — the ultimate
goal. Acirfa, at the pinnacle of the universe, often argued the
universe itself according to the Sun's and Supreme Deities
children, they had arrived. They had done what no other race
had and it was refreshing, it was doing something to them.

Wherever they had explored before, breadcrumbs of
knowledge and information was gathered until they devised
the constellation points to find the Red Sun. Only then could
the coordinates be relayed from the Blue Star reflecting from
the Red Sun.

Down below, deep in the forests on Genapa, a seer with a tongue capturing the future broadcasted a dream she had lived through many nights. A nightmare that would befall Acirfa if not heeded with caution. To whoever's ears she could grab a hold of, to whoever's hand she could clutch onto with a breathless plea, she spoke these words, "from the sky, they will come, a race never seen before and they will kill, steal and destroy. They will not value what we have. They will not understand how things have been. They will try to change it all down to the roots in our earth." The one voice that had dared to wonder past these words, not brush them off as an old woman's stories, a child, "why elder, what have we done?"

The seer's only response, "their planet is dying, they are sick. We have been constant for too long."

"Constant." The young girl asked some more, even when pulled away by her parents. She did not understand the universe, its dual nature. Neither did most. But they would.

Chaos was creeping up on balance.

They descended from their ships oozing a strong green, their pale skin stark against the tree bark. The helmets they wore, a thin blue metal to their necks uncovered their faces and after the deep breath they took in robbing the trees of oxygen, they set their eyes forward. Their steps were giddy, their arms were sure, slicing down the leaves with their foot-long machetes, their minds were the clearest it had ever been. An incredible feat, to have traversed the stars in search of what couldn't be found by any other until now. With this in mind, the first group of Genapians they took them by surprise and sliced every one of their necks. The blood that spilled to the earth, sizzled, it carried a scent. It moved through the earth, with harrowing cries and when the news travelled to those that were quick to not believe, protecting the seer at all costs was a must.

She did not tell them, "see, you should have listened." She just grimaced, allowed herself to be led away.

The Genapians knew life outside of their planet existed, they weren't ignorant to that. Many had taken the courage to explore the depths of the universe and teach upon their return all that they had found. Still, in their innocence, divinely-pure, never did it cross their minds that those who were sick and as such jealous and envious of what they had would descend onto their land bringing such horror. As a result, there was no need to protect Acirfa anymore than the Blue Star and Red Sun already did. The Seer always thought it strange, the lack of effort placed around their planet; just like the opinions and worries she had always had, the Supreme Deities would not be enough to protect them.

Acirfa's first taste of blood ... a poison to the Genapians minds. One that had settled into their DNA, for generations to come the memory would be locked forever in such code. Of a time many feared most and the result, their minds crippling under pressure, their bodies ruined without proper burial and reunification with the Ancestors. The taste of fear, the one hope from the anointed Mother Seer, what a combination.

"Our sisters and brothers lives lost must be repaid with our dedication and conviction to survive. Take control, change our reality as the Supreme Deities decide while gifting I with their tongue."

They were all nodding their bowed heads, pressing their fists in the earth. At her feet like grandchildren, those willing to do more than learn, they filled their hearts with her *truth*, her power. For to take action their minds had to be blessed with water, unearthed from the fearful state being held in captivity. Not one of desperation however, be like the elements; have your calm, your journey, stillness while you plot. While you devise; while you let the fire ignite, then burn, and burn ... till it explodes with its purpose.

What to be done, the Mother Seer's foretelling far less as detailed as the first, "we are at the cycle's resurrection, a clan must rise, many in unity. Leaders commanding what will be born from the Red Sunstones."

"I"

The boys, the males, the men took to their stand. The women too, the girls advised to keep the Mother Seer warm. Those that ventured out, groups to the north, west, east, south, prepared for any encounter with the Albinos, struck them with the full backing of those that had fallen before them. Not an eyelid batted, not a heave of bile up their throat. The mission was set; the mind focused. Petty things such as worrying for their huemanity would come later.

The Red Sunstones, hidden across land and sea by the first men and women; it took many years of searching to gather all six. Their every step had become drenched in death, blood, and their mourning, it was kept up in high spirits till those that remained filled with joy pocketed the raw materials. The less than a thousand that had returned, crept in the dead of the night into the slave compound, the Albinos deep in slumber after belly fulls of liquor.

"The ritual, overseen by the moon and Blue Star, then all will end. All will begin." Her final words, travelled along her dying breath; spell-carried by the wind into the Genapians ears. And so, they trudged to the forest, setting fire to the camp that should have never been.

From east to west, there stood two mountains. They waited, even while the smoke alerted and lit the sky. The Red Sunstones had already begun their cast before the Blue Star's peak. And the full moon high, as were their ships. What had begun was beautiful, it would not be stopped as the Supreme Deities breathed in their life. The sky split as did any surrounding ships, completely annihilated by the fusion of the Red Sun, Blue Star and full moon. The Red Sunstones that levitated from the six elders' hands, who had initiated their responsibility as heads to the breeding clans, melted then reshaped clean and cut into six golden staffs from the metal ores of the earth.

The vow:

"To protect Acirfa. To build a legacy of strength and honour. To symbolise the return of divinity. To be as pure as Ma'at."

The Red Sunstones would reinforce a shield around Acirfa and through generations would be strengthened by six gates and Elite Supreme Warriors.

The Blue Star shone the brightest it ever had that day, pouring its energy into the six leaders who inaugurated the first chain of dynasty rulers and as such the Blue Flame validating this union unlocked in their DNA. By time the Kutawala's arrived unable to halt the ritual, they were blocked off by the energies surrounding the Genapians. A forcefield they could not touch unless they wished to burn to the bone. The dynasty leaders directed their Blue Flame and staff at their invaders and flashes — only flashes.

Whatever happened to the Kutawala's and their Albinos that day, how they escaped perhaps, whoever lived shall tell the tale. Through the stories. Through their scriptures. Through their teachings.

Whoever brave to reopen the sore of huemanity.

"To survive a nation of sheep ruled by wolves owned by pigs you must become a lion."

17

{Calista}

Back in my cell.

The voices are back; a blur of noise, silence; maybe they are all my thoughts emptying through the walls screaming at me. The damp floor my nails caress or claw, I cannot tell. That is not all, my eyes they sting as though covered and marinated in cayenne pepper. And the red tint, the only strong colour to my vision, it narrows to something thin. It's in my hand, I'm winding it closer, spinning the material to its tangled end. But there is no such. It is beyond my reach, far into another cell. Far into where the darkness evades with a strange emptiness. Her presence that lingers, her energy that deflates my lungs; her nails that would scratch along the bars. I squeeze the string at the memory. The imprint she has left, the one initiated by *her*, The Prince ... I will go through it until it is stripped from me.

I see the way they look at me, it was the same way they did Tamika. They inspect every inch of my physical from the walls they chain themselves too. But their eyes, they never leave my hands. The hands, though dirty with sweat, skins of dead flesh, still managed to be live with blood that were not their own. Hands that have taken the bow to sin and turned its head and heart to oppose each other. Those that weep, knowing I the newly elected champion will trample upon them much quicker than they could lift a fist in their defence. I, the one whose eyes they don't see are filled with sand though beyond the surface holds the whole ocean in a drop. I, the one who is engulfed with every death, even if I am not the culprit, in an all-around video. I cannot incline my head to my scarred feet without seeing their shadows, their eyes, the huemanity that had been robbed from them.

So I keep to my cell, to the wall I was chained to when I arrived. The only space I'm worth. Yet, the one who hasn't evaded me the way I wished, she stretches from the shadows and sits facing me. Her eyes are closed. Soon too mine follows. Let's forget, I whisper to my mind. Let us disappear to somewhere far far away.

Against the dead, limp grass, caked-soil itches between my toes. The sun obscured with toxic green clouds, it would have been better if I had a little more control over my dream. Then I could alter its stark semblance to the reality I live — far away from the sun's gaze. The clouds that forever stay the same, talk about being predictable and consistent. Him too, with his back half to me staring off at another. The Prince he clicks his finger, its snap almost like a wake-up call its the only sound

I hear. And the sound waves it emitted travelled with a hazy purple. It deforms from his finger nails, pumping through the scene I had begun to question. Of life, birds nesting in trees that had their branches and leaves. Of nature abundant with its streams and navigating across rock beds to mountains and seas. Of what it means when Mother Nature is as it should be, without compounds and camps of chained Genapians raw with nakedness and shame.

The purple haze it lifts me to The Prince's side who takes my shoulders between his hands and gives me a little shove. I stumble as a shadow; a woman she bandages a leg, then an arm, to a head and hand, walking through me as she colour codes the wounds of those she dresses. Red for those most in danger, a torn ligament, a burst vessel, immediate care was needed. But from their lack of medicine, those able to perform the procedures necessary, not to mention the question of the cleanliness of their environment, it would be difficult to extend their life span. Many of those in such a predicament knew that and fidgeted with the red strips, some even disobedient enough to throw them to the side and curse at the ground. Still, she continued, not a care in the world — actually, with all the care. The sweat on her brow, the fatigue in her muscles, the power of her thought is what she persisted with. That, *I will be of service no matter the lengths.* Her thoughts, loud and clear, not my own. Beyond all of this, she shined as the beauty she is. Her crown though hidden behind thick locks dangling ancient silver jewellery, symbols of animals winged and four-legged, crossed with bold lines and little swirls; neither tipped or toppled off her head. And following the curve of her jaw to her neck, an Ankh, Ma'at's head and small crystal beads wrap into her necklace. Her hair gracefully on her back curls shaving her ankles. As if that wasn't enough and the Supreme Deities had to do much more, her nut-brown skin and curvaceous figure is hugged loosely with a floor-length red dress. Diamante rings her shoulders and arms the length of her torso; very fine material if touched wouldn't hold any weight. A belt is fitted around her waist with the Dynastic Emblem glistening in gold.

Such regal beauty and pure energy, I'm reminded of my mother. A feminine goddess. The kind one would dream to meet, become captivated by in stories but the world overlooks for she is meant to be one step behind never centred ahead. Empowered even though we have never met, energy surges into my body. Her smile stretches across full lips, her bright brown eyes crinkling with satisfaction. During her time of great evil, she still finds the strength to be the light. Undefeated by the poison sown all around.

"Meet my mother."

Simply confirming, I remember his presence. Yes, they do share some likeness.

Her bare feet pad from body-to-body, giving them clean water and dressing their wounds with some type of oil she carries in her satchel. Her hand glows with blue energy, healing those coded with yellows then some red.

They thank her, cuddling together for warmth, bowing their heads for her blessings and continued care.

There's a cough. A chorus of coughs. The painfully, deep-throat kind. The Queen straightens. The Kutawala and his Albinos animated with their magic excreting from their pores, grab what their eyes feast upon. The children, girls in particular, plucked from the embrace of their protector's squeal — their skins scorched at the brief touch. Many cowered, many shouted stirred with the spirit of warriors.

"Leave here."

"The Supreme Deities will curse you."

"Over our dead body!"

This could not happen again, had to stop. A thought free from the darkness, panting with feet doubling, tripling, scaling the distance acted with a gust of debris. His panther roaring with an entrance that stopped the Albinos mid-motion, shape-shifted from his skin. The Kutawala skidded a little back raising his hand. The clenching of his fist and extension cracked into the panther's nose. The magic spread from there, a rapid-fire of venom stretching through its fur coercing its departure. The tentacles from The Kutawala's knuckles, a prism around the panther cuffed it back to Tamari. He all but crumpled, the panther minimising in size, its roar a last dwindling fight. The prism shifts to Tamari broken on his knees — the master at its obstacle. People gasp. Some cry into their hands, bowing to the earth almost wishing to fall soundlessly into their graves. An abomination had befallen one of their own.

As it took its shape and form, I was walking closer. I felt so light though my heart was growing heavy.

Blood drained from his face; skin stripped of its dark pigment transitions to look like them; an Albino. Bleached white, he had become unrecognisable even to himself in a puddle of water. An invader, his people stare at him. An invader in image.

The Prince in his younger years, no longer held back by his mother shoots forward, his third eye glowing a deep purple. An arm pulls him back, it had broken through the prism.

Tamari held him firm; *not him too, not my brother.* Tamari whimpers; his panther slowly fades a translucent-white, then nothing.

"You cannot do this." The Prince shouted in The Kutawala's mind.

"I was young and foolish." He recalls from beside me.

"And brave." It was all true and The Kutawala laughed at the fact. "I can do whatever I want because you allow it and I own you. Now if you know what's good for you, you will keep your mouth shut."

The Prince falls to his knees Tamari slumps against him.

"I could not find a lie in what he said. We had surrendered, my father had bent the knee even if it was to ensure our safety. A king must never ..."

The Queen sees to her people, but it isn't enough when every day The Kutawala comes to take them away. But today, unlike any other she sweeps past her children.

"If you want my people you are going to have to go through me."

Tamari grunts, "no." Many others dispute her decision.

"Anyone else feeling rebellious today?" The Kutawala widens his arms. One-by-one the elderly rise, then the children. If the queen is willing to put her life on the line for them, they will do the same. There is no them without her. Their dynasty has to live on somehow. They beat their chests with their fists and mutter prayers for their queen.

"May the Supreme Deities bless her with strength."

The Kutawala snarls. The beating muddles him, its rhythm off-putting to his chaotic nature. Impulsive, his magic whips around her neck. His eyes beg for a cry, a move of disobedience to aggravate and justify why he must make an example of her. The magic fleshes from her neck and scorches the corners of her dress. She pushes her energy into a cocoon of heavenly light sticking to her skin. The magic repels. Back ten-fold it chews on her supreme-symbols, biting its way through to every piece of the cloth that tore then fell; her body a model of scars.

"For every mark, you become a reminder of what will happen if you disobey."

"So be it. You may have our physical form, but in time you will realise you picked the wrong civilisation to interfere with."

"We picked perfectly, in fact, we were welcomed." His magic slips around her hair. She clenches her fists, her rings cutting deep. The Prince paled in comparison to Tamari soaking up her pain. Like water crawling onto the sand, the magic burned at her hair. Within minutes, it has shortened her hair to her waist. The chanting and chest-beating gets louder. Her energy snuffed; the magic destroys what remains of her dress. Naked and spine in perfect alignment, her eyes challenged she says, "you will reap what you have sown. We will always and forever be protected by our Supreme Deities."

Snap!

We are forced out of the memory to the stars above Acirfa.

"Imagine with all our abilities in two moves he could do that to my brother and my mother, it makes you wonder ..."

"Right."

"Could he be capable of much more, have we already reached the peak of our potential? It has been 10 years and my sister ... now we must rise."

Though said so simply, it's a process. Rising doesn't just tick off like a bomb. This has me wondering, how long has she been with me?

"Ramiyah, how did she ..."

The Prince's image ripples, his purple haze, but like the first time I saw him in the arena. Another stands in his place. Whether conjured by my mind or because they share the same space, same blood, DNA spliced into two. She smiles with his lips, winks at me with his eyes, beckons me forth with his hand. All her or all him, I'm back in our cell.

The child still facing me eyes closed.

18

{Calista}

The following morning, I knew when I sat at the kitchen table, there was something more than my worries in the air. As if I had to hold my breath for if disturbed by sound, silence would be like a parachute with a punctured hole. I being the passenger unable to cease my fall, trigger my leg to bounce and chew the inside of my cheek.

How will Dakarai react?

He hadn't uttered a single word after he excused himself. It got strange right after he guided me away from him. His touch had lost its presence, as did his mind, I wonder most. Did he sleep at all? We could have talked some more about it, I could have reassured him somehow, right?

No. Death was nothing to joke about worse something to engage in conversation at the hours meant for sleep. I pictured him as a mirror, his reflection I could see then couldn't, this distortion. Just like my own. Could he still see me? I wonder again sipping my peppermint tea.

When I tip my empty cup, the single droplet crawling down the side, his bedroom door swings open. I exhale as does the door returning to its close. He's dressed in all black. A little closer I see I was right. His eyes tell it all, not looking at me consumed with a weight they cannot hold. He mutters a good morning — at least I think he does.

The energy we give off, I wait for him to collect himself resting against the back of my chair. If I am to be afraid of anything it would be this; this inability to speak so freely, be my true self and instead of guessing knowing exactly what the outcome of yesterday's brief talk would be. This uncertainty. I hate it.

My back towards him I only hear him turn on the tap, rinse his cup after drinking his tea, turn it off. Silence once more. I assume, facing the window, he is gazing at the sunrise. Being this high up, he like a bird can look down at the citizens of London commuting to and from work, the trees rustling with a light breeze and pigeons using the city as its toilet. The warm glow of the sun pushes his shadow over me and I touch it; distant although always near. His head bows and I return my hands to my lap.

"Were you lying to me?" I wince, my heart thrums with the idea that he thought I would fool him. To answer him, I shouldn't, it would be embarrassing. Offended, I bite my tongue. The counter top sigh and he's in front of me. He does not sit, arms at his side, he connects with my eyes.

"Lately, you have been acting out of the ordinary. The secrets you have budding it has finally caught me in your web. Our two assignments were meant to be kept apart." I lower my gaze. "If what you are saying is true, how did it happen?"

Yes, how did it happen, my fall into this trap? My precious life threatened by those whose survival I sought to expose? How did they do it? Firstly, "I was kidnapped once I reached Kimarr, the rest. A blur of events."

But what he said 'acting out of the ordinary' did something else happen before that I have forgotten?

"You aren't so sure yourself, how must I know where I must start? My situation here isn't that great either. I cannot be as impulsive as you. Come on Cali ..."

Come on Cali, THINK.

This is what should have been said because I know the same. Have I rushed for help too soon?

My throat dry I mutter, "this time it is different Dakarai. I can feel it. I can really lose myself here."

"Must you always be saved." It stings, his words, his thoughts, this whole situation ... The truth I can take but I'm in the ocean suffocating, my hands I believe are tied. Either I go through with The Prince's instructions, whatever they were, or return home a failure.

Dakarai scratches his jaw, unshaven and the hairs in tight balls. "I know we made a pact to always protect each other, but this ... can you not get yourself out of this situation without my intervention?"

How does one escape the grasps of eminent death?

"I don't know what to think ... there's this SYSTEM ... you being here when you shouldn't ... where is the evidence?"

"I get it ok. My image doesn't match my words. But there are many on the path to death who look ... healthy and fine but up here ..." I tap my right temple. "I'm lost and I'm dying. And in here ..." my left hand massaging my heart, "I can feel what he has taken from me. What is missing."

I stand and point my forehead into his shoulder. The tears are coming, bubbling far too quickly to the surface and I would rather swallow them. But, "my timing is off and I get it, I shouldn't have come."

Come home. Come to where it would be easy to escape and drift away into a fictitious reality where nothing mattered anymore.

"Cali. Don't be like that."

How else should I be?

"Did you know I got put on suspension? Yesterday I wasn't even supposed to be in the station. I am an alleged suspect in a case that is directly linked to Khari and I. I feel like this may be the first assignment I may fail, and now you come to me with this ..."

Failure is present for both of us, a dark cloud oozing with static and rain, will the sky ever clear and let through the sun?

Our sighs are heaved into our space. He places his hands on my shoulders, his warmth seeps through my clothing.

"If you are really dying, how can you be here right now?"

The question that should have been asked long ago. With how portals are set up on Acirfa, stepping through one in the state that I should be would only accelerate my death. My cells would be zapped with its energy and I probably wouldn't have made the trip here but –

I don't feel like myself.

Should I tell him?

Must he know much more?

The vow we've made to protect each other, must it be upheld?

I am not the same. What I've become. A monster.

A murderer.

I know deep down Dakarai wants to face the reality of my situation for what it is. "You know the teachings. *'Evidence must align with one's claims. We must think before we act on something that could be nothing. Evaluate every detail before making a move. Strategy over impulse.* The code Cali, won't you abide by it even if what you say is true?"

Khari may as well be standing here, they are one and the same. And the truth it strokes my back while whispering, *'how can I help you when you withhold what is most important? Be vulnerable. Know that I can only assist when you unveil the picture your mind has fractured.'*

"How are you here now?" His stare penetrates my temple.

I step shoulder-to-shoulder. "The one thing we are supposed to leave as a last resort." His lips part, before he can say, "no you didn't." The words that shouldn't have been given life I release, "Create a double."

"There are no coincidences. Every event we experience and every person we meet has intentionally been put in our path to help raise our level of consciousness."
-Cheryl Richardson

19

{Dakarai}

The mind can be a fragile thing. When it's overloaded with worry and anxious of the future, it can make the body sick. It can play tricks and illusions that one would think is real just because they thought it. Pondered upon that thing. Gave it life through constantly calling it forth into existence. When under pressure, similar to the breath it can choke you up when unable to be released. The mind, my mind how would it look now? Fractured, broken pieces concerning the White Room, the SYSTEM, SARAH ... Calista's arrival, am I even in my right mind to decide on the next course of action for us? For me and Khari? Or. Me and Calista?

The universe works in mysterious ways. The thought triggers a laugh, one empty of vigour and joy. My eyes linger on the door she walked through after our talk. For her to come to me now, when things are getting spicy, confusing, I really wonder if this is the universe's doing or this so-called SYSTEM? Her articulation was mainly through body language, the words she truly wanted to share it went back to the fragility of the mind. I could see it so clearly, we walk the same path in two different worlds. The words if only they had touched her tongue, I would have been pulled from my mind into hers with or without her permission. She was crying, I know she was, why else would she bury her eyes in my shoulder, squeeze the life out of my fingers. Such weight imprinted on her mind, I felt it bury in my heart.

"I'm torn." I breathe pressing my thumb into the side of my finger.

What had Kimarr done to her? The confidence she walked with before we parted, her smile beaming with wonder and exploration in my memory was all but smoke, for my love ...

"I hate to see her this way."

Almost like a stranger.

Unknowing of what she had become on this journey, or she knew too well but felt ashamed to expose herself; how vulnerable she had become. How unlike herself.

Create a double.

Buzz.

I fish my phone from my pocket. Unknown caller. For about three seconds I watched it ring then looked to the door. I didn't want my love to stray too far. The vibrating stops. It kicks off again on my watch. No caller ID. After the fourth ring, I answer.

"Follow me, I have something of yours." The voice is masked.

"Who are you?"

The line goes dead.

I stride over to my window, crack it open and peer down below. The trees on the common terrace, at the centre between two branches hanging low there's a bench. Someone sits with their back to me, their hoodie up. Everything seems normal, especially the residents commuting to and from work. With a sigh, I release the handle and lock the window.

"Ah, it wouldn't hurt to have a look."

My jacket in hand, keys shoved into my pocket, I slide out of my apartment. Outside, pushing through the doors that swing on behind me, the seated figure is gone. I brush a hand where they sat. Something gritty and white spreads on my fingertips. It's like the dream I had, the ball of codes that rolled along my skin. The feeling I can still remember.

Someone brushes my arm; something drops into my hand. I go to grab him with my other. His hood slips off, his wavy hair streaming black towards me.

"Hey?" I shout.

He skips forward, the black lifts him off the concrete and into a tree. He disappears like a drop of water in a puddle.

It looks like magic, the kind I've seen before when I was on the run from The Kutawala's Albinos, or maybe it isn't magic at all. There is no green glow. I unfold the note.

I've got the answers you're looking for.

No name, nor address. My watch buzzes again. "What?" I bark into the phone. The masked voice, as if reading my mind, provides a location and hangs up before I can press the person further.

Damn it.

Deptford high street. The bell chimes as I push the door to a cafe. An aroma of coffee and cupcakes fill the air, at once pleasant and sickening. The seats are arranged in booths along the right side of the shop with a few spotlights over the counter. I walk around the centre stairs leading to the basement catching a few wondering eyes from their conversations.

"Please take a seat anywhere you like and when you're ready to order just wave a hand or press the designated button at your table."

I give the young man a nod of the head. He never smiled once as he repeated his dialogue to every new customer he passed almost like a scratched record. He kept his hands under the white apron tied around his waist, it had the shops logo printed along the hem in bold red. I drew my eyes away from it as it flashed, I was not going there again with Earth's tricks. In the far corner, a woman opposite a mirror is at a table with dark shades on. The cafe is bright enough, all artificial light rather than sun, I couldn't figure out why she would bother. It didn't look like it was for the sake of looking cool or to hide from those that might recognise her. She readily blends in with her orange floral t-shirt and black trousers but those shades she removes a hand from her opened newspaper and tips it to her nose. Unlike Sarah, she looks a lot younger and sane. Her eyes, well the one I could see glows. This is enough to pull me to the vacant seat before her. My hand graces the top, its pushed out. She gestures to join her, meeting the top of her cup to her lips.

"You found me easy enough."

She continues to read today's newspaper. I wouldn't really call it reading as her head doesn't dip instead stays upright.

"What's this about?" I hunch a little closer. She folds the newspaper into half. I only see her throughout. One of her eyes is partially glazed over like fresh ice, the same one I glimpsed in the mirror. Even with this deformity, she moves like she has 20-20 vision, unbothered by my stare. Her other eye, I can't quite pinpoint where it directs whether at my throat or my chest. Whatever it assesses, the other eye reveals glowing in and out like a light bulb being fed electricity.

"Not quite what you were expecting ay?" What she picks up, I beat four fingers on a menu tablet. She's no Earthling. She's tugging on my aura; I'm seeing hers too. The same blackness her messenger carried. Pulsing around her silhouette, even in her shades. Her soft laugh I feel through the table as a low thrum. My eyes skim over the trucker hat pushing her tight curls onto her shoulders. She appears mature but it's clear she's in her late teens, maybe even early twenties.

"Are you in a rush?"

"You could say that."

"Well lucky for you so am I." She glances at the clock by the cashier. I look too the minutes slowing then the seconds. She's outstretching her aura; it crashes over the cafe. I don't see her power just feel it tickling my skin, when she clicks her finger then directs them to her eyes, the room is electrified. The walls are hazy. Everything is blurred apart from us and the table.

"Have you decoded Sarah's message yet?" I don't respond, still fascinated by her control. She doesn't bear the mark of the Eye of Horus, so what else could be allowing her to tap into the Ethers like this?

"See I would hurry up with that. Time is running out. Before you know it, you're back in your slumber. I could help with that, but it would only tamper with the purpose of her revealing herself to you."

"You said you have answers."

"I do, which is why they won't kill me. I'm too valuable. They need me."

"Who are they?"

"The person in control of the SYSTEM."

"Do they have a name?" I was drawing up my mental notepad at this point. Whatever connection she has with the SYSTEM and SARAH will be helpful but still how did she know to contact me?

"Maybe, maybe not. I can't tell you that either way. You're not ready. Besides, it will defeat the whole purpose of you coming to know the truth. When the time comes, you will speak their name, and that alone will be enough for you all to break free."

I roll my eyes relaxing on the cushions. Just typical. All that 'I can tell you enough to spark your curiosity but anything more you must find for yourself' crap she should have just kept to herself. What a time waster.

"What's the point of our meeting again?"

She folds her glasses and slips them into their pouch.

"SARAH of course."

"Right, her message. Not your message then. Or your message is to hear her message?"

She gives a flick of the hand, flips it left-right, 'comme ci, comme sa'. "She dropped a bombshell you and Khari are struggling to comprehend. A ESW always needs evidence, right?" She spreads her arms the tassels that drop from her cardigan hang like small berries from a tree. And they sway, light twinkling through the fabric. A few travel up her left shoulder and change to a soft pink, it doesn't appear to stop there as it gathers to generate even more. Maybe something dark.

"You need more evidence. A physical representation of what it is we talk about."

The light illuminates her face, her lips. What she says her pacing is off, far too slow.

"Here I am." She flashes a smile, full of straight teeth. The crinkles around her eyes, she thinks this is funny, a joke. "I've probably alerted them just by talking to you. See, just like you, I'm not supposed to be here, or awake. I've woken up."

My eyelids are drooping, I couldn't tell you when it started. I had to kick my foot to a tap to stay alert or even hear what she was saying. Something about waking up. I swallowed, blinking to look behind her. Through the blur, something was correcting, sharpening. A shadow, average height under 6 foot.

She keeps the conversation up though I'm not engaged.

"I'm still figuring that out, but something must be wrong. She must be getting closer."

"Who?" I whisper.

"The one who will set the bar for your enlightenment. She will destroy to escape."

The shadow has moved directly above her. Icky-black, at its core spikes protrude then retract.

"Does she have a name?"

I had asked that before, right? I press a hand to my forehead, swiping the thin sheet of sweat.

"Calista will have..."

My eyelids shoot back. The shadow, its arm moulds into a solid barrel. A single hole. As small as a marble. Even smaller is the light that crawls through it. Jagged lines. Blue-to-purple. Purple-to-red. Then a straight beam, stamped between my eyebrows. Smoke. Release. I dodge to the side, one arm guarding my face.

"Their tests have begun." Her voice rips, the bullet falls into her hand. A dull silver metal. On the surface, reflecting, Tadaaki's body wavers. His head in my hand. His blood. I jump to a stand. Not during the day. It has always been at night. The electric charge that bounces off my skin. Is she doing this, calling my nightmare forth?

"I have no control over your PTSD"

"It's just a memory acting out."

Her thick eyebrows narrow. "It's a good thing I cloaked us." She leans forward and whispers, "they're testing you through me."

"What do you mean?" I shift my hand to hover over my Eye of Horus. Any sudden moves, any weird appearances, I won't hesitate to act.

She stirs her tea. "The virus, it's attacking me. The ones in control." Her glazed eye shimmers, ants of intricate codes running like a Temple run game, every turn shows something different. Ones and zeros are the usual. But ones.two, two.ones, I've never seen before. As I get lost in them, Tadaaki's dead eyes I stare into again. She dangles a hand, I bend closer to her, they press into my temple. My fist knead into my thigh. His eyes they're bleeding, my mouth is spazzing open, close, loose with my jaw. Such pain, I don't want to remember. Relive.

"Make them stop."

The codes continue to float through her eyes.

"Make them stop."

"It's all you, your choice ..."

"No this is your fault," I swat her fingers from me, then point a shaky finger at her coded-eye, "you tell them, stay away from me. Get out of my mind."

The codes in her eye speed up, dancing, hopping over each other. Building a bridge, then collapsing.

"Can't you see I'm fighting back?" The strain in her voice, her teeth clenched. That's not good enough. He is still here. Tadaaki is still in my arms, his presence enveloping my senses.

"Are you messing with me? Is that why you called me? Not to tell me about the SYSTEM but to expose me to them,"

"You may not remember." Her nails jab into the table. "What that moment truly meant, what was covered up that you have forgotten. Your back there every night and still only see the horror, not the crack in the image."

"You wouldn't know. You wasn't there." I ram my fist into my eyes. I plead with them to dig the images out.

"I'm inside the SYSTEM. I was there."

"You did nothing?"

"I did everything. You forgot. I came to remind you. Right now." She stands, plucks my fists from my face and shoves them into my chest. An x around my heart. She pulls my wrists to her, then pushes them back into my chest. Every push, her energy pounds to my heart. A signal.

"There's a white room you're trapped in. Find the white room,

Dakarai."

Another gunshot ripples through the air. She disappears into black light.

"Do not listen with the intent to reply, but with the intent to understand."

20

{Calista}

In two minds or only one; bipolar, I just might have developed the condition. Ever since my split with my double, the other side has been cold. I don't know what's going on wherever she is, on Earth, with Dakarai maybe. I can't know, my nails scratching at my walls, tugging on my plaits, my condition is much worse now. Immediate, desperate. Everything is so heightened, I have nowhere to escape. Not in my mind, not through music. Even the dim specks of light around the cells, they can't do the damage I require. To go blind, to tear the colours from my eyes. For the red to dissolve with the white. The nights that I cry into my arm, I feel like a baby in need of her mother. In comfort. With a lullaby of safety, security.

The Prince spoke of darkness, I must step beyond, from the light into its territory. To what end, for what purpose? I cannot see what it must reveal. Yet, I didn't see this move they would pull on me.

Ramiyah, her rebirth.

A hand appears in my face. Bangles around the wrist, silver, brass and golden metal tight around fingers.

"Mother?"

"Follow me my child."

There's a golden glow. I looked down at my bloodied hands with cuts and bruises covering my knuckles. Tears spilled onto my black shirt. It was coming back to me, how I got here. Where this memory continued from.

In my rage with the ignition of my Blue Flame, the training room meant for everyone to share no matter if we were ESW's in training, Tech N9nes, Scholars, all factions; it had almost burned to ash. My fault. They all pointed with their eyes. My lack of control. Discipline. A princess had disrespected the very space they all felt safe in. And Father, I was embarrassed because of the way they laughed at me, mocked me. Father was the one to blame I believed; he should have talked to me in private. Helped me save face. I cannot remember what he did exactly, I just thought what kind of princess wasn't respected by her own people even as a child?

"Wipe your tears." Mother barged through my bedroom door without a care in the world. Of course, news had travelled to her, it probably reached as far out as the villagers too. What a mess! Her waist-length locks raised into the air like Medusa's snakes gliding against the wind she created. The royal stones, Jasper and Lapis Lazuli, were laced into her locks. She thrust her red scarf tightly around her arms. Her two-toned Ankara red and blue strapless dress hugged her figure and stretched out behind her.

"Look at you, is this my child?" She gestured for me to get up. I resisted at first, but when her stern look intensified, I felt a greater need to do as she asked. "You are a girl-child growing into a woman. Be in control of your emotions." I sniffed. "Let no man pull you low enough to hate him and what the universe gave you, that includes your father. Who are they to judge you, just because you are a woman and you carry the Blue Flame? Right?"

"Yes," I muttered between sniffles.

"That does not sound convincing."

"Yes Mother, I hear you. Loud and clear."

"But do you feel me?" She straightened my back and tucked a plait behind my ear. "Let no one break your spirit. You are strong, beautiful, and intelligent. There is nothing you cannot accomplish. Remember your teachings. Remember you have come to this plane with purpose. Accept yourself first, then your peers will too. If not, attract those that will. No daughter of mine will buckle under pressure." Mother smiled wide and proud. "Forget about how your father moves. He loves you and is pleased with your improvement even if he doesn't display such. You are doing great, not every woman is built to withstand this initiation, but you are. Look beyond your desire to please others. Keep pushing forward. Go through whatever becomes your obstacle."

Mother fades to smoke.

The hand that holds mine, I follow to Myah's face.

Change. Such a minuscule yet daunting thing. I have already changed so much. It's like I wear a mask, I struggle to find who I truly am with the constant battles that keep me submerged in their barbaric mentality. If I am not happy with myself, I must change, I must rise to the occasion and seek better. But isn't that what I had started out doing. The blood that smears my hands reminds me that I have become a monster but this is only a small sign of how low I have sunk. I take lives for the thrill ... but also to release my people from this animalistic life that has been bestowed upon them. Can I be redeemed? Can I still rise?

"Anyone can. From the Lower Self you can either sink or swim as goes the expression. Rebuild yourself Calista. The Savage Games, Tamika's death was only meant to knock you off your square. Find a new one."

Is this Myah talking to me? Her mouth isn't moving, her eyes are still on mine. She pulls herself closer while tugging on my hand. This is the closest she has ever been in my space. My breath touches the top of her head. She lets go and pushes her left hand then her right to my cheeks. I duck into my neck.

What is she doing?

The one thing I hate is people touching my face, especially if dirty and I hadn't given my permission. I latch onto her small wrists and begin to slide them off. But she coos. Like an owl at night. And I freeze, muscles tense. My body obeys a secret command I am unaware of. A sequence of vibrations spoken in a language unknown to me.

Her cold hands are warming. I jolt like I have been shocked with a defibrillator. What she shocks into me. I see memories that are not my own. I had glanced these in my dreams. Three different stages of one's life.

Childhood.

Teenagerhood.

A dreamed of adulthood.

As the images rush by, I come to realise that The Prince may have had a point after all, and one of the most unexpected truths is disguised as a child; the embodiment of one's previous existence. It all makes sense, why I see her. Why I felt the need to protect her against Tamika. Why she waited for me in the dark the first time we met. She is here for me.

The mirror above our sink, I look into. The body of a child, yet the symbols on her scalp, they are shifting. I had seen them before. In a different world, around a neck perhaps. Her body however, it's becoming transparent.

"Where must we start?"

"At the beginning, where the dynasties pulled on hell's reins and got burned. The Civil War." Myah nods, Ramiyah nods.

From the mirror I watch her become a casket of light and process our diffusion. Only the first five seconds, as my eyes flutter with more of her memories ambushing my brain. When the memories stop. The heat transfers back to cold. She's gone. Inside me. Inside my mind. Inside the home she nestles in. A piece of herself reunited.

Her parting gift: *we are all but reflections of each other.*

It's a good thing Tamari shows up. I need him to take me to the person with all the answers.

"To what do I owe this surprise?"

"I'm beginning to understand why you need me so badly ..."

"Like I said..."

I don't want to hear what he has to say. He needs to listen and not respond. "But first, I need to know what really happened during the Civil War. All details. Leave nothing out."

When I was eleven, I learned about the Civil War from the man who supposedly played a big part in it. I was in my history class when Father decided to grace us with his presence and provide us with first-hand information. History from time to time bored me. After all, it was the past, but if we do not acknowledge it then how do we expect to find who we are and our place in this world. History teaches and prepares us for the future. Provides us with information to continue the cycle or break it through change.

He never told us the initial cause of the war, but rather the gory details along with its aftermath. Although he did mention critical aspects that were vital to understanding how they survived such a devastating attack. Now, all of that changes. The Prince will either confirm Father's story or discredit it altogether. Two different perspectives; the one from outside it all in a kingdom untouched. The other, a kingdom that became more than ruins, a site for a new world. The Kutawala's world. It's time the truth and I meet.

"I thought you'd never ask." The Prince claps his hands together after clicking his fingers like a drummer does his drums. "Step into my office." The walls shuffle to a living room-like setting that resembles an underground lair. Brick walls box us in with the overwhelming sweet scent of frankincense. Upon instinct, I breathe in its purity. The Prince offers me a seat on the only sofa in the room while he perches on a stretched-out table. I don't like how close he is. One move and we could bump heads. His eyes, with his long eyelashes, stare back at me. I feel to clear my throat, even that I cannot do.

"Shall we?" He picks up a tray of the frankincense and blows the smoke into my face. Our minds merge; light rips through my brain.

21
THE CIVIL WAR

{Calista}

At a table, long and round all the heads to their dynasties sit upon hovering chairs. The back of it curving to their spine in an ergonomic design, a spongy black material around their arms and head. Many have their legs raised with the retractable footrest, others have their legs folded in a yogi stance: either the base of their feet connecting in a cobbler's pose or a half lotus pose, one foot crossed over the other. Above their heads projecting from their arm rest are their identities and avatars. Only kings and the Emperor.

The room itself, branches cover the ceiling almost as though asked to. To protect the conversations that were to be held in private and confidence. An open space however, the plants continue to the single door tightly locked with thick roots. Windows fill the whole room letting in the sunlight, illuminating their gathering around the table with its slight hue of blue; to whoever was brave enough to observe from the outside their images would be blurred.

"...we propose a treaty. One that will ensure we forever have each other's backs, as long as it stands. This also means we should share our resources. Emperor Rameses, since you have the greatest empire, we feel we could learn a lot from you, as you could about our spirituality along with other things."

Pause.

All eyes shifted in unison to where he was positioned at the top of the table. He was rolling his bracelet around his wrist, never stopped for a second even when all attention anticipated his interjection.

"It is safe to say the offer stands as it always does, a lifeline amongst we huemans for the betterment of our planet. Do you accept?" From the Sixth Dynasty, King Amare was confident enough to make the statement everyone thought at some point. But as the only dynasty with their roots and present still deep in the practices of the beyond, with an alarming attachment to the ancestors and the higher powers invisible that be, many would argue they were far too inexperienced to be proposing such a thing when it had seemingly lost its value. The past spoke for itself, the First War locked and pushed to be forgotten, the regal families were far more aware than any other Genapian — the need for separation from such.

When the Emperor raised his eyes to the centre of the table where the hologram of Acirfa spinned on its axis, he all but smirked. The answer was self-explanatory really, their reality had since incorporated technology into huemanity. Though nature was still present within its calculations and calibrations, spirituality, they would all but ignore. Technology and the art of what could be broken through in terms of limitations is what gave him the highest power amongst the rest. As one of the leading sources to his vast empire of multi-talented individuals, any changes needed to be made he held rights to the final decision.

"Do you truly believe your foundations in spirituality is enough value for such a treaty? Shouldn't we keep matters concerning our kingdoms private?"

"Is it not that you don't wish to share, horde all that you have gained? By the tongue of our Supreme Deities that is not the Ma'atic way, neither should it be for any Genapian. We are all brothers and sisters despite our differences."

"If I may ..."

Emperor Rameses pressed a hand into his jaw. The king of the Second Dynasty continued, "King Amare does have a point and as we all should know, through separation comes destruction. What if we had another invader into our world, would the whole of Genapa survive or only parts? Our ultimate goal should always be, protect Mother Nature first and she shall reciprocate. You have every right to hold back on whatever knowledge you decide but still think of the overall picture. We need each other and sometimes we must lower our pride. Despite our material gains and so onwards, we are still only huemans."

He couldn't have put it better. Those who agreed amplified their individual hues, even the Emperor couldn't resist making eye contact.

"Even still, a treaty, we are not children ..."

"No but we are no longer a heartbeat."

"The past ..." The Emperor did a little flick of his hand, his Jasper beads shook like cowrie shells in a basket.

"Will always repeat in the future, if we aren't careful. If we forget ourselves." King Amare closed his fist against his heart. "What about brotherhood and sisterhood scares you so much? Won't you consider the possibility of total security without jumping to dismiss any idea that could possibly threaten your hierarchy?" Emperor Rameses gives him a stern look. "Yes, I've long recognised your disdain for our art which has caused us to not live the way you prefer. To live by traditions that ultimately frighten you because you've been brainwashed into fearing true spirituality."

"Are we really going back there?" Around the table, the other kings spoke their thoughts almost immediately. Their voices rising, their frequency shook the leaves. To the room adjacent to theirs, the walls shook with a ferocity that had the queens and Empress Nubia halting their discussions. Those that stood put their ears to the wall; Empress Nubia crossed her feet at the ankles and sighed.

"This is nothing new my sisters."

"Still, this cannot continue ..."

"Maybe if the Emperor could just listen not to respond for once, we would get somewhere. I'm growing tired of these meetings having no resolution. If this is how it should be maybe we should just —"

"Now wait their queen, don't be like my husband and assume separation because it is easy it must be the path we should all walk."

"That is easy for you to say Empress Nubia, your kingdom is flourishing. What about the rest of us?" Queen of the Fifth Dynasty folded her arms, as she pressed her shoulder to the window by the door she glanced two teens. "Ramiyah and The Prince still haven't learned their lesson."

The door to their room opened; their mother joined them.

"Aren't you two supposed to be studying?"

Normally they would jump to her side. They were always caught red-handed in these situations. She crumpled her dress in her hands, the hem skimming her ankles.

"Did I not speak?" Their eyes were only on the small crack of light peeking through the door to the royal lounge.

"Ramiyah? My son?"

When The Prince turned, Ramiyah squeezed his hand, his third eye was glowing. Purple. Red.

"A storm is coming."

22

A month after the meeting, the twins' parlous feeling clouded Genapa. It started with a bang. The sound of a gun ripping through the air, a massive round ball following it. It looked like a grenade of some sort with a greenish glow seemingly nuclear and toxic. Dangerous enough to poison and kill anyone within a mile radius. An anchor at its base separated mid-flight disintegrating a shower of electrified metal. Lucky enough for Kimarr, it all began on its outskirts, so the warriors on duty had just enough time to blow their horn. Those that ventured out beyond the wall returned later on with notice that the indigenous people of the rainforests and mountains had perished before making it to safety. The footage that they showed from what they observed, King Amare without a moment's pause entered his study, found a papyrus scroll buried in his bookcase and coded a message stamped with his blood. The two messengers obeyed the command to portal to the land of the First Dynasty, Aelburn. As King Amare watched them leave, he couldn't see where they were going. Usually, it mirrored Aelburn's walls but as the portal spiralled to a close it was pulsing. Like something becoming unstable. And the colours they were polluting with something murky.

"King Amare ..."

Pulled from his thoughts, he tapped a button on his desk for the transmission network to the other dynasties.

"The others are struggling bad, especially the Fifth and Third Dynasty."

"Whatever is out there, in less than a sunset half of their empires have been annihilated."

Finally, static.

"Report." King Amare stepped on the disc opening from the centre of his room. He reopened his eyes and almost squeezed them immediately shut.

The fire.

The blood.

Of weeping women and child.

Of hands reaching to the sky, of those same hands burning to ash.

And the sky, the green painting the Blue Star invisible. Twisting like a tornado, destroyed the trees and their leaves, spinned the water from the lakes dry and dumped them on the huts.

"Save your people. These creatures, my brother, they come with the anger of hell. The desires of temptation. They ..." It was his voice, the king of the Third Dynasty echoing through the fires, his figure guarded in the shadows, wherever he had managed to shout from King Amare cursed as he was sucked back into his room.

"Any word from my messengers?"

"None and the birds sent with them," A hand lifted one with its neck sticking out of its ruffled feathers.

"No hologram has shown up of the Emperor. No message has been returned."

"Just as I thought back then. This is what I wished to prevent."

"What are our orders my king?"

"Evacuate to the south bunker and prepare the transmission to the Second Dynasty."

His warrior bowed and disappeared to gather his peers.

"Us too Father, how must we assist?"

He turned to them bowed behind him. Only children, not even adults yet. Their training, their abilities, they still had much to learn.

"This is the real test. We as the prince and princess of this dynasty must rise to protect our people. This is war Father, we will not be exempt."

"Tamari keep them safe." A step behind them he crossed his heart with his sword. "As for you two, the children help them first and using whatever equipment you can find prepare a route for the adults and everyone else to take whether it is to the walls of the kingdom or near the palace."

The third day.

King Amare managed to provide sanctuary for the Fifth Dynasty. The one portal he could open after trying all morning it was small enough to fit a ball but with the energy he had poured into a crystal, had also been blessed with the Supreme Deities after prayer, it kept it stable enough for all who could be saved to make the trip. Sadly, their daughter who had an artery ruptured and her lungs filled with more than smoke passed on in the arms of her mother. She too, almost as if she asked to be taken instead, her heart gave out just as their kingdom fell to dirt. Her husband, King Kala at the time was with King Amare and news only travelled to him when he returned at nightfall. He held her in his arms, loose, too tight and she just might decompose before him. So he closed his fists in her skirt, his eyes trained on her open palm. The ring he had gifted her for their union, the glow from the blue stone blinking in and out, he removed and joined it with his own.

"What is our strategy King Amare? Such force and lack of precision, they've hit the mark in so many areas. Our kingdoms, our resources, how can we be no match ... how can thousands and thousands of our brothers and sisters within a couple days just crumble, just like that. Our Supreme Deities, what is their excuse now?"

King Amare nodded carefully.

"Keep the faith my brother, this feels different ..."

"Whatever the feels the circumstances still ..."

"Reporting!"

King Amare held a hand at the six warriors that had stormed in, they were to take it easy, after all the dead souls were still tormented. While King Kala placed his wife on a sheet for the Regal handladies to take care of, King Amare beckoned one to his ear. "Ready to brief on intel acquired of our invaders."

Ramiyah and her brother noticing as they passed by tailed them as their father stopped in his study. They darted through the shadows and narrowly avoided the warriors on stand-by.

"They are like Albinos allergic to the sun. Their eyes look lifeless, a blue that is lighter than the sun's reflection on water." On the projection the kings drew in a deep breath at the sight of them swinging their machetes, leaping like animals, set on their mark.

"The machinery they use has a power source coming from their Life Force. But whenever they are separated, with the dial of a button in their palms it implodes even catching them in its catastrophe."

"Self-suicide? For what purpose." Ramiyah nudged her brother to be quiet.

"What are our countermeasures?"

"The impact can be contained singularly but when they all self-destruct at once, more than a kingdom can fall. The Earth could become uprooted. The only tech powerful enough to offset some of the damages is the Red Sunstone."

Everything went black. Then white.

Then Ramiyah perched behind her father on his window sill stared at the clock that had stood still since everything changed. Until now. A digit flipped to zero. Midnight. The hour of the owl. It came with a recording, her father hesitated to listen to. His hand hovering over his desk where the object jumped into the air, rattling with importance.

"Not even live, has he no guts to face me?" King Amare banged his fist squashing the digital envelope flat.

"Still, a message is better than no message."

King Kala lazily reached from his chair and tapped the play button. White light streamed to the ceiling.

"...as it stands, chaos is around us all. Our hearts and minds are with you. But the only assistance we can provide is through preparing your travel to our kingdom. We will open our gates to you."

"And allow my kingdom to fall, you would love that?"

"A king without his kingdom may be powerless but no king with no knowledge of his past is far worst if one ever wishes to rebuild their legacy."

"Yes, but his value will be displaced, disgraced he will be for he has failed at his single most important job. His people."

"What are you saying, you reject this opportunity?" King Kala was on his feet, his vigor restored.

"My brother, I will not lower to where he wants. There is only one other way for us to survive."

He swiped the Emperor's projection back into his crystal orb and fiddled around with the lock to his desk.

"There you go again ..."

"Don't you wonder, amongst the six gates and the impenetrable shield around Acirfa, how they got in?" King Amare smiled, he had found what he was looking for. "While he sits comfortably in his kingdom, lives are lost in Genapa. Heirs to the throne are slaughtered. If not him then who?"

All of the dynasties have men and women who protect the gates with their lives. But the second layer of protection has always been from the First Dynasties Elite Supreme Warriors. How did they pass them, the most sophisticated, unless they were let in?

"You might have a point. There has not been word of the Albinos moving north, which only means that they have their eyes set on a specific target. If they want to take over Acirfa, why not challenge each of the dynasties? But for this to reach this level of success, they had to have help from the inside. But these are all fleeting conspiracies. One that can be uncovered when our people are safely guarded."

"The bunkers are secure. We just lack weapons. And the Red Sunstone, you know how that goes," King Amare tucked his secret through the arms of his shirt Ramiyah craned her neck to get a better look at. It wasn't glowing and it wasn't small either but it disappeared with him like it was nothing.

A week later, the Second Dynasty sent through a live recording.

"Stay safe my brother. We have persevered for this long but whoever leads them is too capable. Our kingdom we imagine must be the same as yours, our defences are far too primitive to withstand the kind of tech they hold. Just a heads up, protect your staff at all costs and your children. Keep the faith, if not in this lifetime, then in spirit, we shall meet again."

As the twins watched they remembered hearing of the underground passages to the River Elin and the other kingdoms spoken of by their parents. They only hoped it wouldn't go to waste and just like their mother, prayed while watching the warriors defend them on their feed. Only they know of the passages, everyone else believed it had caved and been sealed.

"Those Albinos don't appear smart enough to see what is in front of them." The few warriors in the room were nodding, but one could never tell when their leader was still in the dark.

At the tunnels entrance, their only son Dakarai, hand in theirs, his parents looked back at the wave of Albinos pouring in through their kingdom's walls. Their speed. Their agility. It was quickening. And their steps it was heading in their direction.

King Adebayo pressed his forehead with Queen Jendayi uttering a prayer. The tunnels opening began to crumble.

"My queen."

"My king."

Their people rushed forward, the little energies they had they tried to pull them through. To not get swept behind in the chaos. To save what they valued more than their own lives."

"Don't sacrifice yourself." Their last plea but they had already turned their backs on them and Dakarai with his custodian squeezing his shoulder. Ramiyah must have muttered the same too pinching her thighs.

"Help us find another way Custodian Tadaaki, lets also divert their attention."

"We can never return."

"We have no hopes to."

23

It is the autumn season on the verge of winter. The Albinos barge through King Amare's walls with a force that stabs the twins in the chest. They keel at once, at the windows they half-turn their heads to look at.

"It held up for quite some time."

"Clearly not long enough."

Custodian Tamari gives Ramiyah a hand lifting her to her feet, she squeezes his hand but her eyes they are white filling with a blue.

"No Myah." Too slow to tug her back she has fazed through the glass and drops three stories into a bush.

The warriors scattered, shield up around the palace, she slips through a gap between two.

"Ramiyah." The Prince shouts, "come back."

"There are still more children. I must save them, their parents must be worried."

"Where? Let the warriors find them."

"They are in the pipes near the walls that have caved, they are crying for help. Don't you hear them."

She's running.

Custodian Tamari is running.

The Prince is running after him.

"Myah, all the children are safe in the bunkers. What you are seeing, there are ..."

"An Albino aims at a young boy crawling through the earth. I can reach him."

The Prince and Tamari breeze past a few warriors shouting for them to get back.

"This is no time to be playing games."

"Get behind the shields."

One catches The Prince in a sweeping motion; the other Tamari evades darting to his left then rolling away.

"It is not real Myah."

The boy with a red laser to his forehead she spins him onto her back and takes off back to where she came from. Smoke lifting from the red dirt at her feet.

"Ramiyah hurry."

She took a second to look back. The one albino had formed a group, and all of their lasers was on her back. Those without their guns whip their blades from behind them, the magic cracking the earth. The cracks moved so far they had bridged their distance in a blink of the eye.

"You have got to protect her, in a couple seconds they ... they ..."

"Don't say it."

The Prince's third eye shifted purple.

"She will make it." Tamari brushes the palms of his hands together; no portal was opening. He continued the friction, only sparks sprinted off.

"It's their magic. It does something to the portals."

The moment the warrior holding onto The Prince diverted his attention to Tamari he ducked under his arm and raced to meet Ramiyah. He locks his mind with hers, "faster, faster."

Ramiyah across the distance skidded to a stop with a, "stay where you are, I'll handle this. You too Tamari." Their link broken The Prince shook his head, if there was one moment he wouldn't listen to her. It had to be now, now or never, especially as they lock her in a circle. Before, she set the child down and teleported him behind the warriors. But as soon as she did, she threw her wrists up at the blades weighing down on her. They scraped against her metal gauntlets, as sharp as they were they wouldn't get through. Drawing strength from her thighs locked in a squat, she clenched her fists and flipped them. The Blue Flame she harnessed erupted at once, the Albinos stabbed each other.

More move forward.

She doesn't see the marches of Albinos at the warrior's front banging ferociously with their heads and weapons, only the ones that nip at her side, drunkenly hopping from foot-to-foot, smashing into each other as they rushed at her. The few that they were, they quickly multiplied and quadrupled with a dizzying affect.

Wringing her wrists, infused with Blue Flame, then explode. She did this, over and over. And over again. Each time their weapon melted; each time they burned. Each time they became ashes and formed a tornado around her. But when the next jump to her, their machetes a ceiling above her head, her arms they feel a little less strong.

Her heart, it beats a little bit too hard.

Her eyes, they are closing.

Her Blue Flame, the flames are getting shorter and shorter.

And The Prince still charging, still finding their distance not getting any closer, his eyes are wet. The image he is seeing, through her eyes and his. Her recurring fate he tried to punch from his mind.

"Supreme Deities give us strength."

While he wiped the tears, something far off strained at the crumbled walls. Something black being loaded. Something taking off into the air. The thing that had started this all.

"Get back!"

The warriors that had ended their fights had caught it too; they were calling to The Prince; they were calling to Ramiyah. Everyone was calling to her. But The Prince was the loudest, his lungs burning, his eyes stinging against the wind that too tried to hold him back.

"Lend me your flame Ramiyah." He reached out his hand.

"Too exhausted," she croaked, caving to her knees.

The black ball showered its metal then fractured into a series of balls. They bounce into each other mid-flight, mixing their energies with the momentum they had from their launch. They bang one final time.

Vibrate.

With the last bit of her strength, she exhaled. The Blue Flame boiled onto her skin, melted her gauntlets to her fingers, down her arm. Covered every visible inch. Then ash. The Albinos. Their weapons. She pressed her hands into the earth, the Blue Flame dived in then layered a circle around her. It stretched beyond. To where The Prince stopped.

"May we meet again."

Ramiyah lifted her head, the black ball smashed into her back.

It breaks like glass.

Each splinter jabbed into her.

As slow as film sticking with an internet connection being cut off, everything slows. She explodes. The Blue Flame, the metal, the black pieces. Her limbs become an abstraction of colours and sparkling pieces. From her to everything she touched, the earth quaked to The Prince's feet.

Tamari seconds before the shield falls grabbed him.

Out of harm's way, escorted into the palace, he struggles to contain the depth of loss that bulges from his throat. His eyebrows twitch with an anger he hasn't felt before. His hands quiver with a need to be buried in something deserving of all the emotions building in him. The force behind his voice is enough to crumble the remaining kingdom walls, and kill a few Albinos, but not all of them. As he screamed in their heads, blood drips from his nose.

He couldn't keep this up forever or he would pass out. Any second longer and his mind would have split.

Tamari understands his pain all to well, hanging his head to his chest. He wouldn't allow the tears. He wouldn't allow the desire to go back out there and let loose on the remaining Albinos clawing at the last door standing to the palace. His arms hanging lifelessly by his side. Out of the Prince and Ramiyah, he could only save one.

"They and their leader will pay."

"Hide here." The warrior that had helped them inside pushed them into a corner where they could see into the throne room.

King Amare was in there. So was the queen holding her stomach, it was taking a lot out of her not to fall to the ground. The warriors around them with their spears and lightweight armour are of no match.

"It is about time you surrender, don't you think?"

Tamari, searched and searched until he found the man with his back to him move to waunder around the room. The feature he can see, the clearest, is a look of satisfaction. Of joy and reward.

"The Kutawala." King Amare yawns his name out, eyes trained to the ground, though his head is still sure and upright.

"Kneel."

"Strength, not weakness. By any means, don't accept defeat." The Prince had collected himself and pressed a hand to the window.

"That is my only demand in response to sparing you and yours."

The King bowed sweeping both hands to the tail of his shirt. The flaps fly up.

"For a king to admit such disgrace ..."

One knee folding.

"For a king to be disrespected by the likes of a Kutawala ..."

The other knee following.

"For one to be so foolish as to accept defeat ..."

The Kutawala's arms fold, legs square in a stance of dominance.

"I, King Amare, am no such." Two crystals rolled from his sleeves to the ground. They clink together. He picks them up and smashed them on the tile. The only one that was black out of the whole floor pattern. At The Kutawala's feet thick smoke spiralled to his nose. It crystallised. Filled the room. Spread to the glass, travelled to where Tamari and The Prince stood.

Far beyond.

To the palace steps.

To the crumbled huts.

To Kimarr's walls.

And as the smoke fanned out, they disappeared, banishing themselves to a dimension, only a few have travelled to.

Rimorr. The place of mirrors.

What remains, stays concealed by a liquid-solid barrier.

24

{Calista}

Back in The Prince's lair. The walls are hazy like visible heat waves climbing to the ceiling where they pool together. He taps his fingers along my jaw, the sensations stable me a bit and with a final shake of the head the fog in my mind has cleared. He lifts from the table and when he's back the thing he needed to retrieve is placed in front of me. It whispered loud and clear, *your move.* The revolver, it didn't clunk with the weight that it should have.

A test?

Just silence.

Just ready eyes.

Finally, the only intrusion to what had my heart skip a beat is Tamari starting the engine in his throat, he must have felt it too. The three of us uncomfortable waiting for one to relax so the rest could follow. The Prince I wanted him to be that person, ask questions, probe my mind, not hand me a weapon. The sleek design tempts me to touch what I've never seen up-close. It was their weapon, the intruders of our planet. Pure metal, jagged, harsh by nature, nothing circular or pleasant about it. Things that come so rigid, squared, rectangle will always be dangerous and as a result against

nature which only operates in motion. In circles and spirals
— the continuation of life. I feel the fear to lift such a thing, —
do it anyways. It's snug between my thumb and index finger.
I raise and point.

"Why should I believe you?" It propels me to a stand as if
it required a straight back and the stance of a bull. It wasn't
a question that I had been burning to ask, just the easiest
to start off with. "You blow some smoke in my face, your
retelling, is it the truth?"

*"It feels real, but is it? I saw what you wanted me to see but is
there more beyond what you wanted?* See, Calista I am a man of
principle, we are on this journey together. The stakes are high.
You, ignorance must be wiped, truth must be welcomed, the
darkness must be embraced. The Civil War ..."

As he moves, I notice the lair is much brighter than the
last time I was here, there are definitions, alcoves, a bit
of character rather than a boring dug out hole for a door,
couple chairs and a table. The walls especially the one I broke
through it has patched itself back up like my force through
it never happened. Funny that, I wonder, what else can be
broken but reappear as its perfect version? The single light
an umbrella above me, The prince is in my space nudging the
gun to his forehead. "If I wanted to tamper with your mind, I
would have done it a long time ago. And, you wouldn't have
noticed." The cockiness in his gaze, one penetrating, dark and
full of mystery, it is quite the insult I roll with my eyes.

I knew the gun was empty before I picked it up. Still, I pull
at the trigger feeling its spring. How relaxed he is knowing
this fact, part of his weight pushing into me, I wish to conjure
something resembling a bullet to give him a fright.

"My father, you have no concrete evidence he had an alliance with The Kutawala."

"Only a fool would eliminate him as a prime suspect. But the question is why, what has he gained since?"

"My father's telling, your telling, they are only perspectives. Is it not that your ..." My spine feels the full weight of words that if heard by the ear would be a cause for an argument of some sorts.

"Spit it out."

I shiver as his hand wraps around mine causing him to straighten a bit with the gun even higher, to his right temple. The unravelling of his third eye beams to me in waves. And the smile that gives, my eyes water a little.

Jealous.

Envious.

My father was able to protect his people; he didn't rely on the Supreme Deities to intervene with huemanity when they needed it most. There was nothing wrong with that.

"You sought his approval for this long, Cali. He is not so high and mighty as you think. For you to see and still be blinded, you truly are your father's child." My stomach quivers. It is a fact but no one had dared, I had always decided we were nothing alike right down to my Blue Flame. "He is the monster you call yourself. He is the cunning man who betrayed us, brought in the enemy to exterminate us like rats."

He's pushing me back, mentally and physically into a dark corner where an alcove curves to the ceiling. I stop us with a hand to a brick, fingers sprawled for further reassurance.

"You have no proof." He bats an eye at the increase in my voice.

"His kingdom is better off. His warriors and Tech N9nes and all the other specials are safe, cultivated. But beyond his wall, the earth *weeps*. The Kutawala *creeps* in this prison world my father created. Who else created this state we share now but him? If you believe his lies over the truth, you are as you say you are. A monster."

My Blue Flame spins around my wrist. "You don't know what you talk of." I push back against him, he flings the gun off his face, losing my grip it flies to the ground. It dissolves into dust without a sound. I flow from a closed fist by my side to a open hand gripping his throat. He elbows my arm away smacking me into the alcove's wall, his hand to my throat and the other in a monkey grip to my wrist.

"It stings doesn't it."

My hair drags as my feet leave the ground.

"To know the truth and still deny it."

I half-swallow against the tightening of his fingers.

"Before you save anyone else's face, first take care of your own. You are an open book Cali though you play as if you are the author." A jab straight through the chest, my heart squeezes.

"And the only person who can help you believe is the one you harbour inside."

My Blue Flame crawls up his arm and illuminates the space between us, he slowly releases me with a nod. "See and she knows it too." I crumble to a crouch as he steps away.

My Blue Flame stays as it is and that's when I remember, this is the first time I've been able to call it since Tamari and I met despite the little trick I played on the battlefield. And it's as full and certain as ever. With no limitations, I close my eyes just to experience its return. How I've missed this part of myself. To feel and not always know what I feel. To breathe and know that it is not something harmful that will turn me inside out. To understand how complex I can be even with a newly acquired status. It's deep and light blue with curls of black, the innocence, the purity between yin and yang. It could only symbolise the rise, the truest form of oneself through imperfection. Could Ramiyah have really called this part of myself out when I missed it most? Am I to feel comforted that she understands what this means to me? Though she invades she restores, I brush off the thought with a smile. I note to The Prince, "my father has done many things but until I speak to him myself, we are done with this conversation."

As I stand welcoming my Blue Flame back into my heart, it is not The Prince I see with his arms crossed, but beside Tamari a shadow. The shadow whose face is forming the features that were prominent before they were destroyed. Painting with flames and light, Ramiyah, *I will talk with you now.*

25

{Calista}

S tanding on the same ground that has become like home, my opponent gives me the look 'today is the end of your reign'. I hated that I had to return to this place. The Prince when I asked if he could do something about this, he all but took a step back as if he was completely powerless in this world. After all that I have to deal with mentally, I can't just stay in my cell and dive into a cocoon to process and decide?

"Damn I cannot get a break."

Being out here again, with the memories and the energy the spectators bring, I taste bile on my tongue. Nonetheless I ease into a squat and breathe, "let's get this over with."

The horn blows and the commentator rambles on in the background. The crowd cheers for me like they did Tamika, maybe even a lot more.

A foot comes crushing down. I dodged at the last second, dust spraying into my mouth. He jabs thereafter, to my top half, the bulk of his arms swinging with such precision I just about elude every move. As I duck to work around the thickness of his waist, he lifts a knee into my stomach and a fist cracks into my head

"Woah there, our champion is in the fire so soon ..."

I see the stars. The darkness in my mind; in front of me. It comes in flashes. Blackness I can comb my hands through. Still just able to make out his torso I spin a roundhouse kick into his chest.

"Is that all the mighty champion can do?"

"Here we go again." I mutter but instead of coming closer as he gestures to, I pivot. A full one-eighty. At first, I walk then skip into a stride, to a run, but her words I knew would come plays to the beat of his feet.

Is that what we are doing now? How cowardly.

Tamika cackles almost behind me, but I know it's him, with his breath metres from my neck. I dive into a lunge as he nears, blow dirt into his eyes. The moment he stumbles, his stability wavers like an infant not sure of their feet. The hunk that he is I slam my foot into his knees, then kick up into his chest.

The crowd cheers masking his fall onto his back. He's up too soon, rolling over his shoulder. Reaching for my neck, he catches my hair instead and as the reigns she mentioned they would become; as I tried to unhook and run, he reels me in as his bait smashing his forehead into mine. I buckle, losing the strength in my neck. He sweeps me to the ground, asserts his weight on my ribs. A punch, two punch. I snap my head from one side to the other. An arm shields his next, pain shoots through to my elbows.

Get up! My ears ring. From Ramiyah's shout. From his elbow. And the blood that leaks, it gushes into the pool of water around my head. The rain is getting heavier now, the sky is darkening, but he is the darkest. His face squashed with desire, tight with a winner's streak, knowing of what it means to crush a life. He's not the same as Tamika, he doesn't want to be freed, to be redeemed by his Ancestors. He's quite comfortable where he is, what he's become, I am, "you are nothing like they say. What a waste."

He picks me up as he stands, my shoulders between the vice of his hands.

"I thought you were supposed to be strong? Have a courage to survive." my opponent shouts at me. "You are ..."

You're not weak.

"Pathetic."

Don't let anyone break your spirit.

"I see it now; it is all a shell. But there is ..."

You're strong, beautiful, and intelligent, there is nothing you cannot accomplish.

"Only one way out of this game. It's you, not *me*." The pressure he applies I clench my abs, my fist, my heart. I needed to resist.

"It's game over."

"I will not accept defeat."

"Any last words?"

He lowers me to my knees gliding his hands to my neck crossing under my jaw. I hadn't engaged with him before now. He was as I had set myself up to be: a nobody. He was there when Tamika and I first interacted in the prison house, they would sit together but his eyes somehow from time-to-time found mine. It wasn't a simple look, though his expression was plain he appeared to be reading. Taking me in but not. I never felt any type of energy from him, not even now. He's just absent though I feel him pressing his desires into me. But these games were never so simple: to just take life.

Something else goes with you.

Something more dies.

And if there is nothing, you just I suppose, escape with the dead.

Only for a moment, as the crowd acknowledges you.

Just like I said, I will not be next, I will continue on through and my eyes closing, though it looks like I'm tapping out. To my breath releasing between my loose lips with the droplets of rain slowing their descend, it is my body that understands the assignment. To be as light as a feather, to forget the weight of the heart and become the light transitioning despite any resistances. The light that as bright as it can be chooses to dim. Then disperse like the bats I had seep into my skin my first day here.

I only feel him fall forward.

It's the lightness that makes me giddy, with excitement, with wonder. That lightness slams me back into the ground, however, the exhilaration that flares through my veins, something more is going on. Someone has fused into my arms, become the second body in me.

The legend of Bluka is real Calista.

"Is this it?" My thoughts come like the cosmos in the universe, I want to know everything, forget where I'm at, just, "tell me more!"

From where Ramiyah speaks to me it's like I'm trapped in a glass box. She echoes, she coos, she vibrates but the images I see unwrapping on the surface. They are shifting with a madness. The arena has completely dissolved somewhere in between. I spin as they do, they move even faster, a blur of colours, of faces. His face. A shadow. Morphing as he does to hers with brown hair cornrowed down past the shoulders. Ramiyah rubs her hands over her bare arms like one should over an open fire. Her eyes they are to the ground and her lips are pressed. The Blue Flame that slithers through despite their tightness they are unlike mine. They carry marks along her jaw then fingers, blue swirls horizontal in the pattern of a 9 constantly repeating up her arms. Beautiful. They still the blur of motion around her. Mesmerising I reach out a hand. I want to know how these feel. I want to share with another bearer of the Blue Flame.

A pain sears through my hip forcing me to my knees. I search the ground then the air for what has attacked me. I can't see, not even feel. It's all dark. Too dark. That when a door opens with a cowering light I feel the full effect of blindness. Ramiyah, Myah is given a little push inside, her fists are balled. The widening of her eyes, the tears are near but guarded. She shouts something I strain to hear but they're forgotten, dismissed. The light snuffed; hands squeeze my throat. The sounds that trickle, stab my ear, my brain, bring back the memories. They're chanting as they always do.

"Finish her."

"Kill. Kill."

My hands are sticking to his fingers but what's missing is what's vital. He's just squeezing. My head lighter and lighter and my hands — numb.

This must be it. The end.

"Death."

A massive inhale cuts through the noise, simultaneously my vision slaps clear — the darkness gone. His hands gone. The thing that did it, the thing that shouldn't have pinged through the air with a trajectory aimed where I am. The seconds that it took, it was minutes for me. The shiny needle gathering momentum against the rain. Where it ends, blood spats in my face. He toppled over my right side, his eyes still. I quickly push him off, my heart a maniac against my ribcage. That was close. Too close. And the culprit, the bullet he secretly hid, the gun that is like it never existed. I find him like I always do amongst the crowd, his hand now lowered. His whisper, "that was your only get out of jail free card."

"What the hell happened out there? This was not part of the plan. I was not supposed to intervene," he curses under his breath. The Prince throws a glass at the wall.

Even after Tamari gave me a blanket, I shiver. Every time I try to stop, using one hand to soothe the other, it only gets worse.

"It was Ramiyah ... she ... memories."

"He is probably suspicious of me. I may have alerted The Kutawala." I focus on the table in front, he's doing too much. Walking back and forth. Stopping. Starting again. We've both been shaken up pretty badly but —

"You didn't hear her. Ramiyah."

Tamari had that effect. As soon as he spoke, everything became still. All that needed to be realised was.

The Prince is stooping in front of me at once. He lifts my head to the light, inspects my eyes to my ears as if he could find her that way. Still, what he said amongst his ramblings something dawned on me.

"Why would they be suspicious of you?"

He shakes his head dropping into the seat beside me. I suppose the question shouldn't have been asked.

"I am not really here."

Right, that's how he only appears at specific times. He takes off his dashiki scarf, folds it and slips it into a pocket.

"Like you, I created a double. The only difference is mine is solid. I am the double whereas I'm really in a different part of Rimorr. This mirage appears different to them; I allow you to see me for who I am."

Right. The mirage he keeps up in public.

"How did you do that? Move through the particles," Tamari asked.

As per usual, The Prince has all the answers. "That was Kundalini energy. I'm still trying to figure out what the trigger was."

I furrow my brows, he looks like a kid up to something mischievous.

"Why do you have that stupid grin on your face?" He rubs his hands together.

"I confirm you are now activated."

"Just like that?"

"With Myah your process is a lot quicker than one who is inexperienced."

"So your kundalini you know of from your mother right?" He barely allows me to reply, so I just nod my head. "Now. It's coiled at the base of the spine where you find the Root Chakra. When the Kundalini is activated, it performs the merging of male energy Shiva: infinite Supreme Consciousness, the Yin, and the female energy Shakti: infinite Supreme Consciousness, the Yang. Together they allow you to transcend the physical laws that confine the hueman body. You were able to shift through the particles in the air for a split moment because your Kundalini is fluctuating between your lower and higher self, moving through your chakras at a rapid pace but unable to maintain a higher position such as the Fifth Chakra. For whatever reason, this could be..." he shrugs "...because you're unable to express yourself and communicate the way you wish to."

"And what purpose will I serve once I'm no longer confined to the physical laws and I've unlocked the essence of my being?"

"That," he jumps to a stand with his arms wide, "you will have to take up with my sister."

The passenger within. With the darkness drawing closer, when I step through where would that leave her?

Tamari with a basin wrings a rag dry to disinfect my wounds. He starts from my ankles. The heat eases the sting a bit. Every ache to my knees to my wrist and neck gently fades. The heat that stays in my cheeks, The prince leans in and waves a hand. The single hand halfs then my eyes are rolling back.

"Calista ..."

A shock runs through my body. The corners of my lips twitch, my body jerks with an uncontrollable energy. My insides feeling like an explosion trying to force something out. Tamari holds down by my feet, The Prince, my shoulders. Suddenly I stop, roll to a straight-back. Well, I move but it isn't me.

"Zaire. I am here."

26

{Dakarai}

I don't know how it happened and what happened, once we were separated, I reopen my eyes and I'm outside my apartment. The night lights are on, dim that they may be, it's for the better. To any neighbour walking on, I don't know how I'd look. Probably like a mad man, my eyes still feel stretched from all the tests the SYSTEM put me through. His face, the ladies face, lets just forget it all. I stuff a hand into my jacket pocket, there's a metal plate. The inscription, code like what's on SARAH's spine. I rub my finger over it, parts smudge with something red but then collect back into the indentation. The numbers are only sixes and nines, the parts that curve, straight lines protrude from with tight curls. It's a weird pattern I shove back into my pocket deciding some sleep away from all of this stuff would be needed.

I unlock the door.

"Right so how would you read it?"

"Well, the numbers are in a matrix pattern, divide them alongside the alphabet. That's the first solution to which the answer would be Infinite Industries. Her barcode is registered to them. But I could be wrong and this code is far more complicated than should already be recognised."

"I get you, my brother. Let's bank on the first option. Keep this quiet for the moment, I'll be in touch."

I leave my coat and shoes at the door and find my way to the kitchen.

"Dakarai where you been?"

The projection he had open spins to a close in his palm, a guess, he must have been consulting a Tech N9ne. From what I overheard a part of the code had been deciphered. Infinite Industries. If it's the company I think it is, we may have a problem.

"I was called out, it was weird. I'll tell you about it another time."

I throw him a bottle of water as I join him at our board. I finish a whole bottle, all the while he looks at me funny.

"That thirsty?"

"Water cleanses the mind, it has been a long day."

"Yeah, and it is about to get longer. Did you notice this before?"

SARAH's barcode shines a locked symbol asking for FID.

"All of a sudden, fingerprint identification. Whoever she belongs to, some Infinite Industries, they probably still have access to her and know of her whereabouts or something."

Not quite, I figured. If they had such authority, they would have traced her to us already, probably even came knocking. Unless they were playing it safe, surveilling us from a distance. But what the lady I met said about her, about the SYSTEM, this should be bigger than a company. Be like the Ethers. Something unseen. Something that could be tapped into beyond the five senses and it all starts with code. I stoop and circle around her spine. The flesh is warm when it should be cold, soft with blood still pumping beneath.

"An android inactive still operates like she is alive under her skin."

"Strange isn't it, it's like she really is human."

I look up at our board, what more are we missing?

"What about the mark she left on you, figured it out yet?"

"It looks like half a logo, the same one used for Infinite Industries. Tell me, what you know about that place?" He takes a seat on the arm of the chair, a hand to his jaw as he looked from the board to SARAH to his display unfolding on his arm.

"Infinite Industries is the top company in London. Anything you can name, from robotics, to experiments on the human psyche, body, pharmaceuticals. They really are ... infinite."

"Robotics, androids, clones. That sort of stuff. And a SYSTEM ..."

He pulls up their website and there it is four lines and tight curls on the end of them. The only thing missing are the upside-down numbers and letters from Khari's mark. A simple design but not, it hid a lot along the straight lines through the tiny circles. When blown up are filled with the primary colours and single, double, or triple dots. I look back at Sarah, her lock is jumping at me, I slide a few fingers closer. To the top, just below the middle of her neck.

"Dakarai ..."

Straight lines box over her coded name, the *s* bold and in italics I dip to get a closer look. How it paints, how it shifts, the lock reminds me of a message. Could I unlock it?

"What are you doing?"

The voice that had called, she swats my hand away.

"What kind of trouble are you guys in that an unconscious girl is lying on your floor?"

The split second I find Khari, he's shaking his head at me.

"It is not what it looks like."

"Is she even breathing?"

Calista is moving the sheet and turning her onto her side, two fingers on her neck. I try to pull her away, refocus her attention on me.

"My love."

"Dakarai do you know how —"

Her hand grazes SARAH's cheek, static jumps off. She powers on and before she head-butts Cali, I pull her into my arms.

"Here we go." Khari slides to the floor leaning in. Calista lifts a hand to point, drops it back in her lap. I know the feeling, speechless.

"Hello Calista, at last, you have arrived." The android crosses her legs. "I understand this will come as a shock, but I know you guys, and you know me. Just not in this form. The SYSTEM isn't safe. You aren't safe. For now, Calista, you have all the answers."

"Backtrack a little, this is?"

"What found us on our assignment. She was killed, in some way, later we found out she was an android and ..."

"This all has something to do with a SYSTEM she knows everything about that we are trapped in. This," Khari gestures with a finger in a circle, "is potentially not real. We must get out."

As Khari explains, SARAH's eyes move like the ladies did. Scanning, then relaying a series of code together, apart, doing their own thing. Still a language neither of us could read.

"Right, your assignment? She's the reason you were suspended?"

"Essentially." I loosen my arms, Calista falls back behind me pressing a shoulder into mine.

"You shouldn't still be here though Calista."

"Your point?" Her voice is small, not as forceful as it should have been. From the corner of my eyes, she picks at a nail.

"You've already welcomed the darkness. The answers to the SYSTEM will appear soon, you will be able to leave. Ramiyah will be reborn. Here, is the last place you should be."

"Ramiyah. Daughter of the Sixth Dynasty?" Khari clicks his fingers. "What does she have to do with anything, didn't she —"

"She's the reason I'm dying, why I created a double to find you two. Why I will fail my assignment."

"I must go now. You too Calista, she will be here soon before you do though."

SARAH's skin shrivels again, she falls onto her back.

Khari is still staring at Calista. I told him she had returned with such news but the added information SARAH provided things were starting to make sense. But Calista's assignment, it had led her to Kimarr, to the Sixth Dynasty, to a princess who ... survived the Civil War?

"Where is Ramiyah?"

Our history lessons hadn't told us much about her, all we knew she had sacrificed for her people. The same people who hated her. She was a bearer of the Blue Flame. For that fact, she was to be treated with caution. But the Sixth Dynasty as a whole, they perished, or they disappeared, whatever happened of them, only my love could share what she has discovered since travelling to the ghost kingdom.

Calista has not answered. I turn around, her chin is dipped into her chest, one of her hand pulls on a part of my shirt.

"My love."

"Ramiyah, she's ..." All choked up, her other hand massages her heart. Khari picks her up and places her on the settee.

"Take your time sis. Water, I should ..."

She catches his hand as he gets up to go but that's not what makes him stop. It's what has me forcing my hands into the carpet.

"Ramiyah ... she's inside of me."

"You'll never be brave if you don't get hurt."

27

{Calista}

I no longer hear the android's voice, but The Prince's. He's the shadow whose face I have seen many times but stays hidden. I shout, "no, stay back." I know my mouth has not moved. It's all in my mind. While Dakarai and Khari engage with me and I respond, I'm elsewhere like I've been pulled back to my original body but before I could stay, I waver in some limbo.

"Step into the darkness Cali."

"You cannot be here." Surely, I must be dreaming. This is still Earth, it has to be.

"You have nothing to fear Cali. The real enemy cannot harm you here."

Who, The Kutawala? You, The Prince, should it not be you I hide from?

I press my hands into my head; something sharp cuts through my mind. As the feeling swells, an image pushes me to my knees in some black substance. Along the surface my face blurs, shifts to a woman's. To mine. To hers. Ramiyah's. This twist in features becomes half my face and half hers. And the memories that form between the eyes that have no resemblance, from the left I revisit that moment.

Father in his black robe under the colourful sky at the edge of a cliff urges me to take the leap. The leap of faith every initiate must. Personally he had sought to clear his schedule. Be here for me. Be here for the process. Be here to ensure I went through with it. His warriors were tight in a half-moon around him. The small spaces between them, if I could get through, this thought fell into my shaking hands. Of course, it wouldn't be possible. They were far skilled, far ready for any coincidences, any sudden moves. Everything was already pre-calculated. And Father, he was the final line of defence.

The small turn I make, the waterfall gushing to the lake's bed, how powerful it is, to make the jump, "Father, maybe you were right. I can't ... this ... I can't ..."

"There is no turning back. Princess Calista, to be a warrior, you must face your fears or else they become a weakness many will target."

I begin to rub my palms together, begging, maybe we could postpone this to another day. My hands warm as I speed up, "please Father."

"Fear is an illusion of the mind. Go through it."

He flashes to me, throws me into his arms, as my legs lift, I squirm like the fishes do on their bait. He's hugging me but letting me go. We're moving further, he is going against my force, if any. Until, when I reach out, his hands leaving me, I tearing his sleeve, I fall against the wind. A shrill bells from my throat. I claw at the air. Flipping onto my front, then my side. When I plunge into the waterfall, gulping salt and sediments, my eyes wide, chest feeling tight, the face pulls from the rocks terraforming. Our face, my eye to her eye on the right.

Our heads shake with a force that hurts my neck. As we kick to swim to the surface, the hand's that force us deeper, I feel the tightness in my chest stabbing into my throat. In my eyes that leak with tears sting. Bubbles, each time bigger than the last release the oxygen I want to keep. It is slow, it is fast, our deterioration but it will not end with us drowning. The light pouring in blinks to darkness. We're yanked out of the water like an anchor. What bangs against our chest, is more than hiccups and oxygen rushing to rejuvenate us. The Blue Flame it's generating, growing, giving what it must.

"We don't want you to die now, just fear for your life." The boy who holds us by the hair, his laugh that is like a donkey whistling through its nose. Him and his boys that taunts us, water skating down our face. "You are ... pathetic," we utter between breaths.

"Sorry, what was that, I couldn't hear what you were saying through all that hiccupping?"

I'll show you something to laugh about. With one scream, an earthquake from our chest, the Blue Flame erupted snuffing their taunts. Their voices gurgle in their throats. They roll into the sand. From our periphery, through the cooling flames, Tamari running down the beach at the speed of a vampire, he does something with his hands.

"You beast." The nasty burns they suffer as consequence for messing with us, they stumble to their feet, scurry out of sight. Their last echo, "the princess is psychotic."

I start to black out. Before I touch the water Tamari catches me.

Back in the living room, a whisper into our darkness, "I deserve much more."

"Body of a woman, soul of a child, mind of the free and heart of the wild."
- Ashley Lemaine

28

{Calista}

"R amiyah."

I awake calling her name, forcing myself to the bathroom where I now press into the mirror on the wall. The lights are off but I see myself clearly, my eyes glowing; our eyes.

"Ramiyah." I whisper this time, my lips skimming the cool surface. "Won't you stop?" These memories, they torment me. Anger me. "Why must I see this? Why won't ..." My nose itches. On my lips something wet continues dripping to my chin, the taste; blood. Suddenly, I'm coughing, banging a hand at the sink, the next at my throat. Blood spats into the drain, both dark-red and black. It moves into a cork plugging the sink. Then it rises, bubbling, steaming. Along its tide, it curls from one side to the next. Their voices stream in. Their faces paint.

"What have I told you about rallying up the villagers? It is not your place to dictate who needs punishing from who does not? Now, this is your third strike and no matter what I tell you, you don't seem to be listening. You are a princess so act like one, you are not a warrior like the boys. Know your role, play your position." His stern look is enough to frustrate me.

Why can't he understand? Why can't he see what I see, is our perception so different that he solely believes what I am doing is wrong?

"What about your position, you have all this power and you do nothing, you should be thankful that I am doing what I am doing?" He raises his hand and is seconds away from cracking me up the side of my head. Regardless of his halt, I feel the blow that should have reached me. I feel the anger that leaks from his pores; I have overstepped my boundaries. The bad thing about it, I am not even sorry. He steps back and thinks of the best way to punish me since all the others aren't working. The scars that are left on my hands from constantly being struck with a cane aren't enough to deter me from the path I have taken.

At the age of thirteen, borderline fourteen, I know what I want to do for my people. I believe all this suffering has to come to an end, one way or another.

When he approaches me once more, I feel this would be my worst punishment yet. With my mother out of the kingdom, seeing her friend Empress Nubia, I know no one can save me from the nightmare I am about to endure.

"Since you like the dark so much, how about you take some time out of the light to self-reflect and see the error of your ways?"

"What — no."

"I'm not asking you." He grabs my wrist and twirls us to the underground basement. No matter how hard I try to worm out of his hold, his word is final. The door has already been unbolted, there is no escaping this. When Zaire arrives, I am half in the dark, half in the light. Tamari watches from afar, his hands clenching and unclenching.

"This isn't fair!" Ramiyah shouts at her father; I, at me in the sink.

My hands are numb.

Dakarai bangs on the door. "Calista, what's happening, why you shouting?"

"Father you cannot do this, she could have serious traumatic issues later on in life," Zaire says.

"Listen, son, there is nothing ..."

"Put me in there with her." I'm shaking my head at him, he's not listening. He hasn't done anything wrong, why should he suffer just because I've decided to take on rebel characteristics? Whether I agree with his move or not, we are one. Whatever happens to me happens to him.

Pushed inside, the door bolts trapping the light on the other side. The darkness immediately I fall blind to. My eyes open. My eyes closed. The difference couldn't be told.

Still, as the days or months continued, the cycles of the moon journeying through the sky, it is not my Blue Flame that enlightens me. It is the thing I fear, the thing I have no choice but to fear. Myself. The darkness. And it speaks to me in ways — the light could never.

Dakarai bangs on the door again. "My love, open the door."

My vision blurs and then refocuses. He breaks the latch, is at my side immediately pulling my face into his. He strokes my jaw, looks into both my eyes, notices the flushing of my skin.

"What's happening?"

I turn to the mirror. One of my eyes is glazed over with darkness swirling within. I cannot reply. It's happening, what they planned. The pacing has increased and my disconnection from my main body on Kimarr, I am out of the loop. Out of sync. Is it too late?

All the while in my mind, Dakarai had picked me up and brought me into the living room. I took over from there slipping a pillow under my head, on my back, staring at the ceiling.

"Where should I start?" In the bubble on Kimarr, time moves more quickly in comparison to Earth. So if I'm to take a wild guess it has been about seven months since this all began.

"What was your assignment?"

"To uncover the truth to the Sixth Dynasty."

I know what Dakarai thinks, something this simple I could have shared before we separated but for once I wanted to do something on my own. Later on down the line I figured I would clue him in it's just unfortunate things didn't go to plan.

"The truth although I switched the assignments, this trip was already designed specifically for me."

"What do you mean sis?"

"The Prince, Zaire, he has a plan with Ramiyah. For me to be enlightened. For me to step into the darkness where all will be revealed. Where my ignorance will be wiped and replaced with truth. All in all, I must awaken the Legend of Bluka."

Their eyes are only on me, Khari squints a little processing all the details, I would imagine. Dakarai the closest his shoulders slump a little. As I take him in, things starting to blur again, this weight I cannot describe I know he has one too. Our assignments what has it done to us?

"And this mention of you dying?" Khari's voice is small.

"They hold my life force until everything is complete."
Everyone is complete.

The rest they should probably know I tuck under my tongue. Of what I had to do for my survival. Of 'Murder not Mercy'. Of the lives I have taken, yet freed. Of Ramiyah, the one that hides though is sprinting to the light.

I have this fond memory of my own bubble. It kept certain things near and others far. My own protective mechanism which came with my birthright and being present in Aelburn. And it had no weight, practically invisible it worked how it should until it smashed to pieces. Like the crown that has slipped from my head borning a monster, it represents the lows that have to be met, the comfort zones that have to be challenged, and the person I must seed, water and grow to ascend as they would like. But what should matter most is me, what I think, desire, the authority I hold over my domain. My true form whatever it endures, whatever I couldn't see it opens up to me now. On the ceiling in pieces.

"Zaire, I am here."

They embraced with my arms, they smiled and joked. What they talk about, cordial and carefree is what sticks:

"She's the perfect candidate. I just need to borrow her while I complete my task. I'm doing this for us."

"We should have been more transparent what if when she realises this ..."

"Tamari what I can give to her no other can. What she needs it must be put in motion from now. She may think I am bad, will harm her far worse than those snakes beside her, I couldn't care less. This is the way." The hand she admires, my hand, it swirls with blue energy through darkness. The truth. The essence of power. Melanin. "Soon enough she will be asleep in the land of truth, prosperity, justice, righteousness, reciprocity. All the principles of Ma'at. And when I'm reborn, everything will reconnect."

Huh?

My breaths come out faster and deeper and as my chest rises and falls, it is no longer wise to stay on my back. Clenching a pillow to my leg, I feel it now. How I should have felt when she kicked me out of the front seat then, forcing me to some place in my own mind.

"Ramiyah, you dared. Without my consent, to override. This is my domain. You cannot just do what you want!" I shout half-choking through the tightness in my chest. My eyes water even as she says, "you will understand why soon enough." Though it taps my mind whatever follows after is like a punch to my forehead.

She comes shrouded by darkness with the moon's light illuminating her face. Her hands balled up in fists, the owls cooing outside, the fireplace she slithers up by crackles with more than fire. The heat she warms her body with, preparing a deep inhale and an exhale that slows, the man she turns half-closed eyes to, sleeps unknowing of her intrusion. Under the thin duvet, he is barely her height which isn't tall, a plump man with a belly befitting for a pregnant woman; a tongue sticks out catching the hairs around his mouth.

Not far from him, his family there they are — a woman huddled under a thick blanket between two children. They stick to her front and back like bees to their queen bee.

Ramiyah moves, no sound to the wooden floors that should creak and her ankle beads that still their rattle. The man stirs. Soft snores escape his mouth with a raspy undertone. A little too close a raw stench burns her nose.

"You, sir, have been accused of rape." Her voice follows after the click of her fingers. Another step, this time with sound only from the shaking of her beads. "You deserve what is coming your way." The second click, energy passes through her hands, the ignition of her flame. "I hereby sentence you to death on the account of multiple rape incidents of poor little children who had their innocence robbed. Tainted by your lack of restraint and vile behaviour."

He jolts awake, the flames heat had penetrated his eyes. Through them Ramiyah mesmerised awes at the flames. It's fiery-red. It's cool-blue. The purple the colours made together. When he rubs his eyes, each time expecting a different result, that she wouldn't be here, that he had been issued a sentence. For it all to be a dream, "Princess," he mutters. "Come na, in the middle of the night, why you disturb my sleep. I am an innocent man."

"The guilty have no right to speak."

He's unable to look away from her glowing birthmark on her forehead. Everyone knew what it meant. The Phoenix is her spirit animal. "What ... please na."

"Murder, not mercy." The tears that had gathered in her eyes spilt. "Burn." He went up in flames, whatever cries he released it was nothing in comparison to how the flames devoured him. Still, his family pulled from their sleep, if they weren't closer before now the three bodies were like one. And they weren't crying. And they weren't calling after the princess as she made her exit. They just followed the ash and bones settling on the floor.

This is not the last of the memory.

This is after her time in the dark.

She was hanging upside down from her bed lost in a daydream, which ended quickly as she overheard a heated argument somewhere in the palace. Her door was locked but through the walls that are never silent, she heard them with their angry voices and accusations. So the person they spoke their hearts out about needed to be present. Zaire and Tamari knew better to hold her back and instead followed her to the throne room where the doors were wide open as if awaiting her. There's a small crowd in front of their father. He was not on his throne. Their mother stood beside him observing, ready to jump in if necessary.

"Your Highness, this is getting out of hand. The people are scared."

"She is a monster."

"You can't have her running loose, killing people she feels have disobeyed the laws of nature."

The King huffed, shaking his head. "My people, that is hardly a matter."

They talked over each other, not giving one another a chance to fully explain their concerns.

Some feared her for her raw power; others worshipped her as protector of her people. Most importantly, a lot of villagers believed death was not the answer. But if death was an illusion, why did it matter so much? One of the villagers, the same boy who tried to drown her, looked in her direction.

"She's out of control." He was firm, pointing at the burn on one side of his face. She resented the way she was treated by her people. All she wanted was for them to see that her actions were done out of love. Love of justice. Love for her people.

She entered stopping just short of the crowd. "Discussing me, again? Don't you see I'm trying to help our people and relieve our society of injustices that go on without actions from any of you? My methods meet the purpose. Why should I be outcasted because I choose different methods to deal with certain situations?"

"Your methods are ruthless. You are ruthless!"

"I! Am strong. If it were not for me the villagers would have still been at each other's throats catching little children in their wrath. I am your saviour. Your Princess. What more do you want from me?!" As she moves to them, they step back with a shaky breath.

"We want nothing from you."

"It would be better if you were gone," someone shouted.

"You need to be put down. You are an animal!" The boy shouted.

How dare they? Anger bubbled. She hanged her head a little. What would it take for them to understand? Though she wanted to relieve herself of the heartache and pain they were causing her through tears and to perhaps fight them all, they were not worth it. They also weren't the ones to go against. Some were officials of the royal court, others held positions in society that were for the progression of our kingdom but many were misguided, corrupt, sat on their wealth. Became lazy. Became of no value if not for their empty titles. Still her flame of a purpose of its own sprouted from her fingers, pushing her people more to the door.

"Ramiyah," her mother called. "Don't give them what they want." Her birthmark glowed, though it was not meant as a threat they took it as such.

"Why should I care about that? I have been selfless. I deserve more than this!" The flame grew, encasing her whole body. Though her heart raged, it doesn't burst like it should just stays as a shield around her. But to the ones that did not understand they pointed, jabbed even more, saw this as further evidence to support their worries.

Zaire behind her pulled on her wrists. *You are better than this. Don't allow negativity to bring you down. It is not your fault they can't see the goddess that walks among them. Not everyone is going to accept you. The only thing that matters is that you accept yourself. Your flaws and all.*

She dropped to her knees. They jumped into the air like cats and hyenas as if she had sullied the ground. But she knew how powerful she could be, how the palace could fall if she proved them right. That she was out of control. That she needed to be exiled. That she was not worth the title of Princess of the Sixth Dynasty.

So to release, it would be better all her pain be in tears. And so, they were. No longer bottled. Free. Tumbling down her face. As they fell, like a vacuum her hands bit-by-bit sucked her flame into non-existence.

"What were you saying about lack of control?" Tamari smiled.

"Sometimes you put walls up not to keep people out but to see who cares enough to break them down"
- Socrates

29

{Calista}

"My love." Dakarai pulls my hands to him. They're encased with my flame. Glowing so bright I'm sure I see the blue fade to black to red. The strange arrangement I know something more is happening. I see it in Khari's eyes, he's standing by the wall his arms crossed. This look of concern yet wonder, it was different to Dakarai's when I first told him. A man building a plan, seeing through me to what Dakarai had asked for, there is something he knows. Something he has found and with Ramiyah, with SARAH, with this SYSTEM he just might have to make a move he won't regret. To act without evidence.

On the mirror hanging on the wall, I see it, the change in my physical.

"Your eyes are black. Who are you, Ramiyah or my sister?"

It is the smile that jumps to a stand from my lips that answers him; she has really started to take control. But it is my voice, "I'm me," that stays the same.

There's a rap at the door.

"You came here for help, has that changed now?" He could have asked anything, anything else beside that. But one thing he never stops doing is making sure I tell him how I feel. I have had the habit of second-guessing myself, so I'm relieved when he comes to me it is in the most comforting way possible.

As simply as he worded it it sounded like he's saying, 'I got you little sis. If you decide to go through with this, I got you. If you decide this is far too cruel and you want everything to return to its natural place, I got you. Though the decision is in your hands, I will stand by you. But if it turns out this will mean you more harm than good …' from the sureness of his eyes, the lifting of his eyebrows as his eyes widens. 'I will exercise the full right I have as Prince of the First Dynasty and your big brother.'

This way we communicate, it is never just words. Just like I had bonded with Dakarai when we first met, Khari is like the umbrella that has always sheltered me no matter the weather. Even when I was wrong, he would correct me in a better more accepting manner than our Father; even when I had risen, challenged and determined, he was in my corner. He was my friend, my supporter, my only brother I would war with and go to war for.

My response to his question, "I am incomplete, whatever happens on Kimarr is out of my control. The double that I am, I know nothing of what I truly desire. I just know, I hate being deceived." Tears spill onto my cheekbones. "I hate now knowing she will take over."

Khari kicks off the wall, activates his Silver Ring and with one sweeping motion scans the mood board. Every detail copies, paste, upload, then he packs everything into the box. He spins his ring half a turn, Acirfa's map projected, he points to the south.

"Kimarr is here right, Cali show Dakarai exactly where you are?" The authority in his voice, the conviction in his demeanour. The whisper caught in my throat, 'don't even bother, your efforts won't change anything now'. But knowing of my brother, when he sets his mind, when he demands a certain response, it's better for me not to resist.

There's another rap at the door as if done with two sets of knuckles then an attempt at a forceful entry.

"I ..." My look back to the door, are they not hearing what I'm hearing?

"Cali, we have no time to stall. Your location, now."

"Kimarr, yes but there's a liquid-solid bubble, you won't be able to get through ..."

"And it's already too late."

The person on the other end fazes through the door, walks straight through as if it was non-existent.

"Maliyah, what are you ..."

"Hello Dakarai and Khari." She performs a waltz bow with one arm delicately flipped to her chest. "Pardon the intrusion but I have come to collect." She speaks in all forms, verbally addressing the eyes that lock onto her and mentally to me and just something tinkling in the air. Its presence growing stronger, more apparent and colourful by the minute.

"Maliyah is your cover, right? See what I've gathered you are not a club waitress and you, are ..." Khari is a foot away from her now. "Not even human."

"I knew you would catch on soon enough." She caresses her throat, the symbols that were something to think about before slide to her fingers, up her arms to her face. In a constant motion they flow along her skin.

I am a reflection of you, as you are I. A variation whose whole is within you. The sooner you realise this, the better.

Who said that?

Images.

Myah?

"Ramiyah." I breathe. The colours burst into blue and shower down as stardust, comets, everything chaotic yet immersive as if dangling in space. They fall into the ground; fall from the ceiling. Still, as if by design they curve around our energy fields.

"You know why I am here. All that is left is for this version of Calista to disappear."

Khari lifts an arm. "You are going to have to go through me."

"You have been exposed to a SYSTEM, right?" She's close enough to be in his ear. "First it's Calista to awaken, second it's Dakarai, then you, your time will come."

He hasn't said anything more since she came, his eyes focused on my hands.

"You possessed her without asking. No wonder why your people and spirituality were frowned upon. You have no respect for the living who have every right to disallow any entity from entering their vessel."

"Well check this." She places a soft hand to the side of Khari's head. "She begged me to." Her head tilts, her breath a whisper to his ear but her eyes they twinkle and they stir a knot in my stomach. "When she needed it most, right before she was about to die. You thought you saved her. You could never. Only I could, as a bearer of the Blue Flame."

"At her lowest moment, you preyed on her. Have you no morals?" Khari locks eyes with her gripping her wrist.

"You make it sound so bad. You forget, you don't know me Prince Khari, the stories told about me, they are pitiful lies from people who only feared. Lived, buried themselves in their Lower Selfs, and I, in comparison on the rise to my highest. They only sought to bring me down. It is the misunderstood who values much more than the truth. I am that person. So is Calista. So ..." She jerks her hand out of his and replaces it back where it was on his head. "She may not remember as she and you and everybody else would like, to make this complication a little easier to swallow but. It happened. Our exchange. She took the opportunity. To be free and I as the one owed has come to collect."

"Just tell me this one thing. She supposedly gave the right to possess her when she was tested on the waterfall?"

"Calista and the SYSTEM both. You will understand this all soon enough, just like Dakarai is beginning to, isn't that right?"

Still, he doesn't move, says nothing. Their whole conversation, had he heard a thing? I know for sure I have and though there are gaps in my memory, I feel it. The truth, not just from her, but from me. My heart. My mind. Me.

And the confirmation she required to continue, she pushes off Khari in a dart to his left, he catches her by the arm. She spins, pressing into his back. "She will find you Prince Khari." He tries to lift a leg. Like stuck in the mud there's this extra pull, it comes from behind and below him. "And she will open your eyes but for now ..." Part of her stills against Khari, the rest, like an elastic band stretches with a sticky black.

"Dakarai." I nudge him. To snap out of his daze. To do something as my final line of defence. His hands though tight, he is loose, detached. Distanced. "Dakarai!"

"Let's go home, Cali."

In a flash I see the bats. I see the face that was mine but not. I see Ramiyah, the black substance, the thing representative of the darkness. She dives through me and as a cocoon takes over every inch until I finally become translucent.

The darkness I welcome, for now, I am whole.

Wakey, wakey Cali.

Are you woke yet? A shadow runs by. The overhead lights flicker with its passing.

Wake up!

Woke.

At the threshold where light and darkness stop to never mix, there I feel the full attack of voice. Whispers. Shouts. Coos. Everything right down to their pitch and density increasing with a mighty boom to a volume so low its disrespectful they thought my ears would be that way inclined. Either way at my feet, the lines that were meant not to be crossed, fade to wriggles, eventually to nothing at all as the darkness skitters over the light. I appear to be under the frame of a door. And far but getting closer is a crystal black mirror with her on the other side. Her hand pushes against the glass made of darkness which moulds around her. Bending to her will. Stretching with the purpose to be broken. Her hand pushes and pushes, mine now on the receiving end. The tipping of scales. This competition of who will win. Who is the strongest? Who dares more? Each time, the back and forth, the darkness thins. Then as if something inside of me pops. Like a burst water balloon, she squeezes through. Naked.

We meet again.

She straightens and presses her thumb against my third eye, as I do hers. Images flash by. What are they, the present, or the future? I am unable to decipher them. A feather-like touch of true enlightenment. A bunch of codes laced with melanin: its core power.

I jolt awake, heaving as if my lungs are soon to be pulled through my throat. My body feels like it is folding inside out, like all my energy is being squeezed out but simultaneously being replaced with something more fulfilling. Alive.

"Ramiyah?"

"Are you ready for the finale?"

"We must let go of the life we have planned, so as to accept the one that is waiting for us."
- Joseph Campbell

30

Footsteps approach my cell.

Foreign in the sense that they don't pat or click, they just move with a sureness. I have no time to listen to their sound as before I know it it stops. I lift my head. And there he is once against, his allure much different to when we last met. Like a true king he commands strength and power the same way Prince Zaire does with a presence that would make the insecure and low self-esteemed cower. Yet my head stays levelled, my eyes to his neck. Deep where she resides, I knew I was waiting on this moment. The strong lines and definition to his body, I wonder if unlike Prince Zaire and Tamari he is really here.

"Princess Calista, it is time for the next step."

"What might you mean?" I croak.

He slithers in and positions his back to the bars. "This." A mirror liquifies and solidifies in the palm of his hand. The screen blackens then bursts with my last fight. It shows Prince Zaire pulling the trigger, the sound of the bullet released shushed the crowd and The Kutawala's Wingman was in his ear. It isn't that I know him but that she does having glimpsed him some place other than at her death moment. With his nose nodding up to the top of the stands, The Kutawala followed with a small drone dispatching into the air. The mirror switches to its lens as it surveys the crowd, specifically the man Prince Zaire hid as. He winked, something I had missed then as I held a hand over my chest. I suspected they wouldn't be able to uncover him but still his figure was scanned and then mine. Whatever that was found, The Kutawala issued an order, his men immediately blocking all the entrance and exit.

King Amare squashes the mirror deep under his skin.

"It was only a matter of time before my son made a mistake in your defence." He rolls to one shoulder and looks down at a man watching him from the ground floor.

"It is time we leave."

The man walks up the stairs slowly, his shoes scuffing the ground. With every step, the ground moans. The king outstretches his hand. I look at it but don't make a move. The man is now at the end of the hall, quickly approaching. Long strides, with his eyes focused on what I presume he knows is the king.

"Take my hand." Again, I hold back. The man is one cell away from us. The king, on impulse, strides over to my bed, just as the man reaches my door forcing his hands on to two bars pushing his head in like he had found his prize and he wasn't about to let them escape. "King Amare, it has been a while." The Kutawala's Wingman bares his teeth looking sinister with his half shaven eyebrows and a bite out of his left ear. "Don't make any sudden moves." I look at them both from the corners of my eye.

Choose wisely. She speaks in my mind.

The king reveals both his hands on either side. The man seems oblivious to what's happening.

"No sudden movements from me, sir." The word 'sir' sounds weird coming from his mouth. He's a king addressing his captor with respect as if he deserves it. The more I watch the king in action the safer I feel with him. My hands reach out.

"This applies to you too, young lady." He steps closer. "Have we met? Hold on. You are —"

The king grabs my hand, twirling us out of there before the man could call upon my true identity.

"Zaire, we need to leave, now." Zaire was half asleep when King Amare smacked his leg. He moaned a little as he worked the sleep from his eye, hunching over his legs. Tamari in a corner stood to attention so fast, he knocked over his opponent's king on the chess board.

"The Kutawala's Wingman has found us."

"What are you talking about? I handled it, didn't I?"

"Let's not get lazy just because she has stepped into the dark. Now move, it is time she leaves."

"I know I know." He slowly rolls his neck, cracks a few knuckles and as he stands stretch his arms to the ceiling then works his waist. "Running once again like cowards with our tails between our legs, we are supposed to be royalty."

It is funny seeing this sulky side to him, if only I could laugh I would.

"Fast fast Zaire."

The mirror the king adjusted his sleeves in, Tamari stands behind me and then Zaire beside his father. The glass liquifies gently like water down a bamboo shoot pooling to the ground.

"Cali. You've got mail."

Her sudden intrusion, like a snap into another world, the floor grows cold. My breath becomes foggy. Everyone freezes. Ramiyah walks around Tamari and settles, cross-legged, in front of me. Our eyes meet and neither one of us backs down.

"I come bearing words of wisdom. We have both suffered a lot. I'm going to set you free. You deserve peace, and knowledge shall bring you there."

"And what gives you the right to redirect the path that I'm walking down?"

"You gave me the right the moment you called to me. Let me remind you of the waterfall."

Her head becomes transparent and there I am submerged in water with her face waving at the bottom of the waterfall. It is the face that split between mine and hers and then fully hers. And as the memory made its way back to me, I remember what she did that made me feel so trusting of her.

"I designed the rest of my body with the Blue Flame. You spoke through the bubbles leaving your mouth, questioning who I was, how I could do that even in water. What did I say?"

"I understand how you feel. I have been pushed to the brink of fear. I have hated what I was. I have also been forced to become what I am now. But if you want, I can assist you. I can show you you ..."

"To which you shook your head but still raised a hand. You was losing oxygen, seconds away from blacking out. I met your hand and said, I can show you the truth to who you are. I can save you from this reality. Would you like to become one?"

"I pinned my eyebrows together. I did not understand but you smiled and you said I would because together we would awaken the Legend of Bluka. And after I would know the truth to who I am."

"And after, I would borrow your body as you find yourself."

"Why do I only remember now?"

"The timing was uncalled for. Now let's contact the Neter within."

The room grows excessively warm; our Blue Flame manifests around us. It bounces off the walls. Walks among us. Laughing in our presence. It is home, at peace, I don't see why I shouldn't be too.

"Why am I still awake even though I've stepped into the dark?"

"We are missing one final component, a full lunar eclipse. It should be on the horizon soon. Any more questions before I depart?"

"What's your plan once you take over?"

She gets up with a smile. Slowly she turns, and whispers over her shoulder. *"I'm going to destroy the SYSTEM, but first I require something from your father."*

She disappears, wrapping her arms around Tamari's waist. The Blue Flame continues to bounce around in the background. I see a golden light spread from my fingertips. It travels all over my body and stops at my lips.

"What the hell?" I whisper. *Your Life Force never left you.*

"More lies, Zaire." Surprisingly, I feel nothing. Anger is absent. My words sound more like a statement that reaffirms what I should have already known.

"I'm sorry, what?"

"I'm sure you know what I am talking about."

"I see. It was all a part of the façade. No harsh feelings, Cali."

The liquid glass joins our feet onto one platform. One moment we are stable, the next we are twirled outside. My hand covers my face as a gust of wind sprays dirt. Tamari gently presses me on, a hand to my shoulder. And as we walk, I at the centre of their perimeter, the faces that observe from outside and inside the buildings, the soldiers that await their commands I can't help but think. They'd be fools to mess with us.

The Kutawala and his Wingman exit the waterfall. We need to turn right, but they are blocking us.

"Who knew we were harbouring the Emperor's daughter right under our nose and we didn't smell a thing?" The Kutawala has a slight high pitch to his voice.

"That is funny isn't it, how you missed the bigger picture? You are supposed to be in control, but one thing you missed. You underestimated our talents," King Amare laughs.

"It is going to cost you in the future." Zaire snickers and proceeds as they planned. The Kutawala stands his ground, with a whistle his little soldiers round the corner and surround us. They hold small bombs which I assume are a remake of what they used in the Civil War.

"You're on your last strike, King Amare." The Wingman pipes up. I couldn't help feeling disgusted, the absolute nerve. Even with his kingdom in ruins, his people still live scattered throughout this world, his son too, he shouldn't be treated as though a child.

"You still don't know who I am." King Amare tuts sweeping one hand into his pocket and the other crossed over his torso with his fingers rubbing. "Farewell."

The Kutawala flicks his wrist, a tsunami of bombs spiral towards us. Through the moment I blinked, my Blue Flame repels from me. It smashes a dome around us, deflecting their weak objects with very little effort. They disintegrate at once and in his eyes, I see a flicker of interest, of desire lifting his eyebrows.

"So, it's true."

The soldiers rush at us, but in another blink, I've been shifted.

To the edge.

To the bubble I tried to escape through as a double.

To her who gestures for me to take a seat.

31

{Dakarai}

The steel gates crack open, a blue light whips out scanning us from head-to-toe and lastly our Eye of Horus and Silver Rings.

"Welcoming Prince Khari. Welcoming Prince Dakarai."

The electrified barrier lowers and the Elite Supreme Warriors on duty thrust their spears into the ground bowing their heads in recognition. They swivel their broad shields to their backs. Khari fist-bumps them from the side of his hand. We are all friends, went through the training together. Some days our personalities would conflict other days we were like brothers and sisters. Still, they were family.

"Whatever prompted your return don't let it keep you down."

"Things will work themselves out."

We have all been on assignments, many of them have been challenged to a point of questioning who they wanted to be as an ESW but still they held on tight to their duty. This assignment wasn't as hard as the rest, it just required a change in perspective. Almost as if our trip to Earth was all a cover as the true assignment was to discover something in ourselves that needed to be shined a light on. My reply is gruff, one of the guys a year older than me slaps my shoulders as further encouragement.

We take the shortest route. Weaving amongst the villagers who smile and bow.

"Greetings."

"Prince Khari welcome."

"Prince Dakarai greetings."

Women feed their infants seated on wooden stools. Children read books to each other in a circle, very animated in their performance. Others exercise according to their teachers' instructions. The elderly chat amongst themselves, laughing and reminiscing on their past as they rest in the shade under the willow trees. Some men help cook dinner with their wives, others carry bags of rice, buckets of water, and play board games with their brothers and sisters. As we pass the waterfalls, a couple of children rush out of the water to give us quick hugs and high fives. A few ESW's signal a greeting. Women Khari is used to flirting with stroke his arm in passing, some giggling, some smiling, many just entertained with his presence. He gives off the bare minimum, not like his usual self.

The animals do their own thing; lions playing with their mates in the tall grass; giraffes holding their heads high nourishing their bodies; elephants playing tug of war with their tusks.

Aelburn is exquisite in every aspect. From the rainforests, waterfalls, and the beautiful people to the palace stretching across the land ahead — its glass walls reflect the sunlight. It still takes my breath away each time I look at it. We walk up the wide steps that surround its entire infrastructure into the open doors. Lavender hits our nose. The Regal Handmaids with red jasper beads wrapped around their neck and wrists greet us with a curtsy. They wear their hair in an afro and their purple skirts lightly blow in the wind. We kiss their hands before moving on.

A few corridors down, Aziza and her twin Kwame, are mind-linked almost like gossiping women, pulling on each other's arm. Those two are always up to something. Once they see us, they quickly break apart.

"What is so urgent you had to return at once?" Khari with a sigh slings an arm around her shoulder. I fist-bump followed by a shoulder touch with Kwame.

"You will find out with everyone else."

"Ah come on, just a little something something." She shakes her shoulders, cozying up to him.

"I'm serious sis and we're going to need your help."

Her shoulders say fine but her hands cross in front still begging a little for something to tame her curiosity.

Khari squeezes her small neck. She gives him a weird look. She can sense bad news. I keep quiet.

It all happened a little too sudden, before and after Maliyah was confirmed to be Ramiyah. That had been the missing link all along, our purpose for meeting but it wasn't only her who had revealed herself. It was the lady whose face I keep on going back to, it was Tadaaki's whose presence in my waking-dreaming mind I couldn't shake. It was even Calista as I held onto her hand to the very last moment when her double disappeared to black ash and then nothing.

As for the lady, her words floated to me while Calista shook my hand, as Maliyah bonded with my love. She said, "find the white room. Follow your heart."

My heart holds many things. It holds guilt. Pain. Disappointment. My growing strength which came from her love. From Khari's. His sister. His brother. His family. Aelburn as a whole. But the largest part of my heart, I felt it squeeze as she was taken from me without resolution that she would be alright. That Ramiyah's invasion wouldn't break her and we would not be reunited. It would be like that night I left Tadaaki without a proper burial service. And so, Calista, the love I cannot stand by and do nothing to protect, to reach out, to seek through the blinds of Kimarr, I will disobey my own mind. I will disregard what was found on Earth — for a moment.

"I will find my love."

Khari steps forward to one knee, his arm crossed over his heart. I've already acknowledged my parents with our formal bow upon entering the throne room now I spin to offer the same to the Emperor. He sits on his throne, braced against its wide oval backing. Empress Nubia has her body half to us by the window behind him, a delicate hand on her forearm.

"Prince Khari greets the Emperor and requests an audience."

"You have the floor."

"Upon our assignment on Earth, a growing concern was presented when Princess Calista showed up as her double. We have reason to believe her life is in danger following the confiscation of her life force and Ramiyah's intrusion into her vessel. Yes, Ramiyah first-born to the Sixth Dynasty."

Empress Nubia shares a brief look with my mother, it speaks words and communicates images. Do they know something that could help us?

"And how did she land herself in such a preposterous situation on Kimarr?" Aziza is fiddling with her ankle beads on the stairs. She sighs deeply but not deep enough almost the same as her father who gives no expression — let alone moves with an inch of concern.

"It is not a matter of how but when. Her assignment to Kimarr wasn't the beginning, it's just where she thinks it all began. See," Khari approached the stairs. "Ramiyah showed herself."

"Have you any proof?"

A tap of his Silver Ring, he blows up his findings: of our first meeting with Maliyah and the symbols on her skin, of the last time we met as Khari confronted her. He also managed to catch her stretch into darkness, into Calista, they illuminated together and finally her disappearance.

"She may not remember ... to make this complication a little easier to swallow but ... she took the opportunity. To be free and I as the one owed has come to collect."

Khari's eyes flicker to his father's, waiting on a reaction. He doesn't even blink. After hearing Ramiyah's voice, they should have some thoughts. Even Empress Nubia shuffles closer a hand to his throne.

"So what do you plan to do, by the looks and sounds of it, she is where she needs to be? Princess Calista could have momentarily tried to back out of a deal she had already made. You know how she second guesses herself."

I couldn't contain my gasp.

"Addressing the Emperor." I join Khari in two strides. "She came to me because she feared for her life, she feared she would not be able to resolve this matter without our help. I suggest we plan a rescue effective immediately."

"Hm, fear." Emperor Rameses lightly chuckles. "Maybe you have her all wrong and this is not a worthy enough reason to put a hold on your assignment for something as simple as a rescue mission she may not want. We all heard what Ramiyah said, Calista took the opportunity. To me this sounds like something that could benefit her."

"Benefit her? She created a double, we all know what that means. She is trapped elsewhere on Kimarr. She even resisted to show me what is happening over there —"

"For good reason."

"Maybe not, maybe she couldn't, maybe —"

"Prince Dakarai you only bring me speculation backed up with emotions. This is unlike a ESW. This is not enough to convince me she needs *saving*."

"Do you not care?"

I have long felt this way. I've seen him dispose of her when she calls for help. Turn a blind eye or look only with a side one. "She is your daughter before she is a ESW. In the hands of the Sixth Dynasty who may be with The Kutawala and his people, do you not wonder of her safety? With all the talents that we have is she not worth your time and consideration?"

"If you want to waste your efforts especially where possession is involved with the hosts awareness, do as you please."

What kind of Emperor, what kind of father ...? I step to challenge him some more but Khari raises a hand blocking me.

"This matter we will handle privately. Whether Calista chooses to continue down this path or not, I will see to it she is safe and sound even amongst the Sixth Dynasty."

I draw in a slow and steady breath. This is how Khari wishes to end this meeting, but it does nothing for us. It brings us no step closer to Calista or Kimarr or a plan to put in motion. I can't even look at my parents, at the Emperor anymore, how could I be the only one so distraught about what she may be feeling? Khari too, he's too collected shows no heat at his father's dismissal. For a man so against spirituality, the Sixth Dynasty, possessions at the most part, he looks like a coward evading the problem at hand. The Emperor a man who pushes through fear, would rather treat it as something he doesn't feel or isn't present in his reality, he sure is hiding it well.

"Aziza I'm going to need you to find a quick route to Kimarr and gather a few Tech N9nes. As a backup find out how to tackle possession."

She stirs to a stand, glances at her father swaying a hand behind her. "How long do I have?"

"Less than a sunrise and sunset."

She scratches her forehead. "I'll see what I can do."

The Emperor walks to where his wife once stood by the window. "Prince Khari I'll leave this to you but before you go, a word."

I'm still reeling but look up enough to catch the exchange with Khari and his mother. She shakes her head but I notice her left hand grips a piece of her dress. At the bottom of the stairs, she squeezes my mother's elbow and together they leave. In a hurry, I continue to turn as they leave and dart to the right wing of the palace.

I decide to wait for Khari outside.

He made his way to his father's side, his hands on his elbows crossed at his back

"What did I send you to Earth to do?" He watches the sky following the birds circling.

"Find the threat to Acirfa."

"So did you not uncover anything?"

"Calista —"

"That's not what I asked."

"The assignment doesn't matter at this moment -—" Khari throws his hands in the air.

"The assignment is everything. Don't you get it?" The Emperor leans in. "Why do you think I kept the two assignments separate. Kimarr. Earth." He holds his hands up balancing between the two. "You should have never abandoned your position out there. Did you really not find anything?"

"I don't remember all I know is Calista is a more pressing matter."

"You don't sound as sure as Prince Dakarai. You found something but you won't say."

"The way you are acting Father, I must agree with Dakarai. Do you not care about her at all? She is with the Sixth Dynasty and let's not forget I know what you didn't do back then before they disappeared."

His father waves him off.

"And you know what else Ramiyah said, when she and Calista developed a symbiotic relationship it was that day you pushed her off the waterfall."

The Emperor clicks his tongue.

"So that is what this is all about. So long ago, why only now does Ramiyah surface? Her assignment to Kimarr, I thought it strange when she switched to this one."

"So you knew, that Ramiyah hadn't completely left this plane and what Calista did?"

"It worked out as it should. Until now they have kept quiet. The ghosts have risen."

Khari looks at him through a mosiac pattern on the window. His father is stroking his jaw with a smile, the first he has seen since he arrived. The only emotion he could bare to display with such confidence and mischievousness.

"King Amare ... Ramiyah ... The Kutawala ... the stage is back after a long interval."

Khari leaves him in his thoughts.

"With the universe, there are no coincidences."

32

Together Dakarai and Khari in a room with Aziza, her Scholar peers and a small handful of Tech N9nes conjure multiple displays. Aziza is on the floor seated with files, videos, page sheets twirling around her. She taps away at her air-keyboard.

Khari highlights Kimarr and zooms in from a landscape perspective as well as footage and images from how it used to look before The Kutawala's invasion to after. The comparison is monstrous, it also brings up bad memories for Dakarai, it being similar to his kingdom.

"I've hacked Princess Calista's Silver Ring."

Khari air drags her recordings to the centre. They view from when she set foot on Kimarr to Lake Myopia where Custodian Tamari caught her. Before there is static, they encounter a dome he vanishes through.

"What do you make of him?"

"The custodian?" The one closest in control of the whole network they have established rubs a hand over his face.

Khari rewinds to where they spoke.

"You're trespassing ..."

"His panther and his skin, there is a lot off."

"It's like the avatars we create and the doubles you manifest."

"But this solid projection it wavers when we still his image. He doesn't have access to the Eye of Horus judging from his arms. But as a custodian there is so much he can tap into."

Khari thought, even from that moment, though he presented himself as an enemy, how could a custodian do true harm to a princess, warrior, let alone a Genapian, one he must serve as a child of the universe and Supreme Deities? From the beginning they set up the trap very distinctly, his multiple projections to how he cornered her it is as he said, *we've been expecting you.* The trinity: Ramiyah, Zaire, Custodian Tamari.

"... hence why he can touch and manipulate not just his spirit animal but Princess Calista's surroundings with his clones and the portal she struggled to spin."

Dakarai points at Custodian Tamari.

"The most important part, his skin is not as it should be. It is stripping."

A notification jumps disturbing their display.

"It's a new upload."

Dakarai flicks it into action.

It's moving fast and a little shaky. What Calista was seeing, the footage is sharp in some parts and blurry in others. The parts that start to make sense, she is in a group. Prince Zaire is on one side. King Amare in front. Custodian Tamari on her other side. Dakarai was right, his skin it's drained of melanin but as a slight sheen shows how it should be.

"So it's true."

The last thing to show, vibrant, The Kutawala beyond the Blue Flame shield. Aziza is at Khari's side. "Is that him? He's really still here, with the Sixth Dynasty, with Cali?"

Khari closes his eyes; in deep thought he licks his lips. "Can we contact Cali?"

"Her connection is still down. The best we can do is send out our drones to bridge the network."

Khari nods. He pulls Aziza back as she enters the display blowing up The Kutawala's face. "I wonder how they contained him, after what he did during the Civil War, Calista should be as far away from him as possible, no?" He clicks his fingers pulling her awareness back to him. "Stay focus, when I get back have everything together for our departure."

"Where you going?"

"Dakarai take the lead."

He's unable to seize him as he teleports.

Khari tries the door to his mother's study; he hopes this is the only place she would be. His mother and Queen Jendayi are the ones who know enough about spirituality, the dark and light arts, what shouldn't be spoken aloud. So Calista's situation, he is sure they have many thoughts.

Queen Jendayi hurries him over all the while placing a finger to her lips.

"Is it a dream?"

"One could only hope a prophetic one."

He understood and would patiently wait until she returns to reality.

From in the throne room, Empress Nubia had felt it coming on. She didn't want them to notice, she wanted them to have her undivided attention, wanted to hear everything and be as understanding and reliant as possible. They were speaking of her first daughter after all. This wasn't just a matter to be disregarded of so easily. But her mind had other plans, and it aligned so perfectly with what was being discussed. The moment Khari declared he would handle this matter, she felt her eyes spin, as graceful as she could down the stairs she alerted her friend. Not waiting a second. The dream played immediately thereafter.

Through the fog that was settling, rooted to her spot, she stared into the distance. Her luminescent deep blue beads around her wrist shimmer under the lunar moon. As the space between her and what had captured her attention became in reach, she knew there were no coincidences. The universe has already scripted and delivered one's destiny. Everything in motion; to stop it now, it would cause a catastrophe.

Calista is alone bathed in darkness. At the edge of the cliff at first, her father throws her into the waterfall. There's a sound of film sticking with light refracting at a rapid pace. The image rewinds and Empress Nubia stands holding onto her daughter's hand. The sky is blood red with the Blue Star stretching across the landscape. The wind claws its hands through both of their hair. Calista screams, "let me go." Bats circle her body under a command she is not aware is her own doing. The waterfall gushes with a black substance. It rises like a beanstalk clawing at Calista's feet, so she thought. After closer inspection, it nuzzles her ankles, builds to the point where it becomes a shadow sticking to her back.

"Mother." Her screams had died down to a whisper against the wind.

"Speak to me my child."

"You need not worry. I am at peace with what must be done."

Even though a tear sweeps to her cheek, her heart smiles with content. Her hold on her daughter's hand no longer feels like a tug, but an embrace. So soft, so light, it becomes like a caterpillar shedding their skin and with one bounce prepares for flight with new wings.

"I understand my child."

The dream ended there Calista all smiles and full of light.

Empress Nubia opens her eyes slowly she admires her ceiling, the stars, half and full moons swirling with blue. The sun had set in the west, the only light were the candles some hours ago Queen Jendayi lit.

"Mother."

She welcomes Khari to the edge of her reclined chair.

"Speak your mind my son."

"You saw her right?"

She pulls his hand to her and covers it with hers.

"How did she seem?"

"Prince Dakarai will not understand. You know it too. Her fate has called her in a strange way, to the eyes that only look from the outside she appears to be in danger. But deep inside, this must happen as it currently does."

Khari hangs his head. He knew it, could see through it all but still felt a queasiness in his heart for the sight of such a union with the deceased taking over the body of the living, his own sister, it seems much worse than it actually is. Everything has a purpose.

Khari straightens.

"You wish to ask about the waterfall?" She pats his hand. "I knew, in fact Ramiyah consulted me too, how could she not?"

"So, there will only be one outcome, despite our efforts?"

"You do what you must Prince Khari, as for my son, you know what to do."

Of course, everything is already set in stone; the universe is in control. Khari bows before leaving.together Dakarai and Khari in a room with Aziza, her Scholar peers and a small handful of Tech N9nes conjure multiple displays. Aziza is on the floor seated with files, videos, page sheets twirling around her. She taps away at her air-keyboard.

Khari highlights Kimarr and zooms in from a landscape perspective as well as footage and images from how it used to look before The Kutawala's invasion to after. The comparison is monstrous, it also brings up bad memories for Dakarai, it being similar to his kingdom.

"I've hacked Princess Calista's Silver Ring."

Khari air drags her recordings to the centre. They view from when she set foot on Kimarr to Lake Myopia where Custodian Tamari caught her. Before there is static, they encounter a dome he vanishes through.

"What do you make of him?"

"The custodian?" The one closest in control of the whole network they have established rubs a hand over his face.

Khari rewinds to where they spoke.

"You're trespassing …"

"His panther and his skin, there is a lot off."

"It's like the avatars we create and the doubles you manifest."

"But this solid projection it wavers when we still his image. He doesn't have access to the Eye of Horus judging from his arms. But as a custodian there is so much he can tap into."

Khari thought, even from that moment, though he presented himself as an enemy, how could a custodian do true harm to a princess, warrior, let alone a Genapian, one he must serve as a child of the universe and Supreme Deities? From the beginning they set up the trap very distinctly, his multiple projections to how he cornered her it is as he said, we've been expecting you. The trinity: Ramiyah, Zaire, Custodian Tamari.

"... hence why he can touch and manipulate not just his spirit animal but Princess Calista's surroundings with his clones and the portal she struggled to spin."

Dakarai points at Custodian Tamari.

"The most important part, his skin is not as it should be. It is stripping."

A notification jumps disturbing their display.

"It's a new upload."

Dakarai flicks it into action.

It's moving fast and a little shaky. What Calista was seeing, the footage is sharp in some parts and blurry in others. The parts that start to make sense, she is in a group. Prince Zaire is on one side. King Amare in front. Custodian Tamari on her other side. Dakarai was right, his skin it's drained of melanin but as a slight sheen shows how it should be.

"So it's true."

The last thing to show, vibrant, The Kutawala beyond the Blue Flame shield. Aziza is at Khari's side. "Is that him? He's really still here, with the Sixth Dynasty, with Cali?"

Khari closes his eyes; in deep thought he licks his lips. "Can we contact Cali?"

"Her connection is still down. The best we can do is send out our drones to bridge the network."

Khari nods. He pulls Aziza back as she enters the display blowing up The Kutawala's face. "I wonder how they contained him, after what he did during the Civil War, Calista should be as far away from him as possible, no?" He clicks his fingers pulling her awareness back to him. "Stay focus, when I get back have everything together for our departure."

"Where you going?"

"Dakarai take the lead."

He's unable to seize him as he teleports.

Khari tries the door to his mother's study; he hopes this is the only place she would be. His mother and Queen Jendayi are the ones who know enough about spirituality, the dark and light arts, what shouldn't be spoken aloud. So Calista's situation, he is sure they have many thoughts.

Queen Jendayi hurries him over all the while placing a finger to her lips.

"Is it a dream?"

"One could only hope a prophetic one."

He understood and would patiently wait until she returns to reality.

From in the throne room, Empress Nubia had felt it coming on. She didn't want them to notice, she wanted them to have her undivided attention, wanted to hear everything and be as understanding and reliant as possible. They were speaking of her first daughter after all. This wasn't just a matter to be disregarded of so easily. But her mind had other plans, and it aligned so perfectly with what was being discussed. The moment Khari declared he would handle this matter, she felt her eyes spin, as graceful as she could down the stairs she alerted her friend. Not waiting a second. The dream played immediately thereafter.

Through the fog that was settling, rooted to her spot, she stared into the distance. Her luminescent deep blue beads around her wrist shimmer under the lunar moon. As the space between her and what had captured her attention became in reach, she knew there were no coincidences. The universe has already scripted and delivered one's destiny. Everything in motion; to stop it now, it would cause a catastrophe.

Calista is alone bathed in darkness. At the edge of the cliff at first, her father throws her into the waterfall. There's a sound of film sticking with light refracting at a rapid pace. The image rewinds and Empress Nubia stands holding onto her daughter's hand. The sky is blood red with the Blue Star stretching across the landscape. The wind claws its hands through both of their hair. Calista screams, "let me go." Bats circle her body under a command she is not aware is her own doing. The waterfall gushes with a black substance. It rises like a beanstalk clawing at Calista's feet, so she thought. After closer inspection, it nuzzles her ankles, builds to the point where it becomes a shadow sticking to her back.

"Mother." Her screams had died down to a whisper against the wind.

"Speak to me my child."

"You need not worry. I am at peace with what must be done."

Even though a tear sweeps to her cheek, her heart smiles with content. Her hold on her daughter's hand no longer feels like a tug, but an embrace. So soft, so light, it becomes like a caterpillar shedding their skin and with one bounce prepares for flight with new wings.

"I understand my child."

The dream ended there Calista all smiles and full of light.

Empress Nubia opens her eyes slowly she admires her ceiling, the stars, half and full moons swirling with blue. The sun had set in the west, the only light were the candles some hours ago Queen Jendayi lit.

"Mother."

She welcomes Khari to the edge of her reclined chair.

"Speak your mind my son."

"You saw her right?"

She pulls his hand to her and covers it with hers.

"How did she seem?"

"Prince Dakarai will not understand. You know it too. Her fate has called her in a strange way, to the eyes that only look from the outside she appears to be in danger. But deep inside, this must happen as it currently does."

Khari hangs his head. He knew it, could see through it all but still felt a queasiness in his heart for the sight of such a union with the deceased taking over the body of the living, his own sister, it seems much worse than it actually is. Everything has a purpose.

Khari straightens.

"You wish to ask about the waterfall?" She pats his hand. "I knew, in fact Ramiyah consulted me too, how could she not?"

"So, there will only be one outcome, despite our efforts?"

"You do what you must Prince Khari, as for my son, you know what to do."

Of course, everything is already set in stone; the universe is in control. Khari bows before leaving.

"Nothing rests; everything moves; everything vibrates."
-The Kybalion

33

{Calista}

Where it all began. Drenched in the waters of Lake Myopia, the consistent tides wash over my body with the sizzling of water knocking against hot rocks. The opium effects it last had is absent. I test the bubble barrier, leaving handprints along its solid-liquid, loving how it bends to my will. It reverts back to its original shape after my hands peel away from its surface.

Today will be the day it will be broken.

"Change is necessary for improvement."

Ramiyah is a flicking light bulb her arms wrapped around her legs. Her eyes focus on the red dirt that swarms on the ground in an array of ants nibbling on its food.

"You say you accept your change yet you make no move to welcome it into your heart. Why do you still linger in your Lower Self?" Her voice sounds like its underwater at first. Her frequency tunes eventually, her vibrations magnifying.

It is not as easy as it seems.

"Things have moved quickly over this past year. I had my interpretation of your people, of you, flipped on its head. Through this experience I don't feel comfortable in the body we share. Though you've given me truth and a sight so potent, my hesitation comes from my uncertainty. From what ifs. Don't I have much to lose? What if your so-called truth is only a twisted version of another lie?"

"If it were, would you have willingly proceeded into the darkness? At first, it didn't make sense, but then you came to terms with it all because it deeply resonated with you. You knew you were missing something; we filled the vacant space. You are not alone. If I lie to you, I lie to myself. I admit I have been withholding some truth but it would be too much of a burden, besides as you slip completely into the dark my soul will be bare to you. You may not like what you find, but in those moments, I will be vulnerable. Vulnerability is not weakness. The first step is to love yourself unconditionally. Survive and everything else will fall into place. You did not come here to be defeated. Draw strength from your past and learn from your mistakes."

In the dirt, she draws a circle around her. It ignites with a red-blue ring. A two-way interaction mini waves meet head on. The same passes through the bubble to me.

"Keep the faith; trust in the process."

My eyes close; I take in a deep breath.

"Let's start with the chakras."

A slow heat begins to surround my back. I feel my senses refine. My ears twitch.

Repeat after me.

In my mind I open up like a lotus flower. My body projects with the chakra symbols dull and ready for activation.

"The Root Chakra. I am grounded with my spirit deep in the Earth. I am calm, strong, centred, and peaceful. I can let go of fear and trust. I am worthy of all things beautiful."

At the base of my spine, the energy becomes a fiery-red and bubbles awaiting its second entrance.

"*The Sacral Chakra. I am creative in all areas of my life. I am open to receive all that life offers. Embrace the past, be content in the now. Rise in positivity. I am secure in myself.*"

Upon the second entrance, the fiery-red roars into a vivacious orange.

"*The Solar Plexus Chakra. I am in alignment with the abundant flow of the universe. I live with integrity and have high respect for myself and others. I allow vital life force energy to flow through me and animate my life on all levels.*"

"I honour the power within me. I am more than enough."

The vivacious orange fuses into an enlightened yellow.

"*The Heart Chakra. I inhale self-love and I exhale peace. I feel compassion and empathy for the pain and struggle of others. I can forgive, let go of resentment, and heal emotionally. I willingly release all fears, concerns, and worries about giving and receiving love. I am eternally loved.*"

Above my heart, a harmonious green forms a cloud.

"*The Throat Chakra. I speak my truth, my voice matters. I own my power. I express myself. I am aligned with my higher truth and communicate this with love and honour.*"

A devoted blue emerges around my throat and meddles with the enlightened yellow.

"*The Third Eye Chakra. My spiritual vision is clear. I always follow and honour my intuition. I invite sacred transformation. It is safe for me to see the truth. I expand my awareness through my higher self.*"

Like an erupting volcano, the royal purple thrusts out of my third eye and penetrates the barrier but doesn't break through.

"*Finally, the Crown Chakra. I am connected, a part of it all. I go beyond limiting beliefs and accept myself totally. I am divinely guided and inspired. I am at one with the universe. I live my life through my Higher Self."*

"I am enlightened."

The royal purple thins into an extravagant violet.

The new energies surging through my veins mingle with my Blue Flame. It visibly travels through my skin in the form of a golden serpent. The Blue Flame assists the Kundalini energy to become one. The individual energies push forward through me and with a body of light swirl in the chakra sections.

A gasp. A puncture through my lungs, that's what it feels like.

I slam both hands to the bubble. A tremble at my lips, a quiver in my stomach. The sounds now, the earth quaking as the soil pulses with Mother Nature's life. The water sloshing, driving me back, forward, all attempts to carry me below the surface.

"Calista —"

Everything pounds. Everything vibrates. Everything is colours, shapes; big, small. What fractures, what gathers. What should be still, pulses, beats. Rings.

"Princess Calista —"

"Breathe."

The voices, the sounds, the sensations; my hands fall to my chest. A slight hover, a light press.

"Accept it. This is all you. The breath ..."

"Is fire."

All that had started at once, in one swoop, finishes with a tingling. Of twinkling stars; of only my breath stilling the noise.

And as my tongue delivers, "I acknowledge the power of my word to create what I intend; I speak with truth. Asẹ̀," the flames that spiral burn. Away at the obstacle before the completion of my awakening, my sealing fate. Away at the final obstacle I focus my eyes to.

Digging my toes into the sediments at Lake Myopia's bed, I taste the air. The difference, it all feels so new yet old. So, refreshing. So freeing.

The universe's Life Force is apparent, something I never could see before. The cosmos and planets surrounding Acirfa look closer than I previously imagined. An explosion of infinite possibilities mixed with creation's blessing. At this moment, life has a new meaning. I becomes us. I am a part of the collective soul, collective consciousness, guarded by creation's warriors. Child and mother of creation.

Ramiyah's hands against the barrier, her Blue Flame and the darkness propel to meet mine: Bluka. I close my eyes and my third eye opens. The world has a purple hue. I awe at every microscopic detail down to the particles in the air. It is beauty unable to be described with the simplicity of hueman terminologies. The energy builds at my fingertips, I draw from the vibrations in the air. Speaking the language Myah once cooed, the kinetic particles bond in a lattice. Floods and pushes against the bubble's resistance. Ramiyah and I exhale together. As we meet, it explodes as glass. The pieces dissolve into my skin, into the air, into the universe.

34

{Calista}

They are here. Her words struck the chords of my heart, then fiddled with the strings of my mind. My weight reduces to nothing as I run.

Seeing is knowing.

Over the hills, the soldiers dispatched immediately after the bubble's destruction, rush through me in passing. From all directions. And through the vibrations I hone in, what they've gathered in images, the only ones that matter minutes ago were spat out through a spazzing-portal. Their reactions quick enough to notice the green fog they protected their front with their shields. Dakarai and Khari side-by-side, a group of four ESW's scattered behind them. Aziza soon after materialises with the help of a few Tech N9nes and their technology. As small as they are, the drones appear much bigger to me, capturing everything as they whizz like bees.

Dakarai makes his way around a group of pebbles falling to Lake Myopia's front. A light flashes amongst the rocks stirring at the bottom of the shallow end. It calls to him, remembering him as its former owner and with a magnetic pulse flies into his hand. The sword enlarges with his immediate touch sheening with a silvery-red.

"We've got company," Khari crouched to the earth, grains of the red dirt stain his fingers as he rubs them together. The grit he salvages for a second longer before blowing them into the air.

"No sight of Princess Calista," says a Tech N9ne in his ear.

"Don't worry, she is already here." Khari lowers his eyes to the shadows forming a triangle around them.

"Come to rescue your princess have ya?" The Wingman boasts from outside of the formation his arms folded. The curls on his head fight to cover his big forehead. He jumps from foot-to-foot, boundless, he only needed a ball now to not look like a fool.

"You hope we will lead you to her." Dakarai slides a finger to the tip of his blade.

"Not at all, she's not the catch here for the time being." He stops, pressing a shoulder into one of his men. As solid as a mountain, he holds up. It doesn't take a keen eye to spot the difference between them and the ones at the forefront of the Civil War. These ones are cultivated, controlled, programmed, they have a flair of discipline, but lack souls. Their eyes still paling-blue are absent of what it means to have life, to have expression. "You know I don't believe we've had the pleasure of an introduction. I am ..."

"The Kutawala's Wingman. Nothing important." Khari clocks his tongue, his legs were falling asleep, he shakes them as he stands even gives them a few taps.

He rotates a finger like a helicopter blade. The first line of defence raise their machetes. "No matter how much time has passed, that which was important then shouldn't be assigned to oblivion now. You get what I mean?"

"Such a desperate desire to stay relevant, you have been locked away ever since. The world has changed much, don't get cocky because of your previous highlight."

He coughs out a laugh. "You're not aware are ya? How it began, how is your father these days? Emperor Rameses."

"He sends his regards."

"As he should, we have a lot of catching up to do as old friends."

His hands to his waist, Khari whips out two sharp daggers with the Dynastic Emblem on the hilt from their cloth.

"The truth your people would be frighten to hear aloud, how the mighty Aelburn still stands without much effort but. Enough of the chatter, show me what their warriors is made of."

The Wingman whistles and his soldier's stoop to one knee. Aim, an arm pointing with some half-open pistol with the size of four marbles in its cannon. Launch, it doesn't steam once triggered, moving through the air so fast. It sheds its black casing, a ball of green energy blazing.

Dakarai's shield is building, so are the Tech N9ne's but Khari his eyes narrow, the skin around them crinkling with a smile.

An abstract display of movement becomes a painting of black and white explosions. My exhale tears and contains to which the Wingman steps in disbelieving his eyes. Their weapons drag to my invisible wall. I push my palm out. Their energy roars to life again, continuing its destination, my energy field cocooning its desires. The repelling force as great as I amp it to be, even greater now the more I stare, in one swoop it disintegrates. The surge too much, the soldiers become dust too. The Wingman jumps back his arm sprouts wings of metal that flutter to his protection. When he lowers, his dubious look of the attack's origin, Dakarai calls, *My love.*

He sees me through my cloak of distorted vibrations. The unwavering frequency taps into the light energies and reveals my physical form. The Wingman grunts and spits.

"The family is one again." The Kutawala. Escorted with more of his men he brings forth a chill that cramps the heat on the earth. The three beads infused with his magic around his wrist glows. An avalanche of hail mixed with snow rushes to the ground with the brisk wind guiding its path. Puffs of clouds escape our lips. Shivers race down our backs. Goosebumps pulse on our skin. We are not used to such weather. Whenever winter descended, we were far from it. Now we are beguiled with its noose. It threatens to suck the life out of our sun-kissed skin. The Kutawala laughs at our cowardice to their inhumane attraction. The cold crawls up his face and solidifies with a reptile-like hexagonal pattern, his eyes taking on a lighter shade of blue than before. "Yes, we have far upgraded since we last interfered with your people."

It is true. They have mutated with deprivation, it is not just a weather thing, it's what comes with it. What rots yet still preserves.

"You have a funny way of describing murder and slaughter." I drag a foot forward, the ice pooling to water.

"Ah Ramiyah, it is an interference when we have help, no?"

It is she talking to him, Ramiyah amplifying her presence as a ghost protruding out of me like an avatar.

"My love." Dakarai tugs on the hand I can no longer feel as she switches our places.

"If you leave now, I'll grant you mercy."

He throws up hands pretending to shake.

"I am not afraid of you princess, I have much greater matters of concern."

"You should be." Ramiyah's voice strengthens with her full weight in my body. The avalanche seems like nothing now, her eyes on his, on the scars that *she* left. As if invoking all the spirits that were wrong, I remember Tamika's memory, other Genapians traumas; Ramiyah's most of all. At her death moment, what captured her attention, the reason she froze. The Kutawala was there. At the carnage of the north wall, the earth ran with lava of blood. Hot. Fresh. He had to have a taste of it.

"That scar is the bare minimum you should have received."

How vile he was, a true abomination to dip and then smear her brothers and sisters across his mouth. The tongue that swiped, savouring, a delicacy, Ramiyah's fists were flames. In my hands, they're Bluka full of Tamika's memory, Zaire's pain after his loss, even her father kneeling before him.

"You must ..."

Dakarai's tug is swatted away as she strides, trippling in speed.

"Succumb to me."

Head-to-head, he grabs my hand. It's like Frost spreads quickly up my arm, gripping my muscles but Ramiyah, our eyes are lit, our senses are tuned to where pain is numb.

"You should have never won the war. You should have never succeeded in wiping out the other dynasties. You should have never taken over Kimarr and killed my people. You should have never killed *me*." Bluka encases one half of my body. It has a duel of its own as it faces off against the frost, slowly restoring its rightful place and crippling the frost's defences. It washes over The Kutawala's arm and I hear him cry out. It is faint, only filled with a speck of what it needs to be. His eyes they tell a story through many blinks, his eyebrows settle, guarding.

"Mercy? Murder? Mercy? Murder?" My head rolls left to right. I favour the former, but the latter calls to Ramiyah to restore the balance. A life for the lives of many. Children, husbands, wives, sisters, brothers, the elderly.

"Cali?"

I draw a fist back.

"Ramiyah!"

I turn from The Kutawala, she is still proceeding and I'm not sure I want her to stop. Dakarai, I realise he is seeing us both from his darting gaze. From my eyes, to my shoulder where the icicles linger. He swings his sword back, charges.

"Don't"

Khari spins to block him, he uses both arms crossed to his chest.

"She is unstable, we cannot just watch."

"Trust her."

"Which one?"

"Both."

Mercy. "I could end you with one thought." We release. The Kutawala's eyes shine, the melanin almost coming back. I witness a challenge in his gaze, he wishes for something more.

"But you cannot. It's too soon."

"Your time is not now."

"I agree." What more he wanted to say, it echoes in his mind, 'I have found what I'm looking for.'

He clenches his fist, extinguishing the avalanche's rays and retreats slowly backing away. His eyes don't leave mine until he steps on his metal board and his soldiers whisk him away.

"Times up. The lunar moon is approaching."

"My love, let's go home now."

Over my shoulder, safe and secure back in my body I whisper, "I will not be returning with you."

"Let's not start with that, we have come for you."

Khari lets him go to me, he warms my arms with his hands.

"What do my eyes tell you? They are the window to the soul, the only truth beyond my voice you must recognise."

He takes the time to look into them. He licks his bottom lip.

What he settles on, "they are not your own," is a squeezed lie. "She is taking over. You are afraid my love, but don't be. I am here."

A portal tears through the air behind me. Black specs of grey dust shimmer with Rimorr. It enlarges in an instant. Dakarai digs in his fingers, the wind getting stronger now. The sky darkens; the only source of light emits from the portal, the stars above and the advancing lunar eclipse.

"Use your ears, Prince Dakarai. The heart that beats out of fear, it is not hers but your own."

The stones on the ground levitate as a foot pass through the portal with the rest of its body barely visible. The king, seconds later materialises, his staff increasing in size and density: a spear with a sharp end and a crystal gold version of the Dynastic Emblem with black engraving. His locks flow down to his waist, lightly patting his royal attire: a thick purple material is slanted across his body with his arms bare and silver beads loosely wrapped around his neck with a tiger's eye stone attached to it. With long strides, he closes the gap to stand just over a metre away from us. He smiles, stroking his full beard.

"You are now the obstacle Princess Calista must overcome." His voice booms across the distance.

"You are mistaken ... your Highness. You cannot begin to understand the affairs between us."

He shakes his head inserting his spear into the earth.

"Too bad I don't have the time to explain. I am only here for Princess Calista and Ramiyah."

Dakarai flicks a wondering eye over to him and then returns back to me. "You're not really here."

"Quite the good eye. What a shock it is you still haven't figured out the purpose of Calista's supposed kidnapping? A guy with your talents should have picked up on it the moment she came to you in need of help."

Khari exclaims over the wind. "Dakarai, this is her decision."

He's shaking his head. I settle a hand to his cheek. The truth is apparent, denial will only weigh down the heart.

King Amare jerks his staff out of the ground and slowly steps forward.

"Tell me, your intentions are different from Ramiyah's, don't you seek revenge?"

"Those with a vengeful heart only twirl a double-edged sword. I see the lessons and messages in opportunities and circumstances. I also deliver the hand and tongue of our Supreme Deities. Keep your ears peeled Prince Dakarai, Prince Khari, your eyes too. Your lesson will come soon enough." The King charges with his staff. Khari steps in front of Dakarai but is met with dust.

"My love ..." Dakarai slips his hand under my arms.

"I don't expect you to understand, but you need to let this happen. It is for the best ..."

"Ramiyah has poisoned your mind and soon she will take over your body. You're not thinking clearly."

"You are wrong. My thoughts are my own. I accept this."

The ceaseless winds begin to suck at anything in its path like a black hole. It targets me, pulling me out of Dakarai's arms. He reaches out, our hands miss and I'm pulled further back. Khari manifests his air element and pushes us together. I blow in the wind like a kite and Dakarai plants his foot, struggling to hold me down.

"You have to trust me."

"I feel like I am losing you. I am touching you but I cannot feel you. I can no longer tell the difference." He grips onto my hand more tightly as my fingers start to slip. "Don't let go," he whispers.

"I am not him Dakarai and you are not your past. I have started my rise and as my other half I wish you the same."

The force gets stronger to the point where we are holding on by two fingers.

"I don't need saving."

Our fingers slip further. Khari wind-turbines his arms giving Dakarai a chance to pull me back.

"I am not ready."

"Neither was I." We're face to face with only a thin gap between our lips.

"Rise, my prince. Rise." I wrap my arm around his neck and kiss him.

When we meet again, I wouldn't have regretted this decision.

A light flashes. I spread my arms to my side, close my eyes, sucked into the portal.

I didn't want to see him fall to his knees so heavily they more than grazed. See his head bowed into the earth's soil he clawed at. This is how change is, it uproots.

The portal patches close.

Epilogue
REBIRTH

{Calista}

I n the darkest corners of the room where the candlelight can't reach, curious eyes dance. They whisper amongst themselves waiting for a legend to become true. The roof opens up, the bricks slowly being removed as they pile on top of each other to the far corners of the room. The Lunar Eclipse with a red ring to it finally sets and the ceremony begins. My feet massage the cold marble floor. A few of the hooded figures separate from the dark, some waft sage and incense around the room, others splash some liquid substance on my body. The smoke quickly clouds the room and creates a misty atmosphere that makes it hard to see. A hooded figure steps toward me and glides their thumb along my face, drawing tribal patterns with red paint. Black candles are lit and arranged in a circle around me. Citrine, black moonstones, quartz, and labradorite are spread out around the candles. The flames lengthen as the eclipse magic enters the room, guiding my energy.

I throw my head back and allow the silk robe to fall from my body. Upon his throne, the king raises his staff. It lifts me into the air, my feet dragging along the floor as I'm brought closer towards him. White strings whip out and circle my wrists and ankles. They hold me suspended in the air. With a mind of their own, they gently squeeze at first. She pushes through the walls of my body and mind, making it extremely hard to breathe. The ring around the eclipse grows in size and creates beams of light that resembles snowflakes. The light dances with the flames, leaving imprints in my shadow. My body numbs. The strings squeeze once more, with the red energy and flames warming it up before its purpose is fulfilled. For a second, I lose consciousness.

In my mind, I am falling from a cliff into a black substance that crawls over me like miniature spiders becoming one. The staff is lowered and my body falls in the air. My hands are off the steering wheel. A shock runs through my body, absorbing the red energy around me. My right-hand smashes into the ground, fracturing it as I fall to one knee. Red and orange wings sprout from my shoulders, shimmering like a ghost. Ramiyah's spirit animal has risen in her revival. It flaps its wings and roars before diving inside my body.

The king's feet shuffle as he rises to his feet. The whisperings in the corners come to a standstill. "What is your name, my child?"

My head rises as deep breathes are drawn in through my nose. "Ramiyah. Firstborn of the Sixth Dynasty." One by one the bodies of the dancing eyes become visible as they step out of the shadows. They're drawn to me like a moth to a flame. In a spiral, they kneel, welcoming her. They watch with awe as my arms slowly rise from my sides to spread in the air, head thrown back, relishing life.

The black substance solidifies around my body but remains as a liquid as it creeps up my face. In a matter of seconds, it covers me, completely taking me to a realm deep in my mind that I never knew existed.

The Ankh around my neck glows brightly and a strong wind knocks out the dancing flames on the candles. Zaire steps forward with a Jasper stone outstretched in his palm. The Jasper rises out of his hand and, like a magnet, embeds itself in the loop of the Ankh. Bluka illuminates my skin.

To some, great evil is reborn; to others, their saviour has returned.

PASSENGERS
WITHIN

CHIEMEKA NICELY

AUTHOR'S NOTE

This book idea came to me within a dream. Initially, it started in the middle of my long-term storyline, which I have decided to compact within a series. So, I had to find some way to backtrack without giving away a lot of information that would essentially shock the reader as I flesh it out as a plot twist.

At times, I struggled to write this novel because I was always thinking about the books ahead, especially when I had already completed the novel in my head and had only half-written it. But once I was able to note down all potential links throughout the series starting with book one, I found it much easier to focus on how I wanted to tell this story. Such as, was I going to fully build my fantastical world in Acirfa or was I going to show a sneak peek and move swiftly on with the storyline? As you can see, I chose the former as it made more sense in terms of establishing a deep emotional connection with the reader. Therefore, when plot twists and other knowledge is learned in novels to come, they will feel more inclined to react the way I wish them to.

In the beginning, I wanted to tell a story that wasn't generic but is unique in every possible way as I draw from knowledge and inspiration that I have gathered over these past couples of months from tv-series/movies and books as well as the events I went to during my childhood. As the first novel has come to an end, I realise it is more than that. I wish to not just present an alternative to the common, but also to awaken the blind to the truth to teach them that they are much more than what others tell them they are or should be. Essentially, the purpose of this book is to remind people of the greatness from which they came and the greatness that rests within.

Everything, the time, energy, and words that I poured into this novel was only me expressing myself in a more suitable way than I couldn't do verbally. With my writing, I began to unveil the world through my eyes. I provided an alternative mindset that is usually a part of the minority.

All in all, with this novel my main message is that you can be whoever you want to be. All you have to do is love yourself and understand that the energy that surrounds you is an external reflection of yourself. And as the title of this novel suggests, in one way you are the master of your peace. You, as an energy life form, are a masterpiece expressing itself in many variations, and until you realise who you are, you will forever be asleep, ignorant.

This novel is only the beginning of me revealing to you my masterpiece, as I write my greatness into existence.

Asè

Chiemeka was born in London, UK.

Her interest in all the sciences, African culture, and issues in society are what encourages her to write stories that hold moral and constructive importance in today's society.

With an active imagination, she blends Afrofuturism with the present in hopes of sparking the minds of those who are capable of turning fiction into reality.

Her business, Nicelypublishing, aims to inspire, incorporate her love for her culture, as well as self-publish her debut novel, The Masterpiece, and other future novels.

Did you love this book? Want to be amongst the first to find out more about the series? Want to know more about this world Acirfa and its extraordinary characters?

For exclusives and updates on future releases:
Subscribe to Seshat's Expressions on Youtube
Follow chiemekanicely on Instagram

N cely
PUBLISHING

Printed in Great Britain
by Amazon

11156899R00174